GUARDIAN

Also by Alex London:

PROXY

GUARDIAN

ALEX LONDON

Philomel Books
An Imprint of Penguin Group (USA)

For Tim, who makes the future bright

PHILOMEL BOOKS
Published by the Penguin Group
Penguin Group (USA) LLC
375 Hudson Street, New York, NY 10014

USA | Canada | UK | Ireland | Australia | New Zealand | India | South Africa | China
penguin.com
A Penguin Random House Company

Library of Congress Cataloging-in-Publication Data
London, Alex.   Guardian / Alex London.   pages cm
Sequel to: *Proxy.*
Summary: "The only way to stop people from getting sick is to get the network
back online. That means reversing the very revolution that Syd and Knox
began"—Provided by publisher. [1. Science fiction. 2. Epidemics—Fiction.
3. Social classes—Fiction. 4. Gays—Fiction.] I. Title.
PZ7.L84188Gu 2014   [Fic]—dc23
2013025938
Printed in the United States of America.
ISBN 978-0-399-16576-4
1 3 5 7 9 10 8 6 4 2
Edited by Jill Santopolo.   Design by Semadar Megged.
Text set in 11.5 point Aldus.

We must love one another or die.

     —*WH Auden, "September 1, 1939"*

[1]

AT NIGHT, THEY DISPOSED of the bodies. There was no ceremony, no ritual, no remembrance.

"They're human," some argued.

"They *were* human," said others. "Now they're meat."

"We have to study the infection," said the doctor.

"We have to contain it," said the counselor and gave her orders. "Burn the bodies."

A work detail was tasked with the burning. One by one, in the dead of night, green uniforms with white masks hauled corpses to the pile. The corpses were webbed with black veins, their entire network of blood vessels visible through the pale skin. Dried blood obscured their faces and each had a single hole in the temple by the eyes, where the killing bolt went in. They were put down like livestock, burned like sacrifices.

As the bodies crackled, the doctor watched the flames, her face half in shadow, half dancing in firelight. "I believe there is a cure for this," she said.

The counselor, standing beside her, nodded, but did not turn to look her way. "Your cure is worse than the disease."

"You believe that?"

"It's the truth. Your way is treason."

"You're in denial," the doctor said. "This is going to get worse if we don't stop it."

"It's a new world, Doctor," the counselor replied. "We can't turn back the clock."

"Even to save people's lives?"

"These"—the counselor gestured at the bodies—"are not people."

"If it spreads?"

"Is it spreading?"

The doctor watched the young members of the work detail tossing the bodies on the pyre. They moved with the assurance of youth, the kind of attitude that allowed them to stare infection and death in the face and believe it would never touch them. "I don't know."

"It is your job to know."

"I can hardly understand it. The blood turns against the body. Itching, burning. Then, expulsion. Half of them bleed out."

"And the other half?"

The doctor clenched her jaw. "They haven't bled out yet."

"They are in pain?"

"They can't communicate, but we have to restrain them to keep them from scratching their skin off with their fingernails." The doctor sighed. "So, yes, they are in pain."

"Put them out of their misery," the counselor ordered.

"But we can still learn—"

"Those are the orders." The counselor walked away, two green uniforms trailing her into the jungle. The doctor took off her white smock, pulled the blue gloves from her hands with a loud synthetic snap, and stood before the flames. She watched her latest failed experiments turn to smoke and ash in the bonfire, every bit of blood boiled away, with all the information it might have contained.

She had ideas, dangerous to share; but if she didn't find a way, she feared, this sickness would go further than any of them could imagine. She would record a message in case she failed. She hoped that someone would still be alive to receive it.

[2]

LIAM WAS ALWAYS THERE, just out of the light, standing in doorways, hovering at the edge of conversations, watching Syd even as he slept.

These were the orders of the Reconciliation: Syd was not to be alone.

Liam tried to give Syd his space, but every inch of air between them amplified the danger. He couldn't do his job if Syd was too far away when an assassin struck. And he certainly couldn't protect Syd if he couldn't find him.

Again.

That was why Liam cursed as he sprinted through the overgrown streets of the jungle city, slashing vines from his face, tearing through thorns, and leaping the gnarly mangrove roots webbed between rusted skyscrapers.

Morning mist shrouded everything, and if Liam hadn't

lived in this jungle city his entire life, he would easily have gotten lost. In overgrown plots, people on clearing details hacked away at the brush; others heaped it in piles for burning. Young Purifiers patrolled in pairs. Clad in their green uniforms, their faces were concealed beneath white balaclavas that let only their eyes and mouths show through. While on duty in service of the Reconciliation, all Purifiers were the same Purifier. The individual was negated by the mask.

Anonymity made it easier to beat their fellow citizens into compliance. Anonymity made it easier for the citizens to submit, made it less obvious that most of the Purifiers weren't even old enough to shave.

Only Liam showed his face, his close-cropped red hair bright as torchlight. He wanted to be visible, known to all. A reputation for violence made violence unnecessary. Mostly unnecessary.

All the Purifiers kept their distance. Liam's orders outweighed theirs: Syd was to be protected at all costs.

Liam reached an intersection and stopped. He rested his hands on the fallen pole across the road, tapped his fingers against it. The metal fingers of his right hand clanged on the hollowness; one of them cracked the surface. Metal and meat, everything rotted; it was just a question of timing.

He wondered, when he died, if his mechanical hand would be recycled before burial or if it would slowly rust beside his corpse, no more enduring than this old lamppost. If anything happened to Syd, he'd soon find out.

The Reconciliation had made it clear to him when he volunteered to be Syd's bodyguard: Syd's death would be answered with his own.

It seemed fair enough at the time.

A few months ago, when the Reconciliation was new, when they still called themselves the Rebooters, Liam had no idea how difficult guarding Syd would be. Syd gave Liam the slip at least once a week. No amount of yelling, scolding, or pleading could convince Syd that the danger to him was real.

Everyone knew who Syd was and what he'd done. Everyone knew it was Syd who sparked the Jubilee, Syd who erased the records of the past, Syd who severed the networks and destroyed the old systems of control. Syd who was the people's savior.

Not everyone was happy about it.

No explaining that it wasn't really Syd at all. His friend Knox had done it, had given his life doing it, in fact.

Syd lived on in the aftermath, just like everyone else.

How long Syd lived on in the aftermath was for Liam to worry about, and he was at the moment quite worried about it.

He bent down and checked the moss on a stretch of sidewalk. Indentations where feet had crushed it, morning dew pressed into the footprints. Recent. On the corner of a building a few yards on, he saw crumbs of concrete on the ground, green and rotted, and he found the spot at shoulder height where they'd broken off. He'd have to teach Syd to be more careful. Rotted concrete breaks easy as dirt and leaves a trail even a novice tracker could follow.

Higher up on the wall someone had carved some scratchiti into the mushy stone:

THE MACHINE WILL

They must have run off before they could finish carving their treason. Purifiers stamped out talk of the Machine wherever they found it. They left the scratchiti—too much effort to erase—but if they caught the scratcher . . . well, Liam had once seen a pile of white Purifier masks delivered to a laundry detail and there was dried blood on every one of them.

He swung around the corner and crept low through an overgrown alley. Plant tendrils and branches tugged at his green uniform and scratched his face. He shifted the brush carefully with his metal hand and followed the path where Syd had passed before.

When he came out on the other side, Liam had gone through a break in a wall into the ruins of a monumental building. A canopy of branches and leaves filtered sunlight through the gaping roof. Patches of marble showed through great curtains of ivy. Daggers of light cut through a high arched window and fell in slashes across two parallel marble staircases, rising to a landing that cut the space in two.

At the top of the landing, there was a figure with his back to Liam, a green uniform, a white mask. The figure was leaning forward, looking down over the railing. He held something in his hand. It caught a glint of light. A weapon?

Liam could hear his own pulse in his ears. He exhaled half a breath and crept up the stairs. Even the change of air temperature from his exhalation could give him away. He didn't want to spook his quarry. If he failed now, when it mattered most, when Syd was in the greatest danger, the best Liam could hope for from the Reconciliation would be a lifetime of hard labor. The more likely outcome would be his own public humiliation followed by his execution.

If he failed now, he would deserve it.

His whole life he had been trained to be a ghost, to slip in and out of secure areas unseen, to attack from the shadows and melt into beams of sunlight. He'd been born a guerrilla, serving the revolution of the Rebooters for every conscious moment of his seventeen years. Now he served the new order, which was the same as the old order, but with a new name: the Reconciliation. He was no longer a destroyer, but a protector.

Step by step, he approached the figure. He fought the urge to shout a warning. Instead, he grabbed the figure's neck with his metal hand and wrapped his other hand around the forehead, quick as heat lightning. He jerked his hands in opposite directions and snapped the thin neck, then shoved the body forward over the railing, where it tumbled end over end and hit the hard earth with a crunch. The metal tube of a blowgun clattered across the floor as it rolled from the lifeless hand.

Liam looked down, where Syd stood just beside the body, staring in shock. Syd's dark eyes, wide as moons, darted up to Liam's.

"You—"

"I've told you it's not safe to go off alone," Liam declared. "If I'd been ten seconds later, you'd be dead."

He didn't add *and so would I.*

[3]

LIAM STARED DOWN AT Syd, looking more disappointed than angry, and the would-be assassin's eyes stared up at Syd through the holes in the mask. Hovering between the two sets of eyes, Syd felt certain even the dead were watching him. All he'd wanted was a moment to himself. Syd felt like he'd been rooted to the floor, his feet locked in place. He fought the urge to scream.

Liam strolled down the steps toward him, and still Syd couldn't make a sound. Liam was pale as fog and moved as smoothly. He had stubbly red hair and patchwork freckles across his nose, a nose that had clearly been broken more than once. He stood a head taller than Syd and had forty pounds on him. Even though his features had a soldier's hardness, Syd couldn't help but think of him as an unwanted puppy begging for scraps. His blue eyes looked perpetually damp.

Right now, however, those eyes were sharp, their dampness frozen to ice.

"You okay?" Liam asked him.

Still Syd couldn't speak, just stared at the masked corpse on the ground, its limbs pointed in all different directions, like it had been stopped in the middle of an elaborate dance.

Liam gripped Syd with his metal hand, held him steady, and looked him over, checking for wounds. The feel of metal against his skin snapped Syd out of his trance. He pulled away.

"I'm fine!" Syd told Liam. He took a step back.

Liam looked at him a beat longer, head slightly cocked, words caught on his lips. Instead of saying anything, he squatted down and peeled the mask off the would-be assassin's face.

Syd inhaled sharply. The killer was young, no older than either of them, and a girl. Her lifeless blue eyes stared straight up at the open ceiling. Around her neck, she had a long line of tattooed ones and zeros, binary code, symbol of the Machinist cults.

"You can't keep running off alone," Liam said. "They won't stop until you're dead."

"What . . . ?" Syd searched for the words. It had been close, so close. This girl was going to kill him. He couldn't take his eyes off her. Other than the tattoos, she looked so normal. She was just some girl. And yet, she had died trying to kill Syd. "Why?" He shook his head. "It makes no sense. Why kill me?"

"You're Yovel," Liam said. "Your enemies believe in you as much as your allies."

Syd flinched at the word "Yovel." He hated it. Yovel was the name his father had given him. It was the name marked in four ancient letters on the skin behind his right ear. It was the name by which the people knew him, the Jubilee in human form, the day when all debts were forgiven. It was the name that should have killed him, and instead it was the lie that reminded him he was still alive, that Knox had died in his place.

Syd rubbed his eyes. "They believe a lie. You were there. You know. The Rebooters—"

"They're the Reconciliation now," Liam corrected him. "A new organization for new times."

"A new name doesn't change anything."

"Words matter."

"Empty symbols," Syd retorted.

"Symbols matter."

"That's glitched," Syd grumbled.

"No," Liam told him. "Glitched is you running off on your own out here. Glitched is you not letting me do my job."

"It's not your job to lecture me."

"It's my job to protect you."

Syd didn't answer right away. He turned his back on Liam, walked along the wall, pulling old vines off a column, crushing his anger inward. He resented Liam's protection, even if it was necessary.

As long as the Machinists believed they could bring the

networks back online by killing Syd, Liam would be at his side, but if he expected a thank-you from Syd, he'd be waiting a long time. Liam was a killer and Syd had to endure his protection; he didn't have to be nice about it.

Liam flexed and unflexed the metal hand. It caught the light, dappling the wall as it moved. Syd had never asked Liam how he got that hand. In this world, everyone had lost something, be it a hand, a friend, a name. Now that the Reconciliation had banned all personal possessions, the only things anyone owned anymore were their losses. Syd treasured his and wouldn't dare inquire about someone else's.

While Syd tore at vines, Liam bent back down over the body. He placed the soft fingertips of his good hand over the dead assassin's eyes and closed them gently.

Syd had stopped to watch him and Liam seemed to blush when he noticed Syd watching. Liam's pale blue eyes had gone soft again, the sad puppy look returned. He stood and placed himself in front of the body, like he was suddenly embarrassed by it. A killer ashamed of killing.

"Everyone's waiting," Liam announced.

"Another speech." Syd sighed. "I guess I don't have much of a choice."

"We all serve the Reconciliation in our own ways," Liam recited.

"I give speeches and you kill people," Syd snapped.

Liam clenched his jaw. Exhaled slowly. Tried—and failed—not to show his anger. "I protect you from killers so that you can continue to inspire the people."

"Uh-huh," Syd grunted, walking past Liam for the main door to the ruined old building. He knocked into Liam's shoulder as he went. Liam followed, staring at the back of Syd's dark neck, the letters behind his ear, his slump-shouldered walk; and he fought the urge to reach out his metal hand and grab Syd, shout at him, tell him to be better than he was, tell him to man up and become what everyone wanted him to be, what everyone needed him to be.

What Liam needed him to be.

But Liam wouldn't and Liam didn't. He clamped his mouth shut, steadied himself, exhaled, and imagined his emotions like a waterfall, pouring down from his head, through his neck and chest, down through his thighs and his knees, pouring from his toes and away into the earth. He was empty again, calm and cold. Able to do his job.

Protecting a person, Liam had discovered, was much harder than killing one.

[4]

SYD STOOD ON THE stage that had been assembled in the middle of a wide avenue beneath the blazing blue sky. Some of the skyscrapers that lined the avenue had been repaired, but most still stood in decay, teetering like tweaked-out syntholene addicts on the verge of passing out.

Below the swaying buildings, the avenue itself was filled from edge to edge with people. There were young women holding babies. There were kids waving signs that said **THANK YOU, YOVEL!** and **YOVEL SET US FREE!**, and a scattering of people throughout the crowd waving white strips of cloth over their heads as they cheered. White for a clean break with the past. White for empty records. White for new beginnings. All those white cloths looked like the flapping wings of birds unable to fly away.

Syd could sympathize.

The people had to be held back by a line of Purifiers positioned between the stage and the crowd, to keep the people from rushing up to touch Syd or tear away a scrap of his clothing. Their ecstasy was religious and it made Syd uncomfortable to see it. An image flashed in his mind: the girl who had been sent to kill him, dressed like a Purifier. He tensed, braced himself as if he was about to be attacked. A bubble of panic rose inside him. Was this the instant they'd get him? Or this? Or this? The seconds stretched. He bargained with himself to stay calm, to stay still, to make it through the next five seconds and the five seconds after that. The panic subsided. Liam stood beside him on the stage and did his best to project the potential for unrelenting pain on anyone with less than generous feelings for Syd.

He wondered whether Liam would throw himself in front of an attacker, would take a poison dart for him, would die in Syd's place.

He knew the answer and it made him even more uncomfortable.

On the other side of Syd stood a bearded old man, stuffed so poorly into his tight green uniform that his belly hung over his belt and his white collar was open and flapping in the light breeze. Puffs of gray hair rose like smoke from beneath his shirt.

"Thank you for joining us, Sydney," the man said.

"Liam made the invitation sound so compelling, how could I say no?" Syd whispered back at him. "How often do I get to stand onstage beside the famous Counselor Baram?"

The man smiled and waved at the crowd, whispering back to Syd through his teeth. "Cut the sarcasm. Sarcastic words hide lazy minds."

Counselor Baram had known Syd his entire life; he had practically raised Syd back in Mountain City, when he was just Mr. Baram and Syd was just a proxy, an orphan living in the slums, paying off his years of debt by taking the punishments every time his patron, Knox, did anything wrong.

Syd had been one of millions, not a thing special about him. He paid for school, he worked in Baram's shop, and he spent his days with his head down, fantasizing about a date with his classmate Atticus Finch. His feelings for Finch, to put it generously, had not been mutual. It hadn't really bothered Syd. He enjoyed the quiet hopelessness of it all. He always figured life would start after he'd finished school and paid off his debts.

Instead, he'd erased the entire system.

He wondered what ever happened to Finch. Before the Jubilee, back in the Mountain City, Finch had been a guy going places, a gamer with sponsors, a kid on his way up and out of the slums of the Valve to live the lux life with the patrons of the Upper City.

Now that the networks were gone and the old tech banned, there were no games to play and no sponsors to pay for the playing anyway. Syd's revolution had stopped Finch's rise dead in its tracks. Now old Mr. Baram was Counselor Baram, deputy secretary of the Advisory Council of the

Reconciliation and now Syd was Yovel, the people's hero, their savior and the symbol of all that was new.

Nothing was like it had been. So, in this new world order, why couldn't Syd be sarcastic? Everyone was in the business of reinvention. He'd even considered growing his hair out.

"Apologies, Counselor." Syd smiled, making his continued sarcasm as biting as he could. "Your sage advice is a boon to us all."

It was too hot for big hair.

Counselor Baram let his eyes linger on Syd a moment, then sighed and stepped forward. He held his hand up in a fist. The crowd fell silent. Baram's voice strained to be heard, but he didn't use any kind of amplification. Although all the old tech had been banned, the Council still had access to things like loudspeakers and projectors. That kind of tech was a privilege of the Council, but Baram liked to be pure, natural, one with the people. If that meant he had to shout to be heard, it was a small price to pay for his ideals. Syd thought it was just stubborn.

"My friends!" Baram declared. "We are here today, six months after the Jubilee—" The crowd went wild at the word and Baram had to wait for them to settle down before he could continue. "We are here to celebrate all we have accomplished! Freed from the burdens of debt and the financialization of our sons and daughters, we are building a new society, a society of mutual care and concern. A society where we are judged by our contributions to the community, not by our purchasing power on the unregulated market!"

People cheered again, even those whose understanding of the new revolution was minimal. Most of the crowd were slum rats who'd grown up just like Syd in cesspools of debt and poverty, where credit was easy but paying for it was a lifelong labor. Even those who had some education, who'd been willing to pay for education—like Syd had—would never have learned any of the anti-market ideas that were the backbone of the Reconciliation.

Anyone who could actually understand Counselor Baram had probably been arrested just after the networks collapsed, when the Reconciliation stormed Mountain City, rounded up the executives and the managers and the creditors and anyone else with whom they had a problem, and sent them off for labor reeducation or confession and execution. Remaking the world wasn't always a stage show and a cheering crowd. Politics was just warfare by other means. The losers didn't get to hold rallies.

So the people cheered, because their side won. These kinds of rallies were a regular thing now, educating everyone on the dogma of Reconciliation: Private property led to greed, so it was banned. Tech produced false luxury, which produced greed. It was banned. Debt was banned and credit was banned and money of all kinds was banned.

But it was better than the old system. Everyone was responsible for themselves. No rich, no poor, no patrons, and no proxies.

Not that the proxies had gone away, exactly. They were the first to be rounded up. They were trained and armed and became the Purifiers. They generally had no interest in reform. They wanted revenge and they wanted power, and the Reconciliation gave them both.

Today, however, the Purifiers were on their best behavior, keeping the crowd under control while Baram droned on about food cooperatives producing record calorie counts—"exceeding all our expectations!"—and about the containment of Machinist factions through "the appropriate application of humane force."

Syd stopped listening. He was a symbol, after all. Symbols didn't need to listen to speeches. He'd get up when he heard his name and he'd say the speech that had been written for him. *Great friends! Citizen heroes! I am just like you!* Et cetera. Eighteen minutes like that.

Funny to think he'd caused the revolution, but he didn't get to enjoy it. Syd was as much a substitute for other people as he'd ever been when he was a proxy. It was just that now they cheered for him beneath a blazing sun.

His memories shimmered like a mirage on the pavement. They waved and sparked the air. And in the sparks, he saw Knox.

Moments before Knox had climbed into the machine that would destroy the networks and vaporize him in the process, Syd had asked him a question: "What am I supposed to do?"

"Like I know?" Knox told him, that lopsided smirk dimpling his cheek. "It's your future. Choose."

Had Syd chosen? Was this it? Was this all?

He noticed a rise in the volume of the crowd and he snapped his attention back to the stage. Baram was pointing at him and the people were cheering and he waved and they went wild. He guessed if someone else had freed him from a life of debt and poverty, he'd have been happy to see that guy wave too. If only these people knew that the guy waving at them wasn't the guy who did it at all. If only they knew it had been a spoiled brat of a patron who'd set them free. Maybe that was the speech he should give?

"That's right!" Counselor Baram continued. "At great risk to himself, he defied the system, fought past an army of Guardians and made his way here, to Old Detroit, to free us all! Thanks to this boy here, Yovel, the networks that enslaved us have collapsed. Thanks to Yovel, the corruption of the corporate fiefdoms has been demolished, and the people have been given control of their own destinies! On the day of Jubilee! The day of Yovel!"

The cheering again, the white cloths waving, and Syd waving back, teeth gritted. He stood.

"Who believes this knock-off story?" he muttered.

"Just let them believe, Syd," Liam whispered in his ear. "They need to believe."

"And what do you believe?" Syd asked.

Liam pursed his lips, didn't answer.

Syd shook his head and approached the front of the stage. No amplification for him either. It seemed he'd be expected to shout as well. He cleared his throat.

He wanted to say, *It's your future. Choose.*

He said, "Great friends! Citizen heroes! I am just like you!"

The crowd chanted, "Yo-vel Yo-vel Yo-vel!"

He had to hold his hands in the air to quiet them so he could continue. Behind him, Liam scanned the sea of faces, his fingers resting on the bolt gun he wore on his belt.

"I am here today!" Syd continued. "To tell you! The story of our victory! Over the—!"

A high shout broke his speech.

At first Syd thought it was just more cheering from an overzealous citizen, but another shout followed, and then shrieks. Full-throated, piercing shrieks sliced through the air and Syd strained into the glare of the sunlight to see the cause.

Liam, on instant alert, shoved himself in front of Syd, holding him tightly behind his back with the metal hand digging into Syd's arm.

"I can't see." Syd squirmed, unable to break the grip. "What is it?"

"I can't tell yet . . . it's—" Liam started and then Syd saw.

A figure clothed in a tattered gray jumpsuit came lurching from the alley to the side of the crowd. She had long blond hair and she walked with stutter-steps. Through the skin on her face, her neck, her hands, all her veins were visible, black and bulging. Through the tears in her clothes, the black lines of veins mingled with red welts and sores, like the flesh had been scratched off by anxious fingernails.

Her mouth opened and she seemed to scream without making a sound.

Another black-veined figure spewed from the overgrown jungle alley on the far side of the crowd, and another and another. A dozen of them spilled across the plaza at the back of the crowd, careening blindly into the sea of revelers. They moved fast, scratching at themselves, opening and closing their mouths, charging forward, bleeding.

The people recoiled, stumbling over one another, tripping and shrieking, panicking as the disfigured bodies pushed into the throng.

As the nearest one heaved herself toward the stage, a Purifier raised his club and with a ferocious blow struck her down. She fell to the pavement with a crack. Her head bounced when it hit. Her long blond hair splayed out in front of her like sparks flying from a live wire.

It was, of course, an illusion.

There was nothing alive about her at all.

[5]

"GUARDIANS," SAID SYD.

"Stay back," Liam ordered, pushing Syd toward the rear of the stage.

"But Guardians are harmless," Syd protested.

Guardians had been the enforcers of the old system; biohacked from childhood, they had more data installed in their blood than the DNA they'd been born with. They were engineered to look the same and act the same and live entirely by the instructions of their programming. They were people without fear, morality, or weakness, hardly human at all.

When Knox had blown out the network and deleted everyone's biofeeds, the Guardians had lost the connection to the software updates in their blood, the instructions from their controllers, the patches that kept them free of blemish.

SecuriTech, the corporation that owned them, was wiped away. Now they had no direction, no purpose, and no control. They'd gone dumb the moment the networks fell. They were still strong, but incapable of taking care of themselves. Some were rounded up, put to work like pack animals, hauling and churning and heaving. Others just wandered, feral.

No one called them Guardians anymore. They were officially dubbed "nonoperative entities."

Most people called them "nopes."

That's all they were anyway.

Nothings.

But these nopes weren't just deaf and dumb; they looked like the stuff of nightmares. The black veins bulged; their cheeks were streaked with bloody tears. They tore at their own skin until it was raw and open.

A few of them tried to come from a side street that was still clogged with vines and they'd gotten tangled in the thick brambles. They squirmed and struggled, bleeding where the long green thorns tore into them. One had scratched and torn out most of her hair. All the veins on her scalp were visible, a network of black wires, pulsing and throbbing. Her face was caught in a thornbush, and in spite of that, she continued to try to push forward, rather than plucking the thorns out. Her cheek tore and black blood ran down. She didn't react. She didn't even have language to ask for help.

A Purifier rushed over to her, swung his club down, split her head open.

Syd saw a tall man in a green Purifier's uniform direct-ing the Purifiers to attack the helpless creatures. At first, his white hood looked like it was made of something reflective, the way it caught the sunlight, but then Syd realized he wore no white hood. He was simply bald, his head smooth and shiny. He had deep-set eyes and long limbs. He didn't appear to be carrying a weapon, but he moved gracefully through the crowd and shoved any mutated Guardian that got near him to the ground, where others came and whaled upon it. He didn't even turn to look at the carnage. His calm was disconcerting amid the frothing crowd. People scram-bled over one another and screamed to get away from the nightmare figures.

"It touched me!" someone shouted.

"Kill it!" someone else screamed.

"Calm down!" Counselor Baram tried to yell over the chaos, but no one could hear him. "They will be quaran-tined! Just stay calm!"

A group of three Purifiers had cornered a Guardian, a male from what Syd could see, and were shoving him be-tween themselves, bouncing him off their clubs. When he fell toward one of them, they'd strike him back, and the next Purifier would wind up to hit him, tossing him around, like a game of wounds. When he finally fell, they beat him until it was impossible to tell if he had ever been anything resembling a human.

The Purifiers whooped and rushed to the next one. Years of terror and humiliation at the hands of the Guardians came out with every strike of a club or swing of a heavy blade at the pained creatures' heads.

Another of the nopes stumbled toward the stage, and a small Purifier, surely no older than twelve, twirled around and around with his machete outstretched to get as much force as possible before sailing it through the neck of his target. The fragile body fell straight down. The head spun off and whirled like a top onto the stage at Syd's feet.

Liam kicked it away. "We have to get you out of here."

"But they won't hurt anyone . . . they're . . . they . . . ," Syd stammered. The images came at him in flashes. Guardians—he couldn't help but still think of them that way—simply stood in place while Purifiers hacked them to pieces, their legs planted firmly on the ground, even after the rest of them was cut apart. They tore at their own skin where the visible veins ran black. It seemed almost a relief to them as they died. The tall bald man strolled through the carnage, his hands clasped behind his back.

Liam had pulled a bolt gun from his belt and held it at the ready.

"They're harmless," Syd said. "The Guardians are harmless."

"They're carrying an infection," Liam said. "Come on."

He had to get Syd out of there. He twirled the gun to chamber a bolt and locked the spring. His only concern was for Syd's safety. It wasn't just exposure to the sick nonoperative entities that he feared. The chaos they had created would be the perfect opportunity for another Machinist to take a crack at Syd. Enemies of the Reconciliation were everywhere. They could dress as Purifiers and put a knife through Syd's back while everyone else was distracted.

Liam would not be distracted.

He tried to drag Syd away, but Syd dodged his grip, ducked around his arm, and jumped from the stage into the melee.

"Stop this!" Syd shouted at the Purifiers. "I am Yovel and I order you to stop!"

They ignored him. Moments ago the crowd had been worshipping him; now he was completely forgotten. Revulsion was stronger than adulation and much harder to quell. The people ran past, trying to get away, as the Purifiers ran forward, gleefully carrying out the slaughter.

Liam waded into the crowd after Syd, knocking people from his path with his metal hand. They bumped him, jostled him, blocked his view. He couldn't see where Syd had gone. He cursed under his breath.

Losing his assignment twice in one day . . . there would be hell to pay for that. And if anything happened to Syd . . .

Syd didn't worry about himself. He charged at the nearest Purifier, who stood over a vein-faced nope with a heavy club raised. Syd caught the Purifier's wrist, spun him around. "I order you to stop this at once. I am—"

He froze. Even with only the eyeholes and the slit for the mouth, he recognized the face beneath the mask. He recognized the sudden twisted smile, and he recognized the devious glint of the eyes.

"Finch," Syd said.

"The name's Furious now, *Syd*," his former classmate sneered at him.

Shortly after the Jubilee, all the kids who had become Purifiers were advised to take new names, names of their own choosing. Their old names had been assigned from databases of stories. Fictional characters. Even Syd's name. Their new names were grotesque fantasies, emancipated teenagers creating themselves in their own image. They were encouraged to think big, so they could aspire to live up to their new selves. "Furious" was doing his part.

On the ground, the wounded Guardian gaped up at them, bleeding black. Finch—Syd would never think of him as anything else—didn't look down at her. His eyes were firmly locked on Syd's. Syd still held his wrist.

"Where's your shadow?" Finch said. "Does he know you're down here with the riffraff all alone?"

"I don't need Liam's permission to give you orders, Finch. Put down your weapon and leave this nonoperative alone."

"Why? You got a crush on a nope now? That breaks my heart."

Syd regretted ever being infatuated with Atticus Finch. He yanked at his arm, but Finch moved fast, stuck out his foot and used Syd's own momentum to trip him. In a flash, he'd spun Syd to the ground and now stood over him. In the chaos of the crowd, no one even noticed their revered symbol of liberation pressed beneath the boot of an anonymous

Purifier. The street was a gory pool of mud and blood, and with one splash from Finch's boot, Syd's face was covered in muck, unrecognizable.

"Some hero," Finch said.

"Let me up."

"I was going to live a lux life"—Finch talked over him, leaned his weight down—"before you glitched it all up, you Chapter Eleven swampcat prick."

"It's treason to long for the past," Syd said, spitting mud from his mouth. "What would the other Purifiers say if they heard you?"

"Who's gonna tell them?" Finch pressed down harder. The weight was agony. A root below Syd dug into his back. He tried to get up and Finch's foot pushed him down again. The front of Finch's boot had a hole in it and Syd made out a filthy white sock.

"I wonder what would happen if the great Yovel was accidentally trampled to death in the crowd?" Finch leaned down. "Would they blame some crazed Machinist? How long would the people mourn such a terrible accident?" Finch licked his lips, his hands jittery with excitement. He raised his voice. "Oh dear me! I tried to save him, I surely did. If only he had let his bodyguard help!" Finch laughed.

"Let me up," Syd demanded.

"Make me." Finch pushed Syd deeper into the mud, grinding his boot into Syd's chest. "I've dreamed about this for a really long time, Syd. The people may worship you, but we both know what you really are."

Suddenly, a metal hand appeared on Finch's shoulder and spun him around.

"And what is he, really?" Liam didn't wait for an answer to punch Finch across the face. Then he lifted the Purifier up by the neck, the metal hand squeezing around his throat. Through his mask, his eyes bulged out. Liam's were calm, and hard as desert glass. "You know I'm authorized to kill anyone who presents a threat to Yovel?"

Finch couldn't answer. His windpipe was squeezed shut. His face turned red. Liam wasn't even breaking a sweat, holding Finch aloft.

"Don't," Finch squeaked out. "Just messing around . . . old friends . . ."

"I fought with the Rebooters while you were sitting in Mountain City playing holo games," Liam continued. "I killed more people before puberty than you've met in your entire life. I wouldn't even remember your name by lunch."

"Stop it," said Syd. The veiny nope on the ground writhed beside him.

Liam squeezed harder. "You can't go running off like that," he told Syd. "You know it's not safe."

"I know," said Syd. "I'm sorry. Just let him go."

Liam looked at Finch, made hard eye contact. "You will leave Syd alone from now on?"

Finch did his best to nod.

"You won't so much as look at him ever again?"

Finch was about to pass out.

"Let him go," Syd repeated. "You're killing him."

"I *should* kill him."

"Don't," Syd pleaded. No one else had to die because of Syd. No one should. This was not what he wanted.

Liam looked back at Syd, took a deep breath, and dropped Finch to the ground. Then he bent down and helped Syd up.

"I am getting you out of here." Liam gripped Syd around the arm with the metal hand—always with the metal hand, Syd noted—and dragged him through the crowd toward an alley off the avenue. Liam took his bolt gun back out.

"Let go of me." Syd tried to rip his arm free. He knew he'd be bruised, but Liam's grip was relentless. They rounded a corner to a quieter clearing. They could still hear the screaming, but not see it anymore. Syd struggled and finally, Liam let go.

"I can take care of myself," Syd told him, wiping the mud from his face.

Just then, another figure in a white balaclava came tearing through thick brush from the other end of the alley, a large serrated knife gripped for attack.

"Drop the blade!" Liam shouted.

The Purifier skidded to a stop. He did not drop the blade.

"I said drop it!" Liam repeated.

The Purifier's eyes darted to Syd and then to Liam, and his arm came forward, tossing the knife straight for them.

Liam did not hesitate this time. He shoved Syd sideways to the ground at the same time as he released the spring of the bolt gun with a flick of his thumb.

The spring unwound and shot a small bolt from the end

of the barrel. There was a snap as it broke the sound barrier and tore clean through the Purifier's shoulder. "Ah!" the Purifier screamed, as the force of the bolt spun him around and knocked him against the broken wall of a building. At the same instant, the knife hissed through the air just beside Liam's ear and crunched straight into the forehead of a nope that had shambled into the alley behind them.

Liam snapped the spring back and chambered a second bolt, bending down to pick up Syd as he did so. The nope took one more step forward before falling against Liam's back with a spurt of black blood, then tumbled sideways into the dirt.

"Liam! Syd! It's me!" The Purifier held himself on his feet, his right arm hanging useless at his side. With his left, he peeled the balaclava off his head and Syd gasped.

Liam cursed under his breath.

The Purifier was a she.

"Marie," said Syd as his only living friend in the world bled through the green of her uniform.

[6]

MARIE ALVAREZ WAS THE only patron allowed into the ranks of the Purifiers, because of her role in the Jubilee. She served the Reconciliation faithfully, efficiently, and with tremendous skill. She never expected to get a bolt in the shoulder from Syd's bodyguard.

"You could have killed me!" she yelled at Liam, shoving her mask into the pocket of her uniform. Her black hair was cut short, her milky tea skin quickly losing color even as her crescent eyes blazed anger.

"Impossible," Liam said, trying to regain his composure. "I was aiming to disarm you, which is what I did. If I'd wanted you dead, you would be. Anyway, you should know better than to come at Syd with a weapon."

"I was trying to stop that nope from infecting him."

"Marie . . ." Syd caught his breath. He looked at the dead

Guardian on the ground, her black blood pooling around her veined face. It was hard to believe she had once been beautiful, that all the Guardians had once been beautiful. "What is . . . happening?"

"I don't know," said Marie. "But our orders are to terminate them. You need to get out of here."

"Syd came into contact with a lot of their blood," said Liam. "I think we need to—behind you!"

Marie glanced over her shoulder to see another nope crashing through the jungle. It moved fast, its hands scouring its body, ripping at itself, tearing its own flesh open as it charged. With one arm limp at her side, Marie grabbed it with her good arm, rolled the nope over her shoulder in a flip, and smashed it onto the ground on its back. She raised her foot to stomp down on the gasping creature's neck.

"Stop it!" Syd yelled. "They're harmless! The Guardians can't even feed themselves!"

Marie brought her foot down, crushing the nope's throat. "They aren't Guardians anymore. They are non-operative entities and they have to be put down. Orders of the Reconciliation."

"This isn't right."

"It is not our place to question the advice of the Council," Marie said back.

"Then I will speak to the Council about it myself." Syd got in her face.

"That is *your* right," she said back.

Syd stared her down. She didn't look away from his

mud-and-blood-coated face; she didn't even flinch. Her face was going pallid as she bled, turning the color of rotted concrete. The gentle slope of her eyelids had caved into steep chasms. The bit of purple left over in her corneas from the fancy gene hacks she had before the Jubilee were hardly visible anymore. Still, she didn't move a muscle. She wasn't about to back down. She'd bleed to death first. Stubborn as ever.

Syd turned away. "Liam," he snapped. "Can you bandage her up? We can't let her bleed out." He turned back to Marie. He cocked his head.

"Fine," she said.

Liam nodded. He pulled out a smart bandage from his emergency kit, not because he wanted to, but because Syd had asked him to. While he packed her wound, Syd took the opportunity to glance back out of the alleyway to the open avenue and the stage. What he saw took his breath away.

Everyone but the Purifiers had left. They were stacking the bodies of the Guardians in a pile in the center of the avenue, tossing them like unsalvageable garbage onto a heap. There were over twenty bodies piled and more on the way. Some of them were just pieces.

The bald man was gone, but Syd quickly saw that Finch was not. He was kicking a severed head up in the air, trying to keep it aloft for as long as he could.

"I got twenty-three!" he shouted when his last kick missed and the head smashed onto the pavement.

Syd took a step forward. He was going to destroy Finch

this time, in front of his friends. He didn't need Liam to do it. He'd take Finch apart and, when he was done, he'd have Finch transferred to sanitation detail. What good was being Yovel if he couldn't settle a few scores for himself?

"Don't go back out there," Liam told Syd. "Or I won't bandage your friend."

"How kind of you," Marie grumbled.

Syd stopped and watched from the edge of the alley. "This is sick."

"Nopes don't feel any pain," Marie said, wincing while Liam packed her wound with the gentleness of a battering ram.

"How do you know?" Syd replied.

"Guardians never did."

"Like you said." Syd turned to her. "They aren't Guardians anymore."

"Syd." Marie shook her head. "Do you really care? Back when they were part of the system, they wanted to kill you, remember? They tortured you. They're getting better treatment than they deserve."

He looked down at the Guardian with the knife in her head, the other with her throat crushed. He thought of the dead Machinist assassin. He felt sick to his stomach. He was Yovel, the symbol of the revolution. And the revolution was capable of this.

"So are we," he said.

Knox's word's echoed in his head again: *It's your future. Choose.*

This couldn't be what Knox had meant.

Syd heard a cheer and turned back to the avenue. The Purifiers stood in a circle around the heap of bodies. One of them lit it on fire and the smell of burning cloth and flesh and hair carried on the breeze. It filled Syd's nostrils, overwhelmed his senses. A plume of black smoke rose from the bonfire, a spreading stain on the cloudless blue sky.

It's your future. Choose.

"Syd, are you okay?" Marie asked.

"He was exposed to a lot of their blood," Liam said again.

"The Reconciliation says the infection can't spread to regular people," Marie told him.

"Still, I'd like to get him to a medic, just to be sure."

Syd heard their voices, talking about him, as if they were a thousand miles away. His ears rang and his vision went red around the edges. Blurred. He felt sick. He tasted black blood on his tongue, felt the mud hardening on his face.

He needed to lie down. He needed to talk to Baram and the Advisory Council. He needed to get some clean air. He needed to stop the bloodshed. He needed to—

He passed out and Liam couldn't move fast enough to catch him.

[7]

"I NEED A FULL medical checkup," Liam snapped at the medics as he stormed into the medical station, carrying Syd. Marie staggered in after him.

"And she could use some attention too," he added.

"Thanks." Marie gave Liam a sarcastic smile.

Three medics, all in the green uniform of the Reconciliation, jumped up to object and, seeing Syd, froze. There was a line of cots along the far wall of the metal container that they'd turned into a makeshift hospital. They'd cut out one wall of the container and used a tarp and mosquito netting to create space for two more rows of cots. All the cots, save one, were empty, as if they were waiting for an influx of patients that had yet to materialize.

"Stop!" A Purifier rushed in, breathless, and Liam's hand went to the bolt gun on his belt. Marie waved the kid off.

"What happened to you?" he asked.

"An accident," she said.

"Is that—?" The Purifier pointed at Syd, his voice cracking. "Yovel?"

Liam looked the boy over. The Purifiers were all young, but this one couldn't have been more than thirteen years old. He had recognized Syd. He'd used the official name, the one Syd hated, and saying it too loudly would bring down more attention than Liam cared for at the moment.

The boy had a Mountain City accent, and had probably spent his whole life in the slums, a proxy taking the punishments for the crimes of the rich patron he'd been assigned. Just like Syd had. Just like so many anonymous thousands.

An accident of birth.

He could just as easily have been plucked from the womb and installed into the Guardian program, and now he'd be one of the nonoperatives, falling prey to some horror-show infection. Or he could have been born rich and ended up purged in the revolution after the networks fell. How he ended up all the way out here, pulling this duty twelve hundred miles from home, was anyone's guess. The Reconciliation didn't run its personnel choices by Liam.

He left his bolt gun in place and raised his metal index finger at the kid, whose eyes were wide blue marbles shining through the holes of his white face mask. "Get back to work and keep your mouth shut."

"Yes, sir." The kid nodded, then saluted—which was not something that was done. He must have seen too many holos before the day of the Jubilee deleted them all. He was a real-life soldier playing soldier from his memories of made-up soldiers. His spindly knees knocked as he ran back to stand guard outside.

Liam was the same way when he was that age, wasn't he? He'd been a soldier for just about all of his seventeen years, but he hadn't been born good at it. He had to be trained. Discipline took training. Proper procedure took training. Learning to kill took training.

The kid would learn, just like Liam had. All it took was the commitment to work hard and to forget your life before. Amnesia was a soldier's best friend, and luckily, it could be taught. Missing limbs still ache, but missing memories never do.

Liam snapped his attention back inside the medical tent as a figure sat up from the one occupied cot, tossed a sheet off himself, and rose to his full height. He stood taller than the rest of the medics and wore a full dark beard, flecked with gray. His head was shaved and the skin around his eyes creased with wrinkles. He was at least thirty years older than the oldest of the other medics in the room and his uniform was white with a green collar, crisp and clean.

"Doctor Rahat," one of the young medics spluttered at the man. "You sure you're feeling well enough?"

The man, Dr. Rahat, stared at the young medic a moment. He opened his mouth and it looked like he was searching for words. "I . . . I . . ." He scratched red lines into the back of his hand, an action that seemed to focus him. "I'm fine," he declared. "You three, take care of that one." He nodded at Marie and then gestured for Liam to carry Syd to a curtained-off area at the rear of the container.

Syd stirred. He felt himself set down on a cot and then felt the cool metal of Liam's hand slide out from under his neck, gently resting his head on a pillow. He opened his eyes and knew he'd passed out in the alley. His nose still held the faint smell of burning corpses.

He looked up at Liam's pale face, the scattered freckles on the slightly crooked nose and the patchy red hair growing in uneven stubble on his chin. His dark red eyebrows were scrunched together with worry, the light blue eyes damp and searching. Memories flashed: Liam throwing the body of the would-be assassin over the railing; Liam holding Finch up in the air by one hand; Liam shooting Marie through the shoulder. How could a killer have such gentle eyes?

Beside Liam, the weathered face of the old doctor looked down curiously. The doctor's eyes were ringed with dark circles, the exhaustion of any medical man in service of the Reconciliation. His face was drawn, pale; Syd made out the faintest traces of the blue of his veins running beneath his skin. Another memory flash. The nopes, the grotesque webbing of their bulging black veins, the silencing of their screams as they were hacked apart. Syd shut his eyes, cleared his head, opened them again to see Dr. Rahat looking to his side, to the spot behind his ear, where the four letters of his name were written. Yovel. Syd bent his neck to block the doctor's view and pushed himself up onto his elbows.

"I'm okay," he told Dr. Rahat.

Liam closed the curtain around the cot area and fixed his eyes on Dr. Rahat. The man wore the uniform of the Reconciliation, but Liam couldn't trust anybody except himself when it came to Syd's safety. No one had Syd's best interests at heart, not like he did.

"What seems to be troubling you, son?" Dr. Rahat asked.

"He fainted," Liam said.

"I can speak for myself." Syd glared at Liam, then looked back at the doctor. "I passed out. I'm okay now. My bodyguard is just overcautious."

"Well, that's not a bad thing to be." Dr. Rahat smiled kindly. "You are the hero of our revolution, after all. Without you, where would we be? Why don't we give you a quick once-over, just to be on the safe side?"

"He came into contact with the blood of several nonoperatives, who were . . ." Liam didn't know how to describe it.

"Infected," the doctor finished for him.

"I swear, I'm fine," said Syd. "It was just seeing . . . what happened to those Guard—the nonoperative entities. It made me sick."

The doctor nodded, stroking his beard. "You're a sensitive soul, Yovel—"

"Call me Syd," he interrupted him.

The doctor nodded. "So many of the proxies have taken on new names, and you, being, well . . . I didn't want to presume . . ."

"It's fine," Syd reassured him. "I prefer it, actually."

"Very well," the doctor said. "You needn't worry about these nonoperatives. They do not suffer when they are put down. In fact, we are putting an end to their suffering."

"By clubbing them to death?" Syd replied.

"Since the Reconciliation has wisely seen fit to restrict passive weaponry, we've found that the most ideologically consistent way to terminate them is through blunt force trauma. That way the labor and its object remain connected. The old ways—press a button, take a life—well, those won't do, will they? If we are to kill, we must do so with absolute commitment. It may not be humane, but it is far more human."

"You ever consider not killing them?" Syd suggested.

"They will die anyway." He sighed. "You saw, I believe, that they are all dying."

"They're sick," said Syd. "What's wrong with them?"

"It appears to be an infection," the doctor said. "Harmless to regular humans, I assure you, but just in case, for the public safety, we must contain their infection wherever we find it. There are too many of them wandering about for us to take chances."

"If the infection can't spread to regular humans," Syd wondered, "then why put down the Guardians at all?"

"The nonoperative entities," the doctor corrected again. "Our society must allocate its resources effectively. If we were to attempt the support of thousands of infected nonoperatives, while people starved, would that be humane? We must make choices."

"This isn't a choice," Syd objected. "It's a convenience. It's easier to—"

"Ouch!" Marie yelled from the other side of the curtain. "You could warn me before you go poking your fingers into my wound!"

"Stop squirming and we'll get this fixed!" the medic treating her grumbled. "Hold her down."

They heard Marie grunt and exhale loudly. Whatever they were doing to fix her wound, they were not doing it gently. The doctor's eyes darted once to the bolt gun on Liam's belt. Then they went back to Syd. "Let's get you checked out," he said. "To be on the safe side."

"Really, I'm fine," Syd told him, sitting all the way up and dangling his legs off the cot. "I need to go talk to the Council."

The doctor set a hand on his shoulder and stopped him from getting up. "Humor an old doctor. As long as you're here, we might as well make sure everything's in working order, no?"

Syd looked at him. The doctor looked back, unflinching. He was determined to examine Syd and Syd decided the easiest way to get out of here quickly would be to let him. He relented with a nod.

"Please remove your clothes," the doctor instructed.

Syd looked at Liam, cleared his throat. "A little privacy?"

Liam hesitated. Syd pointed.

"I'll be on the other side of the curtain," Liam said.

"Oh, how will we ever bear to be apart?" Syd replied.

"Don't run off again," Liam added.

"Or what?" Syd asked.

An answer formed on Liam's lips, but he didn't say it. Staring at him, Syd could swear his bodyguard mouthed the word "waterfall" to himself, then turned and passed through the curtain.

Once Liam was gone, Syd peeled off his clothes and submitted to an entirely pointless medical exam.

He wasn't sick and he knew it. He was disgusted.

For that, medicine had no cure.

On the other side of the curtain, Liam scanned the room. On the cot, Marie lay staring at the ceiling of the tent, while three medics worked on reconnecting the tissue of her shoulder that his bolt had severed. Although most tech had been banned by the Reconciliation to prevent the germs of greed, sloth, isolationism, and inequality from spreading, medics still had some more advanced items. Left without a little old tech, Marie would never have been able to use her arm again. Liam knew how to disable a person.

Through the medical tent, he saw the vague outlines of the Purifiers moving around as people began to gather. Word must have gotten out that Yovel himself was inside. Liam would have to get Syd away from here as soon as possible. The area wasn't secure enough for his liking and this cadre of Purifiers wasn't well trained enough to contain an overexcited crowd, even if there were no Machinists among them.

The people outside formed an indistinct mass. As the breeze blew the gauzy mosquito netting, it distorted their silhouettes. They bent and twisted, looked like a monstrous horde, like another wave of feral nopes shambling in from the wilderness.

The city was changing so much faster than Liam could process. All his life it had been little more than a military installation and Liam didn't like all these new people coming in. Now that the revolution was the government, they saw fit to rebuild Old Detroit and evacuate Mountain City. The people came in as refugees by the tens of thousands. The streets were cleared of jungle debris and filled with human activity.

And with the people came the nopes.

He'd fought them when they were Guardians, of course. That was part of his job. He'd snuck into the Mountain City and tried to outsmart them, outrun them, and outfight them. They were fearsome opponents. Liam flexed his metal hand. He hadn't always won those fights.

But now they weren't Guardians anymore. They were basically dead already. He'd seen them hauling rocks or turning pistons to power spring loaders. He'd seen them fall from the dam construction project and not even make a sound as they fell. Now they were carrying some new disease. It didn't bother Liam to see them put down. Good riddance.

But it bothered Syd, who had no doubt known them better than Liam ever did, who had suffered at their hands and the hands of the system they enforced far more than Liam ever had. Why should Syd care for them now? Was something wrong with Liam that he didn't?

He glanced over his shoulder to a gap in the curtain. He saw through the sliver Syd's broad brown back, its muscle tight as wire underneath the skin. Along the side of his rib cage, there were burns and scars from a young life that had been filled with wounds, but the untouched places were smooth and almost shone gold in the afternoon light.

Liam had a view of four letters behind Syd's right ear that made the word "Yovel," the mark that branded him the savior. The story was legend now: Syd's long-dead father had implanted baby Syd with a computer virus and sent him off to the Mountain City, an anonymous orphan, his name assigned by a database. He was networked and tracked, his debt was purchased, and he was in the system. But hidden inside the official programming in his blood, his father's virus grew.

When it was ready, when it was mature enough to tear apart the network, erase all the records, sever all connections, it showed a symbol on his skin, that four-letter word just behind his ear, *Yovel*. Jubilee: the day when all debts were forgiven. But Knox, Syd's patron, had been infected too by a blood transfusion, and when they arrived in Old Detroit, he also bore the word behind his ear.

An accident of fate.

So Knox stepped into the machine that spread the virus

from Old Detroit to Mountain City and all the wastelands in between. He let it irradiate him, vaporize him as that bit of code overwhelmed every transmitter, every datastream, and every system. The network went down.

When it was done, Knox was no more than a toxic bit of ash, and Syd's symbol remained, a scar, an echo of the name he'd had and the future he'd been spared.

Liam could only imagine what it felt like to carry that mark and all the rest that went with it. He himself had never been networked, never had biodata installed. He'd been born apart and raised to fight. Having no data made it easier for him to slip in and out of Mountain City undetected. There were times he wondered what it might be like to have access to the datastream, but now it was gone; he was one of the few alive who didn't miss it. He wondered whether Syd missed it.

Liam lost his hand for the revolution, but loss was easy. Addition was hard. How do you become something more than yourself? Inspiring others. Manifesting their dreams. It was a burden Liam was glad not to carry, knew he wasn't strong enough to carry. He preferred his role in history to be small, narrowly defined. Keep Syd safe.

Dr. Rahat ordered Syd to turn and Liam caught his breath as the sinewy chest came into view, the scar across his collarbone from a childhood knife fight, the small trail of hair rising to his belly button, the soft skin of his neck, the dark obsidian shine of his eyes staring back at—

Liam turned away quickly. Studied his boots. He felt himself blushing. Had he been staring? Had Syd *seen* him staring? Why was he staring? Syd was just an assignment, and a difficult one at that. Liam had to remember: an assignment.

Syd mattered to the Reconciliation, so Syd had to be protected. Liam didn't have to feel anything about Syd beyond that.

Shouldn't feel.

Shouldn't. Shouldn't. Shouldn't.

Maybe Syd hadn't noticed the look. Or maybe he figured it was just Liam being cautious, making sure the doctor didn't harm his patient. Machinist assassins everywhere; one can never be too careful.

What an idiot, Liam cursed himself. *Focus on the job. No emotion.*

Waterfall. Waterfall. Waterfall.

He sighed and looked up.

And he met Marie's gaze. Lying on the cot, she looked at him with just the faintest hint of purple still in her eyes. And on her lips, the slightest smirk forming around the edges.

In a moment, Syd stood beside Liam.

"Take me to the Advisory Council," Syd said. "I need to speak to them immediately. And someone should bury the Guardians we left in that alley." He turned to the doctor again. "Bury. Not burn."

The doctor nodded, scratching absently at an itch on his

cheek, and Syd stormed outside. Just before Liam rushed after him, he glanced back at Marie.

"Interesting," Marie said, but Liam didn't have time to say anything back. He had to get Syd through the crowd. That was his job. He had to do his job. Keep Yovel alive. Nothing more and nothing less.

[8]

"YOUR CONCERNS HAVE BEEN noted." The chair of the Advisory Council leaned forward on her kneeling mat and pressed her index fingers together in a triangle. Her voice echoed in the cavernous space of the empty factory.

She looked from Syd, seated on his own mat before the semicircle of Advisory Council members in the center of the factory floor, to Liam, kneeling beside him with his hands folded in his lap. Unlike Syd and the eighteen counselors, Liam did not have a mat to kneel on and the hard floor pressed into his knees. Beads of sweat collected on his upper lip, and he could feel several more making a mad dash for escape down his back.

Behind the Council, a ring of white-masked Purifiers stood with their clubs hanging from their belts, ready to do the Council's violence, should such violence be called for, or to protect them, should such protection become necessary.

"I don't just want my concerns noted," Syd objected. "I want them heard!"

"And we *hear* them," Chairwoman Pei responded, her voice hard as stone. She was not accustomed to argument from teenagers during her Council meetings. "Your concern for the nonoperative entities speaks greatly of your compassion, but poorly of your intellect. Nonoperatives are not people and thus, cannot be—what did you call it?"

"Murdered," Syd said.

"Can livestock be murdered?" a counselor to Syd's left mused aloud. "Can feral cats be murdered?"

"The Guardians were born people," said Syd. "The old system transformed them. They're as much victims as any of the proxies you've trained to kill them."

"Mind your tone," Chairwoman Pei snapped.

"I'm just saying, it's not right to kill them like that."

"There is no right or wrong with nonoperative entities," the chairwoman replied.

"If I may," Counselor Baram, kneeling just to the chairwoman's left, interrupted. She glared at him. There was no love lost between Counselor Baram and Chairwoman Pei, that was plain to see. Baram addressed Syd without looking at her again. "The nopes—as some have taken to calling them—have no volition. They cannot act with any intention of their own; they cannot think for themselves, or speak, or even recognize themselves in a mirror. There is no definition of personhood that can be applied to them. They may have been born like other people, but they are no longer. It is a mercy for us to end their suffering."

"I wonder if they would agree," said Syd.

"They can neither agree nor disagree," said Baram.

"So that, like, makes it okay to kill them?" Syd wished he had Baram's way with words. He never was great at arguing. "Because they can't complain?"

"Because they never knew they were alive to begin with," Baram countered.

"How do you know?" Syd asked.

"We will not sit here and argue philosophy with a teenager," the chairwoman snapped at Syd. "We decide the best course of action for society and our decision is made."

"But there are other ways than killing them!" Syd pleaded. "You can look for a cure for what's wrong with them, but you don't want to. It's more convenient to get rid of them because they remind everyone of the past. And the Reconciliation is all about the future, right?"

"And what is wrong with looking to the future?" another counselor asked.

"You can't just erase the past," said Syd.

"You assume the worst of us, Sydney," said Baram. "We have worked on a cure, but found none. For the safety of all, extermination of the nonoperatives is the only viable solution."

"It can't be," Syd said. "Do you even know what's wrong with them? Do any of you even care?"

"We have done our best to find a cure!" a counselor

whose name Syd couldn't remember blurted out. "And all our researcher found was Machinist propaganda and—"

"Pardon, Counselor," the chairwoman interrupted the man with a clap of her hands.

The offending counselor blushed and hung his head. The chairwoman nodded over her shoulder and two Purifiers stepped forward.

"You are tired and speak against protocol," she told him. "Perhaps you should rest."

"I . . . I . . ." The counselor turned pale, looking around the semicircle in wide-eyed panic, but before he could say another word, he was lifted from his place and dragged away into the darkness beyond the circle.

Syd knew he would not be seen again.

"You may not think we are doing the right thing by eliminating these entities." The chairwoman turned back to Syd. "But it is not up to you. We make the determinations that are best for society. These determinations are not made by seventeen-year-olds."

"So a cure isn't good for society?" Syd pressed.

"A cure is not politically viable at this time," the chairwoman replied. "And our discussion of this is over. Our decision is final."

"The Purifiers enjoyed the slaughter," Syd said.

"Purifiers take no personal enjoyment in their duties." Chairwoman Pei recited dogma of the Reconciliation. "Their joy comes from service and it is a joy shared by all. A joy you would be wise to embrace."

Syd's jaw clenched. He looked to the shadowy figures of

the Purifiers, couldn't make out Finch, and felt some relief. If the Council wouldn't do anything about their policy with the nopes, he could bring at least one person to justice today. He would denounce his old classmate. It wasn't much, but at least he'd be doing something. "I know of one Purifier who takes personal joy in cruelty."

"If so," the chairwoman said, "then he'll be brought in for self-criticism."

Syd nodded. "His name was Atticus Finch; now he calls himself Furious. I used to know him at school. Before. He was laughing when he slaughtered the Guardians."

"Nonoperatives," one of the counselors corrected.

"That's all?" The chairwoman rubbed her hands. "Laughter? Laughter is not a crime."

"But you just said—" Syd clenched his fists. It was clear she had no intention of pursuing the matter. Syd glanced at Liam, who tried to shake his head.

"No," said Syd. He heard Liam sigh. "Finch—er, Furious, he also attacked me. Threatened to kill me. I think *that* is a crime."

A gasp rippled around the room. The eyes of the Council then shifted to Liam.

"This is a serious accusation," Baram said. "Treason."

Syd's hands went clammy. The punishment for treason was death. He wanted Finch transferred, humiliated, maybe even hurt a little, but he didn't want him killed. He'd spoken rashly; he'd gotten mad.

"Is this true?" the chairwoman asked Liam.

Liam nodded.

"And where were you at the time this attack took place?"

Liam tensed. In the shadowy heights of the catwalk above the factory floor, a lone figure in green leaned casually against the railing and watched. His perfectly bald head caught a gleam of light in the darkness. Liam pictured the sweat on his back turning into razor-sharp icicles.

"It's not Liam's fault," Syd broke in. "I'm the one who—"

"Each of us must answer for our own failings and Liam will answer for his," Chairwoman Pei cut Syd off.

"I have no excuse," said Liam, keeping his eyes down.

"And you do realize, young man, that the life of Yovel is of vital symbolic importance to our efforts, do you not?"

Liam looked up, but dared not meet her eyes. Instead, he looked at the folds of her neck, the green banded collar of her uniform with eight vertical white stripes around it, signifying her place on the Council.

What the Council was going to do to him for letting Syd be attacked, he couldn't know. In denouncing Finch, Syd had really denounced Liam for failing to protect him. And failure was never tolerated. It could lead to reassignment to a work camp; it could lead to a public whipping; it could lead to a sudden and permanent disappearance. The Advisory Council was unpredictable.

Unpredictability was, in fact, a tenet of their philosophy. They claimed that it strengthened the revolution. A storm cannot be bribed nor can a flash flood be infiltrated. The Reconciliation modeled itself on natural disaster.

Lightning strikes might have been more predictable.

Before they did what they would with him, Liam figured he could, at least, let Syd know whose side he was on, whose side he'd always been on.

He took a deep breath.

"He goes by Syd," Liam said.

"Excuse me?" Chairwoman Pei lowered her hands to her lap.

"With respect, Chairwoman." Liam cleared his throat. "He prefers to be called Syd."

The chairwoman's eyes darted to Syd. Syd too looked at Liam with surprise.

"Yovel was the name given him by his late father in service of the revolution," the chairwoman said. "Sydney is the name given him by the patrons of the old system. It is his proxy name. The Reconciliation does not recognize these names."

Liam shrugged. He gave Syd a small smile.

Syd knew what he had done. Chairwoman Pei, as leader of the Advisory Council, could order the death of almost anyone for almost any reason.

Anyone except, of course, Syd.

He'd been angry and felt helpless and wanted to punish Finch for how he felt. Instead, he'd punished Liam.

"Syd is my name," he announced. He put himself between Liam and Chairwoman Pei. "It's the only name I've known and I intend to keep it."

"I understand you feel attached to this name," the chairwoman told him. "But we are a new organization now, with new structures, and new expectations. Your personal preferences must be subordinate to the needs of all. Your stubbornness undermines what we are trying to build. If the people are to abandon faith in the return of the networks, if we are to stamp out these Machinist cults, then the people must believe in something else. They must believe in *our* symbols. In Yovel."

"I never asked to be your symbol. I'm seventeen. I just want to be like everyone else my age."

"Everyone else your age obeys the advice of the Council!" The chairwoman threw her arms in the air. "We have countless seventeen-year-olds in our ranks—Liam, here, is seventeen. He obeys. The Purifier you are so quick to denounce, he obeys too! Why should we expect different from you?"

"Because"—Syd cleared his throat—"like you said, you need me. I'm of vital symbolic importance."

A few counselors shifted uncomfortably on their knees. Syd might have been just a teenaged boy, but to many of them, he was still Yovel, the savior, and they didn't like to see him get a public scolding.

Chairwoman Pei, for her part, appeared to relish the opportunity. Syd knew by the way she adjusted her posture that she was fighting the urge to have him beaten to death by the Purifiers behind her. Teenagers were moody and demanding. The chairwoman would certainly have preferred a martyr to a flesh-and-blood teen.

"Anyway, what happened with Finch today wasn't Liam's fault," said Syd. "I snuck away from him. I—" Syd had to find the right words here, the words that would undo the damage he'd done by letting his anger cloud his judgment. He had to get Liam out of the bind he'd put him in and had, in spite of himself, to keep them from executing Finch. Syd didn't like having a bodyguard around all the time, but no one deserved to die for it. "I shouldn't have let myself get dragged into a petty argument with a Purifier. I provoked Finch and I deserved to be hit for it. It wasn't treason. Just settling an old score. No real damage was done."

"You provoked him?" The chairwoman looked skeptical. "Yovel provoked a Purifier?"

Syd nodded.

Behind Syd, Liam pressed his good hand into his leg, willing Syd to stop talking. Syd was stubborn and opinionated, and he didn't realize that the chairwoman could always find ways to make him suffer. She couldn't hurt him, but she could make his days very uncomfortable and it would be Liam who would have to enforce her will. That way, both of them were punished.

Syd would hate Liam for whatever the chairwoman made him do, but Liam would have to do it, or he'd be removed from Syd's protection assignment. And he knew that wherever Syd was was where he wanted to be. He couldn't help it. He was just like the people from the crowd. In spite of himself, he was a believer.

"Is this what happened?" Chairwoman Pei asked Liam.

To her left, Counselor Baram knelt quietly, watching Liam with an expression that expressed nothing.

"I can't say," said Liam. "I only saw the end of it."

"Liam didn't do anything wrong," Syd said again. "He—"

Chairwoman Pei raised her arm, demanding silence. "Your objections have been heard, and your testimony noted. In spite of our better judgment, no action shall be taken against this Purifier. Next time you make an accusation, you best make sure you are prepared. That is all. You will be escorted to a billet for the evening."

"I—" Syd looked over to Counselor Baram, who shook his head ever so slightly, a small warning to Syd not to push it any further. Two more Purifiers stepped behind Syd. It was not an idle suggestion that he accompany them. "And Liam?" Syd asked, looking to his bodyguard kneeling on the floor.

Liam didn't look back up at him.

The chairwoman smiled without opening her lips.

"He'll be along shortly," Counselor Baram said as Syd was led from the room.

The moment the metal doors closed behind Syd, the chairwoman fixed her steely gaze on Liam, but it was Counselor Baram who spoke:

"Liam, you have failed, on several occasions now, to maintain watch over *Sydney*." The chairwoman scowled.

Baram cleared his throat. "You allowed him to get into a scuffle with a Purifier. In public. Then you shot another Purifier for no apparent reason. Does something have you distracted?"

"Nothing has me distracted, Counselor," he said.

"Maybe some private thoughts?" Counselor Baram studied him with eyebrows raised. Liam's mouth felt dry. He imagined a holo floating above his head, projecting his every doubt, regret, and desire for all to see. Private thoughts, which kept an individual apart from the community, had also been banned.

Liam shook his head. "My feelings and thoughts belong to the Reconciliation, to which I devote myself fully."

"Purifier Alvarez," Chairwoman Pei barked and suddenly, Marie stepped forward. Liam's heart thudded in his chest. "Do you have any reason to doubt the statement you have heard given to the Council? Do you accept Liam's statement and forgive him for the wound he inflicted on you?"

Liam did not look at her. With one word, she could condemn him. She had caught him looking at Syd. Of course, it didn't mean what she thought it did. He was just a believer. That was all. Nothing more.

But still, he *had* been looking. She knew he had been looking. She knew *how* he had been looking. Private thoughts were hard to keep that way.

"I have no doubts, Counselor," Marie answered. "He did his duty without hesitation or regard for himself. He shot me because to do otherwise would have compromised his duty. If anyone is at fault, it is I, who did not approach my own task with the discipline it required. I am sorry and submit to the mercy of the Council."

Liam exhaled a breath he hadn't realized he was holding. The cavernous factory was silent. After an endless moment, the chairwoman rose and the rest of the Council rose with her.

"This inquiry is complete," she said. "Liam, you will remain at your post . . . for now. Do not fail again. Yovel—" She stopped herself and glanced at Counselor Baram. "*Sydney's* safety is of paramount importance in these troubled times. No more mistakes."

"Yes, Counselor," said Liam, remaining on his knees on the floor with his head bowed.

"As for you, Purifier Alvarez." The chairwoman pointed to Marie. "Your service until now has been exemplary and your role in the success of the Jubilee has not been forgotten. For that reason, you will be forgiven by the Reconciliation. You have disappointed yourself, however, have you not?"

"Yes, Counselor," said Marie. "I have."

"And?"

Liam heard Marie let out the slightest sigh. "And I will gladly surrender half my rations to purge the disappointment from myself." The silence when Marie finished speaking lingered in the air. The Council did not move. "And half the rations of my parents," Marie added. "Who raised me as a greedy decadent patron and therefore bear the shame of my failure as well."

The chairwoman gave one curt nod of approval and left the factory floor, with the rest of the Advisory Council departing in other directions, through other doors, until Marie and Liam were alone.

Liam stood and turned to her.

"I don't know what to say," Liam started. "I guess owe you."

"You don't owe me anything," she snapped at him, her voice barely containing its rage. "Debts are an outdated way of thinking."

"Still . . ."

"Just do your job," she said. "Keep Syd safe." She swept by him and made her own way out into the emerald sunlight of early evening in the jungle city.

"You have no idea how much I want to," Liam said to himself. If only Syd would let him.

[9]

THEY MOVED SYD TO a new room every few nights. He'd slept in old factories and new barracks. He'd slept in a hovercraft and once, under the stars with nothing but a heat blanket.

Tonight's place was the worst yet. Punishment, he was certain, for his disobedience and argumentativeness. He'd heard it a thousand times. His safety was of vital importance to the Reconciliation. His freedom, he understood, was not.

He was in an old school building, and from what he could tell, his room must have been some kind of storage space. There were no windows; the walls were bare concrete, and the door was locked from the outside.

He had a mat, his cot, a side table, a chair, and a water basin. His bathroom was a bucket behind a screen in the corner. He leaned against the wall, with his legs stretched out on his cot, his shoes still on, and his finger absently tapping on the letters behind his ear.

Locked in for the night, he had nothing to do. No holo projector—holos had been banned and there was no network to watch them on anyway; no books—they were hard to come by even before the Jubilee. Nothing to do but sleep.

He was too wound up to sleep.

He couldn't believe what he'd seen at the rally. The Guardians couldn't even fight back as the Purifiers slaughtered them. And the people, *his* people, cheered. No one defended the Guardians. No one would face justice for killing them. They were extraneous people now, lost, living on in a world that had no use for them. They were sick and no one would try to cure them. When they died, no one would mourn them.

A cure is not politically viable? A fancy way of saying no one cared. The suffering of the nonoperative entities was not a priority.

But what choice had they ever had? They weren't the ones who'd programmed themselves and they weren't the ones who'd shut that programming down.

That was Syd. Well, Knox, on Syd's behalf.

Syd wondered why people always abandoned the things they broke. The Guardians were broken and no one was trying to fix them. Back in the Valve, he'd worked in a repair shop, fixing the machines that others had discarded. He could fix anything back then. Now most of what he knew how to fix was gone, and most of what was broken he'd been the one to break.

It's your future. Choose.

He stared at the bare concrete wall. A giant crack ran along it from the floor to the ceiling, zigzagging like a canyon through the desert.

The desert.

He shut his eyes.

Just a few months ago—six months and three days to be exact—he'd left Mountain City and crossed the desert. He'd had friends with him then, Egan, whom he'd known since they were in the orphanage together, and Knox, who had been his patron for about as long, but whom he'd only known in person since he'd tried to buy fake ID off him in a club. Marie came along later, a Causegirl with big ideas about tearing down the unjust system of Proxies and Patrons. She believed in the Jubilee before Syd ever did and she'd have done anything for it. She did do anything for it.

There were also some smugglers from the Maes gang, real criminals, whose only plan was to get paid.

Syd hadn't wanted to change the world, just his own little piece of it. But it cost him, cost them all.

Knox's father killed Marie's proxy, an innocent girl whose only crime was being poor.

One of the Maes bandits killed Egan, whose only crime was being poor and stupid. Well, no, actually Egan had plenty of crimes, but still . . . nothing he deserved to die for.

So Syd killed the bandit who killed his friend. He could

still see her face, sneering, mocking Egan, crumpling dead at Syd's feet. Her face haunted him. She deserved to die. Of course she did. If anyone deserved to die it was her.

But still, Syd saw her face. And the face of the assassin this morning.

It was self-defense.

Each of them died so that Syd would live.

But still . . . what made their lives worth less than his? Or Finch's? Or the nopes? Credit and debt might have been wiped away, but the old rules still applied. A person was judged by their value, their life set against some fixed worth. Those who were useful, like Syd, were worth more than those who were not, like the nopes. Death wasn't an arbitrary event. It was an expression of value. The nopes were worth less. Worthless.

What about Knox? Was Knox's life worth more because at the end, he'd sacrificed himself willingly? Was life the kind of thing that gained value by giving it away? Knox, who had spent his whole life being a thoughtless knock-off patron, in that one moment, found his worth. Syd couldn't help but feel he was letting Knox down, that it was he himself who was worthless.

Marie wasn't much help, even if she was the closest thing Syd had to a friend. She was always gone on some Purifier assignment, proudly wearing the green and white. She submitted herself willingly and completely to the new system, which allowed her to protect her parents from execution for the crime of having once been rich.

Syd had arranged, on her behalf, for her parents to be sent to a farming cooperative in the desert where they would receive reeducation, as if trying to harvest food from sand would teach them to forget their comfortable past, as if memory could be erased by suffering. In Syd's experience, suffering only made memory stronger.

And vice versa.

But her parents were alive, at least. Marie got to see them. She even kept her old name as a reminder to others that, under the new system, even patrons could be reformed. Her friendship with Syd gave her that privilege. The Reconciliation couldn't exactly disappear their savior's only friend because they didn't like her name. And besides, she was a good Purifier. Competent and thorough, with unwavering faith in the new ideas.

Syd couldn't care less about the new ideas. He just wanted to be left to himself, but being "Yovel" made that impossible. He wasn't cut out for this savior-of-the-people business. He was just Syd.

He banged the back of his head against the wall, tapped his finger on the spot behind his ear, mouthed the word to himself.

Yo-vel.

It didn't even sound like a name. It was a reminder of the destiny he didn't want and that he hadn't fulfilled. It was a reminder of what Knox had done for him.

He wished he could forget.

That day of Jubilee, when the system broke down, Knox's

father wept in front of the machine where Knox's body had been vaporized. The man's wealth, all his power, and the last of his family gone in a flash.

Chaos followed.

Syd stood with Marie, shocked, uncertain, not knowing what came next.

Old Mr. Baram, though, he knew. He'd raised Syd, as much as anyone had, all the while expecting that one day Syd would have to give his life so that the revolution could triumph.

Now that Syd lived, Baram had a new idea.

He sealed the factory as the battle outside wound down. Without the network, combatbots shut off, drones crashed from the sky, and the Guardians stopped in place, their minds instantly blank. Nonoperative. Without the network, there was no way to transmit orders and no one to follow the orders anyway. Regular people didn't fight for free and there was no way to pay them. The entire financial system was gone. Deletion was almost instantaneous.

Baram immediately ordered complete secrecy about what had taken place with Knox and Syd and the machine.

"Syd destroyed the networks." Mr. Baram commanded the room, his voice booming from beneath his thick gray beard. "It was Syd, in the face of great resistance, who broke the corporate systems, who erased all debts and deleted the data that held us all in chains for so long. It was Syd—Yovel, as his father named him—who brought us victory, brought us to this new era. It is Year Zero now. We begin again. We begin again, thanks to This. Boy. Here. *Yovel.* Understood?"

Cheers could be heard through the broken windows. Syd could only imagine what the millions in Mountain City were thinking now that all their networks were gone. The patrons would be terrified. Would Knox's friends have any idea what their old pal had done? Would they even notice the network was down, or would they all be too tweaked to notice, partying at some lux Upper City club?

What would all the proxies and the other slum rats think? They were just as networked as the rich. Everyone was networked. Everyone *had* been networked.

Each soldier in the room consented to Baram's instructions one by one. Even Marie, teary eyed, consented.

Syd did not consent.

"Knox died for me," Syd said, choking on the words. He kept his eyes on the machine where Knox had stood minutes before. His friend had winked at him. There was nothing left of him now. The radiation it took to spread the virus through the system had vaporized him. "He died for all of us."

"And we will always know that." Mr. Baram turned to comfort him, but Syd hadn't wanted comfort. "To build a new society, we need new symbols. *You* will be our new symbol. You. Not Knox. It cannot be Knox."

"But—"

"No," Mr. Baram cut Syd off. "The people will need something to believe in. We are taking away all they have ever known. People will be frightened. They need to turn somewhere and they cannot turn to the memory of a dead patron. They cannot turn to any of the old elite for hope. They *must* turn to us, you understand? To *our* symbols. We need them to believe in the world we will create, if we have any hope of creating a better one. *You* will be that hope."

Syd looked back into Mr. Baram's eyes, but he did not see kindness there. The eyes were fixed, penetrating, and firm. This was not an argument Syd could win. His consent was not even necessary.

He couldn't say the words, but he nodded. Mr. Baram patted his shoulder.

"Good boy," he said. "Good."

Syd's mouth twisted, fighting back tears.

"*God gives burdens, but also shoulders,*" said Mr. Baram.

"What?" Syd cocked his head at the old man.

Mr. Baram cleared his throat. "Just an old line from an old book. You could mourn your whole life if you let yourself, Sydney, but you're stronger than that. It's time for the future."

"Ha!" A cutting laugh exploded from Knox's father, who was pressed to his knees, his face still wet with tears. "Some future! This trash is your symbol? Your whole revolution stands on my son's corpse and now you pile it high with lies? You're doomed, Baram! This boy"—he spat at Syd—"always did live in my son's shadow. He's nothing. He's nobody. And he never, ever will be. You'll fail, Baram. You and your empty symbol will fail."

"Eeron Brindle," Mr. Baram said. "You are under arrest

as an enemy of the people. You are charged with the exploitation of debt, with the abuses of the SecuriTech Corporation, and the crimes of every single—"

"You can't reboot humanity." Knox's father talked over Mr. Baram, indifferent to the charges that had just been made against him. "There's no 'year zero.' No starting over." His bitter laughter sounded almost like choking. Knox's father looked at Syd with the same bright green eyes his son had, those green eyes that had winked good-bye the moment before he died. But his father did not wink. His lips pulled back to show the perfect white of his perfect teeth. Even though his hands were pinned behind his back, he seemed to point an accusation right at Syd.

"Your symbol's not even a real man, you know that?" he said. "He'd rather be kissing my dead son's ashes than leading your pathetic revolution of moochers and thieves and—"

A metal fist smashed across Knox's father's face, toppling him forward onto the concrete, blood dribbling from his mouth. He'd lost a few teeth from the blow and his glasses skittered across the floor. He breathed, but did not get up. Over him, metal fist still clenched, stood the boy with the cropped red hair and sad puppy eyes, the boy that Syd would come to know as Liam.

Mr. Baram nodded his approval.

From that moment on, Liam had been assigned as Syd's personal bodyguard.

The lie went out from that factory and became the truth

through repetition: Syd was the people's hero. There was no datastream anymore, so if anyone doubted it, they had no way to share their doubts very far. And no one, really, had any reason to doubt it. Who would imagine that a spoiled brat like Knox Brindle, scion of SecuriTech, would die for his proxy, let alone for some proxy's cause?

The new organization was no longer the Rebooters. They called themselves the Reconciliation and their cadres crossed the desert and entered Mountain City. People were so disoriented at the loss of their datastreams that they put up no resistance. The Reconciliation thickened its ranks from the slums and marched up into the high-rises and mansions of the Upper City. They rounded up the patrons. They rounded up the corporate middlemen and the collaborators. They rounded up any enemies they could find and they settled old scores.

All with the name Yovel on their lips.

Syd pressed the bases of his palms into his eyes, remembering, not wanting to remember.

With eyes closed, he saw the Guardians hacked to pieces, their skin webbed black with veins. He saw Finch gleefully tearing them apart and the crowd cheering him on. The bald man strolled through the slaughter. The pictures popped up unwanted, like old advos in the datastream that you couldn't turn off, but they weren't selling him anything. They were accusing him.

It's your future. Choose.

He'd let the Guardians be murdered. Some savior he

was. No one cared about them. Call them nopes and erase them. Call him Yovel and exalt him. What was the difference really? It was all the same kind of forgetting.

He took deep breaths. He wanted to sleep. At least in sleeping, he could find a kind of peace. At least in sleeping, he could dream about his dead friends and maybe, until the sun came up, feel like he wasn't all alone.

He slept and in his sleep he was still alone.

[10]

OUTSIDE SYD'S DOOR, LIAM stood at attention. Although the entire building was a restricted area, he still felt the need to be vigilant. He couldn't disappoint the Council again. Even if Syd hated him for controlling his every movement, at least he'd be safe. That was all that mattered.

Liam wondered, though, whether that was true, whether he was being honest with himself. Did he want to protect Syd because he was important to the society they were trying to build, or did he want to protect Syd because of some childish fantasy? Was he a believer or was it something . . . else? If Syd lived and hated Liam, did it matter if Syd lived?

Of course it matters, he told himself. *This is exactly why you cannot have these feelings. They are a distraction. You're a soldier. Act like it.*

He snapped himself back to attention. The Machinists

might make another move on Syd at any time. Their fantasy of a machine that could turn the networks back on, restore the data, and undo the entire revolution might be crazy, but crazies were the most dangerous. They didn't care about consequences. They just knew that Syd had broken the networks, so Syd's death should bring them back. It didn't have to be logical to be deadly.

There were other dangers too. That Purifier Syd denounced might want another shot at him. Part of Liam hoped so. It was forbidden, but he'd take his own personal pleasure in neutralizing a petty knock-off thug like Furious Finch.

But professional vigilance wasn't the only reason Liam had to remain alert. He knew, in spite of the restrictions on this building and the secrecy under which Syd was kept, that he was not alone.

Cousin was surely watching.

That exact moment, as if conjured from the vapor of Liam's thoughts, the hairless man appeared in a shaft of moonlight at the end of the hallway.

He moved silently, but he made no effort to conceal his approach. Liam felt as if Cousin's shadow on the wall had more substance than the man himself. Cousin's hands were clasped behind his back and his green uniform was crisp and spotless. His collar was a solid band of white, like a halo around his neck lighting his smooth face. His thin lips were pursed and the folds above his eyes, where his eyebrows would have been, were raised in an expression of amusement.

"Brother Liam," he said, his voice smooth as a python

slithering across the moss. "A most informative Advisory Council discussion this afternoon, no?"

Liam didn't answer. Cousin was goading him, of course. That's how Cousin was.

Liam exhaled through his nose and waited. He tried not to look frightened, but Cousin's presence always frightened him. He hated to be near the man.

No one knew Cousin's age or his origins, or even his real name. He'd arrived just after the victory of the Rebooters, when they became the Reconciliation, and he had immediately made himself useful.

"My past doesn't matter," he had explained, kneeling before the newly formed Advisory Council. "I am here to serve the future."

They too were trying to erase the past, so they took him in. Cousin answered only to the Advisory Council. He had special assignments and obscure duties, some of which Liam knew, and a few of which Liam shared. Even though they had worked together for months now, Cousin still filled Liam with a cold dread. Regular people feared the Purifiers; the Purifiers feared Liam, and Liam, as much as he hated to admit it, feared Cousin.

Cousin rested a hand on Liam's shoulder. It was surprisingly delicate and strangely small for such a tall man. Liam did his best not to flinch.

Cousin smirked. He stared directly at Liam and his pupils seemed too large, like his eyes had no color at all, just black discs in an orb of white. The tiny red veins in the eyes and the slight weathering of the skin around them were the only hints that Cousin was, indeed, human.

"Our young hero shows great concern for the fate of the nonoperatives," Cousin observed. "If only he showed such concern for the fate of his bodyguard, eh?" He brushed Liam's shoulder and then rested his hand against the door to Syd's room. "You could have been punished terribly for letting him run off this morning. Do you think Syd would swoon to see you destroyed like he did for those nopes?"

Cousin spoke just loudly enough for Liam to wonder whether Syd could hear him through the door, but just quietly enough that it didn't seem deliberate.

Liam shrugged.

"One would think mistakes like today's would be impossible." Cousin smiled. "Given how closely you watch him."

"It's over," said Liam. "I made a mistake. I confessed to it."

"I have always been more interested in silences than in confessions," said Cousin.

Liam kept his mouth shut.

Cousin laughed, his face pulling away from his big white teeth. His smile was indistinguishable from a grimace. "I do appreciate your sense of humor!"

He patted Liam on the back, sucking air in through his teeth.

Looking at Cousin's face for too long conjured violent fantasies in Liam. It was the kind of face that made a person want to throw a punch. Liam took a deep breath, thought of the waterfall, emotion flowing down and away.

"We've work to do tonight," Cousin told him. He waved his hand and a holo projection appeared in the air in front of him.

Cousin was one of the few who was still allowed to use the old technology. While there was no network anymore, some databases had been rebuilt for the Reconciliation's own purposes: recorded messages, propaganda broadcasts, surveillance. Liam was allowed to look, but not to touch.

Like so much else in his life.

The image floating in the air before him showed a woman in profile. She had long flowing braids of dark, wiry hair. Her skin was black as the smoke of burning cities. She wore a white smock over her green uniform, her hands were sealed in blue synthetic gloves, and she was working on a collection of holo projections in the air in front of her. She paused, looked straight out of the projection and spoke.

"My name is Dr. Adaeze Khan, and if you are receiving—" she began and Liam detected a Nigerian accent, but then the holo jolted and wobbled; the loop began again. She was working, focused. She turned, looked out, smiled. "My name is Dr. Adaeze Khan, and if you are receiving—" The loop started again. Cousin let it play.

"Dr. Khan," Cousin said. "Reboot High Command, now a chief medical supervisor for the Reconciliation."

"My name is Dr. Adaeze Khan, and if you are receiving—"

Liam cleared his throat. "Why her?"

"Tsk, tsk." Cousin wagged his finger in the air.

"I don't recognize her," he said.

"Curiosity is a form of greed, young Liam." Cousin sighed with mock theatricality. "Acquisitiveness is a thing of the past. We do not lust for material wealth nor do we lust for information we do not require."

"You don't need to quote dogma at me," Liam answered. "I was there when it was written. *You* weren't."

Cousin's face broke again into a smile. "The past is past. Only the future matters now. A future where no one is more privileged than anyone else. Even those who were there at the beginning."

Liam clenched his jaw. He wouldn't argue. Cousin didn't care about the ideological purity of the revolution. He just liked to argue.

"Done already?" Cousin shook his head. "You won't deploy that rapier wit of yours for a parry?" He glanced back to Syd's locked door, ran one thin finger along the frame. "Or do you prefer the thrust to the parry?"

Liam glowered. Why did he alone among the Reconciliation have to suffer Cousin's sense of humor?

"As you wish." Cousin shrugged. He hitched his thumb over his shoulder. "Shall we be on our way?"

"I can't leave my post." Liam turned his face forward, stood at attention again. He'd been raised a soldier. When he felt insecure, he turned back to his training. It was as good a faith as any. Head forward, shoulders back, feet together. The appearance of confidence produced confidence.

"You have a job to do with me now, Liam," Cousin scolded. "This is not an invitation. It is an order."

"My job is to protect Syd and my orders come from the Advisory Council." He didn't turn his eyes to look at Cousin, but from the edge of his vision, he saw the man's pale pink tongue moisten his nearly invisible lips. He stiffened his neck.

"Doctor Khan is part of those orders."

"She wasn't there," said Liam. "I would recognize her if she had been in the factory that day."

"She helped to design the system," said Cousin. "With Syd's late father."

Liam tried not to react.

"You understand?" Cousin asked.

He nodded.

Cousin rubbed his chin as if he were scratching a beard. His face was as smooth as a child's. Youthful bright too. "You see how fond I am of you, Liam? I violated all my revolutionary principles telling you more than you needed to know. Do I ever get a thank-you?"

At last, Liam turned his head to look at Cousin. He clenched his natural fist and felt the fingernails dig into the palm of his hand. He looked at Syd's door.

Cousin whistled and two white-masked Purifiers appeared at the end of the hall. They marched loudly forward, their boots thumping.

"Can they be trusted?" Liam asked.

"As much as anyone," said Cousin. "They're the ones who brought him back here while you had your little chat with the Council."

The Purifiers flanked Syd's door and stood at attention. Liam gave them each a hard once-over. Then he reached out with his metal hand and snatched the white hood off the first Purifier. A pock-faced boy of about sixteen with a nasty scar running across his forehead. Liam nodded at him and pulled the mask off the other. A girl of about the same age, her head shaved. She set her mouth in a frown.

"The hood of the Purifier is a symbol that the individual is not the—" she recited.

"Shut it," Liam snapped. "Now I know you. Both of you. No one else can know where Yovel is staying. If anything goes wrong . . . I will see you again but you will not see me, understood?"

The boy nodded. The girl nodded.

"I'll be back soon," he said and he let Cousin lead him down the hall to the metal exit stairway.

"You enjoy that, don't you?" Cousin asked as they walked away.

Liam refused to answer. He pushed his way outside into the humid night air of the jungle-crusted city.

Cousin took a deep breath and puffed his cheeks out as he exhaled. Liam stood by his side and listened. It was well past curfew. The only sound was the background buzz of the jungle at night.

"Oh yes." Cousin exhaled. "I do love the silences."

He strolled off and Liam followed. There was no real rush. Doctor Adaeze Khan would not be expecting them.

[11]

THE MEETINGS DIDN'T ALWAYS go this late. The large tent in the middle of the barren field glowed and even from a distance, Marie could see that it was packed with people. The tent was the only point of light for miles and she kept stumbling on the dark furrows of dirt as she made her way toward it. One step into a muddy irrigation pit nearly sucked her boot off her foot. Another stumble and she scraped the palm of her hand on a jagged rock.

She squeezed her hand into the cloth of her uniform to clean the small wound and to stop the bleeding. It stung, but she stifled the urge to curse. Even when she was alone, she tried to obey the new guidance about forbidden words. It wasn't arbitrary that many of the old words were outlawed, and it wasn't merely for the Advisory Council to assert itself. They were scholars, after all, and they were attempting to use their understanding to reshape society.

Language formed the world, and if they could reform language, they could reform thought. The new minds that would blossom within the people would never again drift back to corruption and greed. A society would be born based on mutual concern and shared sacrifice. No one would even think to exploit anyone else; they wouldn't even have the words to conceive of the idea.

Marie believed this. She did her best to believe this.

The walk out to the farming cooperative had taken hours, her arm still aching, although the medics had repaired it so well it would barely scar where Liam had shot her. By the time she got out to the co-op, she expected the meeting would be over and she'd planned to find her parents in their barracks.

When she arrived, the barracks were empty, save for one young Purifier, napping against a motorized tractor. His green uniform was far too large for him. It hung like a blouse off his shoulders. He'd taken his white mask off to use the thick material as a pillow. He didn't hear her approach over the whoosh of the wind turbines until she stood directly above him.

When he pointed Marie on her way toward the meeting tent, he shook like a leaf and tried to throw his mask back on at the same time. It ended up backward and he twisted and turned it, frantically stretching the fabric until he was peering with one eye out of the mouth hole.

"Thank you, friend," she told him. "I didn't mean to startle you. If you need to rest, rest. The Reconciliation does not need your exhaustion."

The boy nodded and got his mask right. His eyes were wide and damp through the eyeholes. Marie felt certain he would not be sleeping on duty again tonight. Often a reminder that they served a cause greater than themselves was enough to bring most of the young Purifiers in line. All but Marie had been proxies for some spoiled brats under the old system. It amazed her that they were not all as committed as she to the new way of things. Further proof that the Advisory Council was right: The old ways of thinking had to be purged if there was any hope for the future.

"What's your name, Purifier?"

"Tom Sa—" he said, then caught himself, cleared his throat. "I mean, my name is Arik the Destroyer."

Marie stifled a laugh. Some of the names these kids chose for themselves. Not that she should judge. Not everyone had the luxury of keeping their old name. In truth, the boy looked more like a Tom than an "Arik the Destroyer," but perhaps he'd grow into the name by the time he had hair under his arms. She nodded and went on her way, leaving the boy standing nervously alone in the dark.

As she grew closer, Marie saw that everyone from the co-op was crammed on uncomfortable salvage benches beneath the blazing lights of the big tent.

She saw the lead Purifier of the co-op standing in the front of the room, addressing a man in tattered slacks and a filthy open jacket—what would have no doubt once been fine clothes in Mountain City. He wore no shirt underneath the jacket and his skin had a sickly yellow color, the heavy blue lines of his veins showing through. He stood beside the Purifier with his head bowed, scratching at his arms and bare chest, scraping angry red lines into his skin.

As she drew nearer, the desert wind that turned the turbines carried the conversation to her ears.

"If we had not caught you, would you have stolen food from the central kitchen?" the Purifier demanded.

The man nodded. He would have.

"What would you like to say to your friends?" The Purifier gestured over the crowded tent.

The man coughed and began to speak in a hoarse voice.

The Purifier beside him raised a hand to stop him.

"Louder, friend," he said. "A confession should be made with confidence . . . unless you do not believe the words you speak?"

"I believe what I say," the man confirmed. He cleared his throat and straightened his back. With great effort, he spoke, loudly enough for his voice to carry all the way to the rear of the large tent:

"I apologize to each of you and to the Reconciliation, which I have betrayed with my covetous thoughts. My intention to steal food came from my past as an executive with Birla Nanotech, when I would profit off the labor of others. The desire to take for myself what belongs to all is ingrained in my heart. I deeply wish to purify it, and I thank you for preventing me from following through on my dark desires. With your help, I may succeed in becoming a healthy member of a community of mutual concern and shared sacrifice."

"And do you renounce your greed?"

"I do."

"And do you renounce your past?"

"I do."

"And do you renounce the Machine?"

"I—" The man hesitated. He looked up at his interrogator.

The Purifier punched him in the stomach, bending him double with the blow. Marie flinched, but no one else in the tent even blinked.

"And do you renounce the Machine?" the Purifier repeated, pulling the man upright again by his hair.

"I cannot renounce what is not real," the man said, his voice strained. "There is no Machine. Only fools believe the networks could ever be restored."

The Purifier studied him. All eyes studied him.

"Good," the Purifier said at last, then turned to the assembled crowd. "How best shall our friend purify himself of this greed he has confessed?"

There were murmurs in the crowd. This was a chance for the members of the cooperative to demonstrate their commitment to Reconciliation. As former elites, they were all suspect. Other white-masked Purifiers stood around the tent, watching everyone closely, no doubt noting who appeared reluctant to punish a transgression, who might themselves be tempted to transgress.

"The crime is from the past," a voice called out. "Let the punishment be as well."

The crowd quickly concurred with a round of clapping and stomping. The man in front nodded and stomped his feet, agreeing readily to whatever punishment was assigned to him. Reluctance to be punished would be a sign that he still harbored guilty thoughts.

"Very good," the Purifier beside him said. "In the Mountain City, when a patron committed an infraction, his proxy would be administered jolts from an electro-muscular disruption stick." The Purifier pulled out such a stick. No one needed an explanation. The old system had existed until just a few months ago. The EMD sticks themselves were outlawed, but it was widely known that they still circulated, and the Purifier cadres used them freely.

The Purifier activated his, and through the mouth hole of his white mask, Marie clearly saw a smirk sneak its way across his face. For a former proxy, the chance to shock a former patron this way had to be a thrill. This Purifier was bold to show his enjoyment in front of everyone. It was not supposed to be a joy.

He touched the stick to the man's side, and instantly the man's body jolted. After a second shock, he collapsed and quivered on the ground. Two Purifiers rushed forward to hold him up. Another shock was delivered. And another. And another. The man spit up on himself, his legs gave out, and still, another shock followed. No one dared look away.

Marie scanned the crowd and saw her parents sitting

side by side, together, both of them watching the punishment being administered without the slightest emotion on their faces. Surely, they would have known this man before, when he was an executive. Her father's company did extensive business with Birla Nanotech, who installed much of the biodata into people's bloodstreams.

Marie didn't recognize the man, but she could imagine him standing in their living room at a cocktail party, laughing and telling jokes. Maybe she'd even gone to school with the man's children, if he had any. It didn't matter. He would never see them again.

Marie knew it pained her parents to watch, but they had avoided seeing the suffering that the old system caused for so long, only seeing its benefits, that seeing suffering now served a vital purpose. Facing the pain that greed created, perhaps they could learn to build a world where greed no longer existed. As the punishment went on, her father whispered something to her mother, who nodded grimly.

When the meeting broke up and everyone began to make their way across the fields to the barracks, Marie weaved her way through the crowd to walk with them.

"Hi, Mom," she said quietly, matching her pace to theirs. "Hi, Dad."

Her father glanced at her and held back a cry of joy. He gave her a quick one-armed hug. "You aren't wearing your disturbing mask?"

"I'm not on duty," she said. "And they're not disturbing.

They are meant to remove the individual from the job. All the Purifiers are, in a way, the same Purifier."

"Anything that hides the face of the person with power over you is disturbing," her father whispered back.

"Oh, like a corporation?" Marie replied.

"Don't fight," her mother interjected. "Please. It's so nice to see you, Marie. I'm glad you could visit with us."

"Do your meetings usually go this late?" she asked.

"Who can tell?" her father said. "No way to tell time."

"The Reconciliation tells you when you need to be somewhere."

"Praises to the Reconciliation!" her father exclaimed. "We'd be so lost without them. Or 'us,' I mean. We're all one, no? We'd be lost without ourselves?"

Marie sighed. Her father's bitterness was as disheartening as it was foolish. If the wrong person were to overhear . . .

She looked at him in the dark as they walked. He had on a simple synthetic shirt and DuraStitch work pants. Marie had arranged the clothes. She knew giving special treatment to her parents was wrong, especially since they had been such anti-revolutionary figures. Her father should, by all rights, be awaiting his execution. Instead, he was with his wife, on a food production co-op wearing comfortable pants that fit him. Or at least, that had fit him a few weeks ago.

Now the pants hung off him. He'd used up the notches on the built-in belt and had tied a cord of some kind around his waist to hold them up. His shirt draped around his thin shoulders. He reminded Marie of the nervous kid she'd surprised in his nap. He was not the proud and powerful executive she'd grown up with. As they walked, he kept scratching at his chest and his arms. She noticed her mother quietly take his hand, wrap his bloody fingers in her own. There were marks on his neck and she could see the skin had lost its color, was nearly translucent to the layer of vein and muscle below.

She couldn't deny it, life on the co-op was not being kind to her father.

And now she had to give him her news.

"I made a mistake this morning," she said.

"Everyone makes mistakes," her mother said, rather unhelpfully.

"I let down the Reconciliation," she said. "I put Syd— er—Yovel in danger through my foolishness, and am being justly punished."

Her parents stopped walking. Other figures passed them in the dark on the way back to the barracks, and in moments, they were alone in the field. Even in the dark, she could see the worried glisten in her parents' eyes.

There was little moonlight and her black hair and dark green uniform were almost invisible. The single white stripe on her collar seemed to glow and her parents stepped toward it, leaning in close. They knew, of course, that she was their only protection. Even the other members of the co-op knew who her father had been. Many of them had been his employees. The only reason he hadn't been killed and dumped into an unmarked pit in the field was that his daughter was a respected cadre of the Reconciliation and was a friend to the savior of the people. If she fell from grace, her mother and father would be killed faster than the rumor of her disgrace could reach them.

"Are we—?" Her mother lowered her voice to almost a breath. "In danger?"

"No," Marie said. "But my rations, and yours, are being cut in half."

"I noticed at mealtime this evening," her mother said. "I assumed the cook was stealing from us."

"That doesn't happen anymore," Marie objected. "Personal greed has been eliminated."

Her father snorted a bitter laugh. "As we have just witnessed."

"Your father's not well," her mother whispered.

"Take him to the medics," Marie suggested.

It was her mother's turn to laugh. "You're young, Marie. Even with your uniform and your rank, you are very young."

"All people have a right to medical care," she said.

"You forget that your father and I are not really people." Her mother shook her head. "We are on probation until we can prove our old ideas have been purged. Isn't that right? Isn't that what this so-called farm is for? To reinvent us?"

"To purify you," Marie said. "To reeducate you. To bring out the communal spirit that we all possess."

"Others have gone to the medics." Her mother looped

her arm through her daughter's and led her on, with her father on the other side. "They do not come back."

"They're getting treatment," said Marie.

"They never come back," her mother said. "Better to keep our illnesses to ourselves."

"At least they still belong to us," her father coughed.

"Stop it, Xiao," she admonished him. She turned back to Marie. "Don't worry about us. We'll make do. It's a new world now. You wanted to make the future and so you are. You're an important person with opportunities to rise in the ranks. We're museum pieces. Don't let us drag you down. There's no profit in it."

Marie's head darted around to make sure they were alone in the field. "Profit" was an outlawed word too. Why did her mother insist on using it? Was she so incapable of change?

Marie wanted so badly for her parents to see the good in this new world. It was a harder life, but one where everyone's fate was shared. People grew the food, not machines. People ate what they could grow, not what branding and marketing departments told them to. People enforced the laws, not bioengineered Guardians. People were at the center of the world now and if her parents would just embrace it, they would see all the good it could bring, all the good it would bring.

Soon the dirt would produce enough for everyone to eat. Soon the restrictions on movement and speech and thought would be unnecessary because the Machinist cults would be eliminated. Soon no one would long for the old way of living, because they would come to appreciate the new. There would be a kind of peace that the world had never seen. Her parents would understand that she had been right all along.

"I have to go," she told them. "I'll come visit again soon. Just work hard and be mindful."

"You do the same," her mother said, kissing her on the cheek. Her father stepped around and hugged her. He still had his strength, but as she looked closely into his face, she could see the veins running beneath the skin, like they were swelling, darkening.

Could it be—? No.

The Reconciliation said the sickness could not spread. There was no danger to the public as long as the Guardians were eliminated.

And yet, as she walked away from her parents back across the fields, she was glad for the dark. She did not want anyone to see her tears.

Birthing pains, she told herself. At the birth of a new world, there will always be pain.

[12]

DR. KHAN LIVED IN a housing unit in the secure sector not far from Syd's run-down school building. The housing was newer than most in the city and in relatively good shape. The jungle plants that crawled into the cavernous ruins of skyscrapers from other eras had been cut back, much of the structure restored and an elevator even rebuilt.

"The doctor lives on sixteen," Cousin said. "I suppose she likes the breezes up there."

"I'll take the stairs," Liam said. He didn't feel comfortable in elevators. He didn't like the idea that a bunch of wires were all that stood between him and gravity. Cousin didn't object.

Liam took the stairs two at a time. Cousin stayed on his heels, not the slightest bit winded when they reached the sixteenth floor. It hardly seemed possible. Liam was young and in good health and he had to catch his breath. Cousin waited patiently.

"She's the fourth door on the left," he told Liam. "I'll wait here."

Liam looked at Cousin in the darkness, his smooth skin almost emitting its own light. "Why couldn't you have done this one without me?" Liam asked him. "It doesn't seem like I'm especially needed here."

"We all do our own work in this new world we're making," said Cousin. "And this is *your* work. Not mine."

"We all serve the Reconciliation," Liam countered. "The work of one is the work of all."

"I admire your ideological insights," said Cousin. "But you'll do this for better reasons than the Reconciliation."

"Oh, I will, huh?" Liam crossed his arms and rocked back on his feet. He even tapped one metal finger on his elbow to demonstrate his skepticism.

"As I explained before, Dr. Khan helped design the machine that extracted and transmitted the virus, which gave us our glorious Reconciliation. She is well aware that the process is fatal, so even if she doesn't know about Knox, she knows that Yovel, had he actually triggered the Jubilee, would be dead. She knows Yovel is an empty symbol, signifying nothing."

"He prefers Syd," Liam corrected.

"Yes, he does." Cousin smiled. "And that is why you will do this. Because you *want* to do this. Because her knowledge makes her a threat to Syd's reputation, and without his reputation he has no need for a bodyguard."

Liam didn't say anything.

"And because you can't tell him what we both know you'd like to," Cousin added.

Liam's metal finger stopped tapping. "I don't know what you think you—"

Cousin shushed him. "Please. Your silences are far more honest."

Liam blushed, and he knew Cousin saw him blushing. What good was shame? He also knew that Cousin was right. The woman could be a threat to Syd, and that was all Liam needed to know.

Without another word, he dropped his arms, brushed past Cousin in the hallway, being sure to bump him with his shoulder as he went by. He put his ear to Dr. Khan's door and, hearing nothing on the other side, wrapped his metal fingers around the handle. With one quick jerk of his wrist, he snapped the handle off and gently pushed the door open with his good fingers. He glanced back at Cousin, then stepped in, letting the door shut behind him.

He moved through the apartment without a sound. There were only two rooms: an outer room with a low table and mats strewn around the tile floor for sitting, plus a plastic screen with a hose and bucket on the other side for her toilet, and then the sleeping alcove.

Dr. Khan lay in the alcove on a soft mat, wrapped in a silver heat blanket, her dark braid resting across a raft of soft pillows. She allowed herself that luxury, against the official advice of the Council, but perhaps she had an exemption. Her indulgences, Liam supposed, could be tolerated.

Her secrets, however, could not.

He bent down beside her, and she stirred. One eye opened, then the other, and for a moment she stared hazily at him, perhaps wondering whether he were a dream. He smiled gently, softened his expression, tried to radiate kindness. No need for her last moments to be filled with terror.

But her eyes widened anyway, that inevitable look of fear that they always got when they saw him coming. He wished he could tell her that there was nothing to fear, nothing at all. But why lie, why now?

"Shhh," he soothed anyway, and put his fleshy hand firmly over her mouth.

"Mrrrr-mrrr," she groaned beneath his hand as he pressed her down into the soft womb of her pillows. Her arms came up to scratch him. He knocked them away and then, with one quick chop from his other hand, his killing hand, the hand he told himself was not his own, he crushed her throat.

She gasped and gurgled a moment, looking up with pained confusion on her face, and then she heaved, her lungs filling with blood, drowning her in her bed. In a few moments she would be dead. As he watched her die, he looked into her eyes.

"I'm so sorry," he whispered. A tear ran down Dr. Khan's cheek before that peculiar spark left her gaze, as he'd seen it leave so many others. He matched it with a tear of his own. He was not like Cousin. He did not enjoy this.

He closed his eyes; he thought of Syd.

"For you," he said out loud, only because there wasn't anyone to hear him.

When it was done, he opened his eyes and looked at the woman. She looked peaceful, staring straight up at the ceiling. He used his real fingers to close her eyes as softly as he could and he noticed something underneath her pillow, a smooth thread of some kind. He pulled, and a leather object trailed it from beneath the pillow. The thread was a piece of ribbon and it was sewn into the binding of a book. Books were rare enough objects before the Reconciliation. Those that still existed were public property. No one kept something so valuable to themselves. Liam had seen one or two, but never touched them.

Now he lifted it by the string and rested the object on his palm. Its cover was from the tanned hide of some animal, brown and smooth and soft. He pressed it against his cheek, warm and soft.

He pulled it away and felt ridiculous.

It was smaller than he'd imagined a book should be, but also heavier. He flipped through the paper, smooth and shiny. As his thumb moved along the edge, letting the pages fall, he saw that half of them were blank. The other half were covered in tiny symbols made in a mixture of colors, black and brown and blue. The symbols looked handmade, as opposed to produced on a machine, the old kind of writing. Handwriting. No one did that anymore. He looked at the corpse and wondered about this woman. She was a doctor with access to tech. Why would she keep a book? Being educated, why would she write by hand?

He'd never know the answers, and in truth, the curiosity would only lead him to think more about Dr. Khan when the best thing he could do would be to forget her immediately. Those kinds of memories were the worst enemy he could have.

He closed his eyes, pictured her face, pictured all the questions he had for her, and then he let them pour from his mind, down his spine and his legs and out into the floor, gone. A waterfall into an abyss.

He opened his eyes again, calm.

But the book was still on the palm of his hand.

Syd would probably find something like this interesting. Liam couldn't tell him where he got it, but maybe he could give it to Syd as a gift, something to show he understood how bored Syd was under such strict protection. Something to show that he empathized, that he wasn't an uncivilized monster, and maybe that he was someone important enough to get his hands on a book.

Liam shoved the book into the belt of his pants at the back and lifted his shirt over it, so it was hidden. He couldn't move all that well with it there, but he didn't expect to do anything too demanding now that the threat of Dr. Khan's secrets about Syd and the Jubilee had been taken care of. He'd hide the book until the time was right to give it to Syd.

He left the doctor's apartment. Whatever happened to the dead of her people could happen now. It wouldn't take long for someone to find her body. He hoped whatever else there was to her besides her body would have found its way home by then.

When Liam came out, Cousin was leaning on the wall of the hallway by the door. He didn't say a word. They had shared enough of these moments since the Jubilee that there was no need to speak. Cousin could mock the living and the dead with relentless detachment, but the one thing that put him into a reverential silence was a killing. It was the closest the man came to a practice of faith. He walked wordlessly by Liam's side down the stairs and onto the street back toward the old school where Syd was sleeping.

They saw the white hood of a Purifier in a watchtower, but otherwise remained alone on the street. When they arrived at Syd's building, Cousin didn't follow Liam inside. He did, however, break the silence.

He held up two fingers. "With my blessing," he said and walked away.

Liam sighed and went inside. He didn't need Cousin's blessing. He already knew what he had to do. The two young Purifiers knew where Syd slept and knew that Liam and Cousin had been up to something. They had no need for that knowledge, and no right to it. It was nothing personal. Liam's hand had not yet finished its evening's work.

[13]

"WHEN YOU STEP OUTSIDE, I'll be just off your right shoulder," Liam told Syd as their hovercraft settled down in a cloud of dust beside the churning wind turbine at Soy Cooperative 18, on the slopes just outside Mountain City, twelve hundred miles from Old Detroit. The sun had just peeked up over the desert, a fiery streak that would turn blazing by afternoon. The smell of the crowd would not be pleasant, but everyone would be out to see Yovel wave and smile and give his tired speech. The people wouldn't have heard even a whisper of how badly his last one had gone.

"If anything goes wrong, I'll be the one to get you back in the vehicle," Liam told him. "Do not follow anyone but me."

"I heard you," Syd grumbled. "I heard you the last time you said it, and the time before that. It's a walk through some soy fields. I think we'll be okay. Also, there's an army of Purifiers waiting to meet us."

"I've told you," Liam said. "You have to remain alert and focused at all times. Even the Purifiers can't be trusted. Look at your old friend Finch. There are a lot of people out there who'd be thrilled to see the symbol of the Reconciliation dead."

"I'm aware," said Syd. "I might be one of them."

"Sydney!" Counselor Baram spluttered from across the cramped cabin. "That is not even funny."

"Relax." Syd shook his head. "The symbol. I'm talking about the symbol."

Liam's mouth opened, but he didn't have anything to say. It had been a week since the incident with the nopes, a week since he'd taken care of that Nigerian doctor, and in that week, Syd hadn't been out of his sight. They'd barely spoken to each other, at least not in any way that could be mistaken for a conversation. He still hadn't found the nerve to give Syd the book.

Liam's and Counselor Baram's eyes met across the cabin. The old man raised an eyebrow and Liam gave a tiny nod that it'd be fine. He could keep Syd safe for this event. He could even keep Syd safe from himself, if it came to it.

Counselor Baram pushed himself up off the bench to stoop in the low cabin. He straightened his uniform, scratched an itch around his collar and nodded to Liam. "Ready?"

Liam nodded.

Syd nodded.

The back bay door hissed open and bright sunlight streamed in. The ramp touched down and Counselor Baram stepped out first, followed by Liam, who then motioned for Syd.

Blinded by the afternoon sun, at first Syd only heard a great cheer rise up as he stepped outside. The roar swept through the crowd like an unruly wind, swirling away and back again. Syd held his hand up to shield his eyes and he saw the throngs on either side of a central path from the ramp of the hovercraft. A line of Purifiers in their white balaclavas held the people back. The scene looked jarringly familiar. A crowd like this in an open field seemed like an ideal place for an assassin.

The memory of fear wasn't the same as fear, and this time Syd didn't feel tense before the crowd. Syd understood Liam's anxiety, but the bright blue sky above, dotted with puffy white clouds, soothed him. He'd been cooped up in that schoolroom for days. A walk in the open air was worth the risk.

The co-op's official delegation stepped forward down the center of the path, right up to the bottom of the ramp, all smiles. They bumped fists with Counselor Baram, and Syd went down to them, offered his own fist. Liam took his position off Syd's shoulder and they began to walk the path through the cheering crowd.

"Welcome to our farm, Yovel!" the leader of the delegation shouted over the noise. Syd clenched his jaw at the use of that name, but didn't correct the man. "I am Brother Jenz and it is a pleasure to meet you."

Brother Jenz was a tall blond man with broad shoulders and stunningly healthy complexion. His cheeks were red as sunset, his skin gently tanned, and his eyes a glistening blue. His blond beard was trimmed and the woven clothes he wore looked all natural and handmade just for him. He was clearly living well as a leader of the cooperative. Syd noticed the scar on his neck, however, the echo of a faded gene job from Sterling Work Colony. Before the revolution, Brother Jenz had been a prisoner.

Syd decided to withhold too harsh a judgment. Before the revolution, everyone had been a prisoner in one way or another. Syd himself had been sentenced to Sterling Work Colony too. That was what made him run to begin with.

"I would love to give you and Counselor Baram a tour of our operation." Brother Jenz gestured broadly over the crowd and the fields, toward an area of squat buildings and meeting tents. "We are very proud of what we've built here in just a few short months. We've reached our calorie quotas ahead of schedule; we have a storytelling troupe, a popular athletics as-sociation, and a thriving choir. Our evening meetings are truly joyous affairs. I think you'll find us a model community."

"I believe all our communities are model communities," Syd replied flatly.

"I . . . well . . . yes . . . I meant that—" Jenz stammered.

"Relax, Brother Jenz." Syd smiled. "I'm just messing with you."

Jenz stammered, surprised that Yovel, savior of the people and soul of the Reconciliation, would "mess" with him. Counselor Baram gave Syd a disapproving look.

Liam, however, looked amused. Syd hadn't imagined his goon had a sense of humor. Liam had a lot of secrets, that much was obvious to Syd, but he hadn't thought humor was among them.

As they walked along the path toward the cluster of buildings in the distance, the people along the sides pressed against the Purifiers. They stretched out their arms, craned their heads, cried out to Syd. Some held up babies or thrust out injured limbs, as if even the briefest touch could heal whatever was wrong with their bodies or their minds.

"Yovel!" they called out.

"Syd!" others dared, even though the name was not officially recognized. Syd walked straight down the center and tried to ignore them. Brother Jenz and his delegation walked rapidly ahead. Liam nudged Syd forward with his metal hand. Always with the metal hand, like he was afraid to touch Syd with his real one.

Afraid of what? Syd wondered.

There were at least a thousand people gathered to see him. It was absurd, based entirely on a lie, but to leave them with nothing to show for his visit seemed cruel. These people labored in the fields, after all, while he lived in relative comfort, with all his needs met by others . . . kind of like the patrons had lived in the Mountain City, actually. Kind of like Knox had lived before Syd showed up.

Syd veered from the center of the path and began giving fist bumps and hugs to the people in the front of the crowd, leaning between the arms of the Purifiers, who themselves gasped as he drew close. He wondered whether he'd met any of them before, back in vocational school when he was still just some proxy.

"Syd, this is not safe," Liam whispered in his ear as he pried a tearful young mother's hand from Syd's wrist. Liam was careful not to use his metal hand.

The people were so enamored of their savior that they didn't recoil from Liam's gaze as they normally might have. Or maybe, this far into the countryside, they weren't aware of his reputation for violence. He wondered whether he should make a show of force to keep them in line.

He decided against it. Syd would not approve.

"Just don't slow down so much," Liam urged, guiding Syd along the line. He scanned the crowd, searching for threats, sudden movements, weapons of any kind. At least the local leadership had made people leave all farming tools behind. If Liam saw even so much as a planting trowel, he'd have hauled Syd back to the hovercraft faster than Brother Jenz could spit.

"Thank you for all you've done," a young man said as Syd passed, giving him a respectful knock of his knuckles.

I didn't do *anything*, thought Syd. *I don't deserve any thanks.*

Instead, he said, "Thank you too," which seemed to him ambiguous enough.

Hands pawed at him. He felt his clothes stretching. The crowd was getting rougher. He tried to pull away from them, but a dozen hands had grabbed him and dragged him closer. They called out to him. They begged for his blessing. He tried to be polite.

An old man with rheumy eyes lurched forward, held upright only by the linked arms of the Purifiers in front of him. He grabbed Syd's shirt with both his hands. Every vein on his face was visible, heavy and black, like a drone's view of desert canyons or a map of a blacked-out network. There were weeping sores where he'd scratched himself raw.

"Help me," he groaned. "I—" The man's eyes darted, his tongue lolled in his mouth, wrestling with words that wouldn't form. A memory of the nopes popped into Syd's head, how they looked up at him wordlessly, how they oozed black blood, how they screamed in silence, just before they were beaten to death.

Liam shoved the man back, and before Syd could say anything, the old man vanished into the forest of bodies, their outstretched arms like the creeper vines that devoured skyscrapers.

Syd's eyes scanned through the crowd over the heads of the people in front of him. He couldn't see where the old man had gone, but he tried his best to read the crowd the way he'd once learned to read an individual. What could he see? What did it tell him?

Most of the people were on the younger side, male and female in roughly equal numbers. He couldn't see the old man anymore, but he made out the lowered head of an older woman trying to press her way forward. She was covered in a headscarf and she avoided looking at anyone as she wriggled through the throng. People gaped at her with unmistakable contempt. A few tried to look away, to act like they hadn't seen her. Still others made way as she passed, trying to avoid even so much as touching the cloth of her blouse. When she glanced up, Syd saw that she too was covered with a network of dark lines, her blood turning against her in her veins.

Syd had stopped moving to watch the old woman and, in pausing, had allowed a crowd to mass in front of him. They all reached out, they all wanted to touch him.

"Yovel!" one yelled. "I knew you in the Valve! It's me! We were friends!" Syd didn't recognize the guy, who would've called him Syd if they really knew each other. And anyway, back in the old days, Syd only had one friend.

And he was dead.

"Yovel!" a teenaged girl yelled. "My patron had me punished every day for her crimes! I would have killed myself if not for you!"

"Yovel! Marry me!" a girl barely ten years old shouted. Others around her laughed. They were all young.

Syd let the little girl knock her fist against his. Other hands wrapped around theirs, locking them together. He felt hands on his arms, hands on his waist, on his shoulders. The stench of their bodies, their breath, their need . . . it overwhelmed him. He felt himself being sucked forward into the mass. The Purifiers in front of him couldn't hold the line. It was about to break.

And there was the old woman, directly in front of him.

"It . . . burns . . . ," she said with visible effort.

"What?" Syd tried to free one of his hands to pull the old woman closer, where he could talk to her, but there were too many other hands grasping him. The air around him felt as heavy as wet wool and stank of sweat.

The woman's mouth bent. Her eyebrows crushed her eyes. She turned red with effort but she produced words. "Blood," she whispered. "Blood—burns." She scratched at herself. "Help us to—"

She was cut off by unseen hands pulling her back, and she was gone into the crowd. Syd tried to move in after her, to cross through the Purifiers' linked arms and ask the woman what she meant, how he could help, what he was supposed to do for her, but there were faces in his face, and still more hands on his body and they tugged at him, and they squeezed him and he felt like he was drowning. Some way to die, choking on the breath of his own believers.

He gave Liam a look, and unhesitating, the bodyguard yanked him back, thrusting his body between the crowd and Syd. His metal hand swatted the other hands away, shoved people down, broke their grip. Others rushed forward, a Purifier fell, was trampled, and the rest began wielding their clubs to beat people back.

Brother Jenz cried out for calm, for order, but no one heard him over the panic. A stampede came at Syd. Liam punched someone back, knocked him out with one blow and then his arms wrapped around Syd, practically lifting him off the ground. He sprinted them both up the ramp and into the hovercraft. Purifiers cracked their clubs and knocked the crowd apart.

Syd looked over his shoulder as they climbed aboard. He saw Baram struggling up with people grabbing at his clothes, and behind Baram, as the ramp began to lift, he saw the Purifiers shoving deeper into the crowd, wading into the seething bodies. He saw the old woman. She met his eyes for just a second as two white masks blocked her from his view. At the back of the crowd, he saw others, six or seven people, all of them frail, stumbling, lined with heavy black veins, hauled away by Purifiers. When one of them fell, he saw a club rise and he saw it fall.

"Those are people," Syd said. "They can't do that to people!" But no one could hear him. The ramp wasn't even fully closed when the engines growled and the entire ugly scene vanished in a cloud of dust.

[14]

WHEN THEY TOUCHED DOWN in the alley beside the old school hours later, Counselor Baram left the hovercraft without a word. He hadn't spoken to Syd the entire ride, busying himself in the cockpit with the pilots, even as Syd demanded explanations from him.

"They were taking away regular people," Syd called after. "Not Guardians. Those weren't Guardians who were infected!"

"Syd, let him go." Liam stopped him. "Let's get inside where it's safe."

"Safe from what?" Syd snapped at him. "Stop being paranoid."

"My paranoia keeps you alive," Liam responded. "Get inside."

"You don't give me orders."

"Syd, please. I'm just trying to—" Suddenly, Liam stopped. His hand went down to his belt and came up with the bolt gun, spring locked to fire.

"Don't shoot." Marie stepped from the door of the school in her Purifier uniform. "My arm is fine, by the way."

"What are you doing here?" Liam lowered the weapon. "I could have shot you. Again."

"It went so well for you last time." She smiled, pulling off her hood and running her hand through her hair.

Syd would never cease to be amazed by her guts. Everyone else cowered in front of Liam, even if he had never done anything to them. He'd shot Marie, and still she talked back.

"I need to talk to Syd," she said.

"How did you even know about this place?" Liam demanded.

Marie shrugged.

"I told her," said Syd. Liam gave him a disapproving look. "Someone had to know where I was."

I'm someone, thought Liam, but out loud he said, "We can't talk out here."

Marie opened her arms. "So you going to invite me in?"

Syd didn't give Liam a chance to answer. "*I* am. Come on."

When they got to Syd's room, Liam did not want to leave them alone together.

"Don't worry," Marie scoffed. "He's not my type."

"I'll be right outside," Liam grumbled, leaving the door cracked open while he took up his post. Liam couldn't help the pang of jealousy he felt. Marie knew Syd in a way he never could, a way Syd would never let him.

When Liam had gone out, Marie relaxed a bit. "Cheery room," she said, looking over the blank walls and the unmade cot. Syd's clothes were strewn about, and while he cleared them off his chair for her, she fired a quick glance to his bucket in the corner.

"Don't worry," he told her. "I empty it regularly."

"I'm surprised Liam lets you out to do that," Marie replied.

"Oh, he doesn't," said Syd. "I'm allowed to use a bot for that. The programming is pretty basic, and I had to fix it myself, but they decided it was better than giving me the chance to slip away. Also, how would the people feel if they knew what my bowel movements smelled like?"

Marie snorted a laugh and sat down on the chair opposite Syd's cot. "People know you're human, Syd."

"You'd be surprised." Syd sat on the edge of his cot, directly across from her, so close their knees touched. He spoke quietly, certain that Liam was listening. "I'm a little surprised Liam let you come in here anyway. He's . . . possessive."

"He's just being protective," she said. "But anyway, he owed me one."

Syd feigned shock. "*He owed you!* Why, Purifier Alvarez, debt language is forbidden in this new age of ours!"

"I'm glad you appreciate the irony," she said. "Listen, I'm not here to talk about Liam."

"I figured."

"I need your help."

"My help?" Syd looked around his messy room. "I'm stuck in here. There's not much I can do for anybody."

Marie took a deep breath. She was going against all her ideals here. The girl who risked everything to wipe out the privilege her family enjoyed was about to ask for special privilege for her family. No going back now. She'd come this far and a week had already passed.

"Something's wrong with my father," she said. "He won't survive on the half rations he's taking because of what happened last week. I need . . . I need you to intervene."

Syd shot up like he'd been jolted by an EMD stick. "What kind of sick?"

"I don't know."

"Itching?"

Marie nodded.

"Veiny . . . like you can see his veins?"

Marie hesitated. "I know what you're saying, but he just needs more food. He'll be fine if he doesn't starve. You can help with that."

"I think it's more serious," said Syd.

"You're a doctor now?"

"I just notice things."

Marie stood again, turned her back on Syd. "No. If this infection is spreading, the Reconciliation has doctors. They'll get it under control."

"Like they're doing with the Guardians?"

"I know you think they're being cruel to the nonoperatives, but they're dying anyway and it was just—"

"I get it," said Syd. "You did your job. You don't need me to forgive you."

"But I do," she said. "I need you to help my parents."

"You think I'd let them die out of what? Spite?"

Marie shrugged.

"You don't think much of me," Syd said.

"I do," said Marie. "I want to . . . but ever since Knox . . . you know. You're supposed to *inspire* people. All you do is sulk. People are losing faith in you."

"I don't know why they have faith in me in the first place."

"Don't say that."

"You sound just like Baram and Liam, you know?"

"They're right."

"I went to a co-op today." Syd closed his eyes. "Smiled at people, put on a good face . . . and it turned into a riot. I'm sure people died. Every time I do anything, people die. You were with me from the beginning. You know the body count. I'm not supposed to be anyone's inspiration. I'm a fake."

"So what? Everyone's a fake. At least you can give people hope if you can stop thinking about yourself for one second." Marie regretted saying it as soon as she said it. She knew she shouldn't be antagonizing Syd, but he was even worse than her parents. They had a reason to resist the way things were; Syd was just being difficult. "I'm sorry," she added.

"I saw other sick people today." Syd stood up beside her.

"Regular people and they were starting to look just like the . . . nopes. The moment I was gone, I think they were *dealt with* by some of your white-hooded friends."

"No," said Marie. "That's not what we do."

"I saw it."

"You believe the worst about everything."

"Experience has yet to prove me wrong."

"Well, this isn't what you think." Marie looked around his depressing room, looked at the puffiness around his eyes, the red rims. He hadn't been sleeping. He was a boy who couldn't let the past go. He wouldn't let himself forget any of the bad he'd been through or remember any of the good. "Not everything in this world has to be horrible, Syd. Have some faith. Knox did."

Syd winced at the name on someone else's lips.

"He died so that you could live," she went on. "You can't just wallow in self-pity. He gave you a future."

"Why don't we go see your parents?" Syd changed the subject. "I'll have a talk with the leaders of their co-op and we'll get their rations back up. Maybe Yovel can be good for something more than waving at people."

"No way." Liam came into the room. He'd been listening the entire time. "That is way against the rules. Her parents live in a restricted area. It's a reeducation camp. The Council would have both our heads for going there."

"Liam, this is something I can do," said Syd. "I can get her parents enough to eat. Don't you want to see Yovel make people's lives better? I thought you were a believer."

Liam sympathized. "Look, Syd, I know you want to help, but we need to get approval for this kind of thing. I can't keep you safe if a riot breaks out among all the patrons they've got working on that farm. Most of them hate you."

"I'm not sitting in this room doing nothing while people are dying," said Syd.

"I . . . well . . . ," Liam stammered. He looked at Marie, wished she weren't there, wished he could have just a moment alone with Syd. But it was now or never. He had to try something to stop Syd from this crazy idea. "Look, I've got a surprise for you," he said. "Something you'll like. I've been saving it for you. You see, I found this handmade—"

"I don't want your surprises," Syd cut him off. "I want you to take me to Marie's parents." Syd crossed his arms. He met Liam's eyes. As hard as Liam's face was, the eyes had that pleading dampness. His cheeks were flushed, chastened at being cut off in front of Marie. Strong as he was, he looked terribly vulnerable at that moment, and Syd realized then that he had never really looked at Liam before, never closely. Liam had been more like a piece of furniture than a person, even as Liam looked at him all the time. He saw Liam's eyes widen with expectation for what Syd would say next, what this long, lingering stare could mean.

So Syd told him: "You will take me or else I'll have the Council remove you from my protection assignment. For personal reasons."

"I don't know what you're . . . I have no . . ." Liam blushed bright now, the way anglo boys did. Syd just stared at him, his own features showing a practiced indifference. Marie raised her eyebrows, waiting.

Liam felt like the ground had fallen out from under him.

"I'm not sure I can take you there." He looked away, standing up straight, returning to his military posture. Now was not the time to fall apart. "It's not an area I'm authorized to be in."

"But you will take me anyway," Syd told him.

It wasn't a question so much as an order and Syd had no doubt Liam would follow it.

[15]

IT HAD TAKEN A few days, but Liam finally found a way to get them to the cooperative on the edge of the city without getting in trouble. When they arrived, morning mist still hung over the fields and the high dirt berms and low-slung buildings. With the rattle of a prerecorded holo projected on the side of a building, a glorious sunrise over the jungle canopy, and a swell of music, the workers rose to a new day of labor for the prosperity of the Reconciliation and the benefit of their community.

Or they should have.

Other than the music and the holo hanging in front of the meeting tent, the co-op was dead quiet when Liam, Syd, and Marie arrived. The fields were empty. The dining tent too. They picked their way over the uneven dirt toward the barracks, a knot of anxiety clenching in Marie's stomach.

Outside, leaning against the tractor in the same position she had seen him in before, was the young Purifier, sleeping soundly. He didn't have his white mask on, as it was again pressed behind his head for a pillow. His face was dotted with zits, his mousy hair tussled and unruly, and a slick of drool hung from his mouth, dangling precariously over his chest.

They stood over him. Marie put on her white mask.

He snored.

Marie coughed and the boy's head snapped up. The thread of drool broke and dripped onto his uniform. He hopped to his feet, looking around frantically for the white mask, which had fallen behind him and on which he was now standing.

"Purifier! Where is your community? Why are they not preparing for the day? Why are you sleeping on duty again?" Marie grilled the boy, flashing anger through the eyeholes in her mask, and doing her best to amplify the terror the boy was obviously feeling.

"I . . . they . . . ," the boy stuttered. "Is that . . . Syd?"

Liam clenched his fist, but the boy didn't even seem to notice.

"Syd!" He almost jumped. "It's me! Tom? From school? Remember me?"

"I thought you were Arik the Destroyer," Marie said.

"Tom!" he said again. "My name was Tom! We were, like, friends?"

"Uh . . ." Syd had a vague memory of the kid's face and a

broken holo projector he'd wanted Syd to fix. They'd hardly been friends.

"Have you come . . ." The boy looked conspiratorially between Syd, Marie and Liam. "Have you come to save me?"

"Save you?" Marie grunted at the boy. "What do you need to be saved from?"

"You mean . . ." The boy was perplexed. "You don't know? The infection?"

He pointed to the barracks, shaking his head. Marie moved toward the door.

"Don't go in there," the boy warned. "It'll take you too."

"Where are the other Purifiers?" Liam asked.

The boy shook his head.

"Sick?" Syd glanced at the dark doorway.

"Ran off," the boy said. "I'm the only one who stayed." He cleared his throat. Stood tall. "I'm not a deserter. I'm loyal to the Reconciliation."

"Why didn't you report this to your guidance counselor?" Marie whirled around on the boy.

Tom looked at his feet. "I did," he said.

"He ran off too?" Syd asked.

Marie was disgusted. How weak these cadres of Purifiers were. How cowardly. How could they build a better world if they were afraid of some sick people?

"No," the boy told them. "He's inside. The infection got him." The boy finally met Marie's eyes. "I know who you are, Marie. It got your parents too. It'll get everyone. It's our punishment. We never should have changed the way things were." He looked at Syd. "You never should have broken the—"

Marie didn't stick around to hear the frightened boy's rambling. She plunged into the dark of the barracks to find her parents. Syd followed her. Liam hesitated.

"Wait, I—" But wherever Syd went, Liam went. To the ends of the world if he had to. So what if Syd didn't feel the same way about him. He didn't have to. Loyalty wasn't a transaction.

As they entered the barracks, the smell almost knocked them all back outside again.

Marie pulled off her mask and used the balled cloth to cover her mouth and nose, but even so, she couldn't totally stop the smell of rot and sweat and human waste from rising to her nostrils. As all their eyes adjusted, they began to see the source—or rather, sources—of the smell.

The barracks was one long room with a door at the front and the back, leading out to the latrines. It was wide enough for four rows of sleeping mats with an aisle between each row. Slatted walls and high open windows webbed with wire let in some light and allowed the air to circulate. The meager openings, however, were no match for the powerful smells of over three hundred sick people lying on their mats beneath thin blankets, groaning, coughing, and crying out. Even in the low light, they could see the toll the affliction was taking.

People were covered in the black webbing of their own

veins. Some lay tearing furiously at their clothes and hair and skin, opening sores with their scratching. Others lay motionless, unable or unwilling to move. Some had begun to bleed black blood.

While their symptoms looked just like those of the nopes, they did not suffer in silence like the nopes did. They made their agony known in unintelligible groans.

Except for the ones who had passed beyond agony.

There were more than a few of those. They looked as if all the black veins in their body had burst. They lay covered in dried blood, all over their faces, necks, hands and feet. They were ageless, genderless, faceless. In death, they had attained complete equality. They were indistinguishable.

Marie shivered. She both longed and dreaded to find her parents and hoped the boy outside had been wrong, that they weren't here, that they had taken the flight of the Purifiers as their own cue to leave.

And then she feared they were out in the wilderness, sick, or picked up by another patrol of Purifiers who had not abandoned their duty and had executed her parents on the spot.

Her mind searched for a scenario that did not end in her parents suffering an agonizing death. She wandered down the middle aisle, scanning the gaunt faces of the dying and wishing that she could offer more than her gaping stare and her rising panic that she was now no one's daughter.

Liam kept himself at Syd's side. "Keep your head down," he said. "Maybe no one will recognize you."

No one did.

The savior of the people did not visit places like this, and there was no reason any of these formerly privileged pillars of society would have recognized some dark-skinned slum kid. It's not like they could have looked up a picture of Yovel on their datastreams. As long as no one saw the mark behind his ear, he'd be anonymous.

Strangely, this was the first time in months Syd had been able to truly let down his guard. He felt, for a moment, like himself.

As they moved down the row, those who could reached out to Marie.

"Purifier," they called out.

"Water."

"Excuse me."

"Help me."

Fingers clutched at Marie's pant legs, tugged at her without enough strength to slow her down. Dark eyes pleaded. And the voices, male and female, too weak to distinguish:

"Water."

"Water."

"Flaaa . . ."

Some had lost the power of language altogether. There were too many hands. Too many people. Too much pain.

"Gaaa."

"Water."

"Oooo."

"Marie."

A flood of terrified relief crashed over her at the sound of her name. Marie saw her father and her mother beside him on the same small mat, leaning on each other. The veins beneath their skin were visible, but not bulging out, not black. They were not well, but they were both alive and they were better off than many, worse off than some.

She knelt down in front of them and resisted the urge to throw her arms around their necks. She didn't want to hurt them. She didn't want to infect herself. It occurred to her, far too late to do anything about it, that maybe she already had. Why did she rush in here without thinking about contagion? Why didn't the Advisory Council warn people that a plague was spreading? Why had she let Syd come?

Worrying about her parents had clouded her judgment. Five minutes ago, she would have berated herself for betraying her ideological purity and unwavering commitment to the Reconciliation. Now all she wanted was to make her parents better.

"Mom," Marie said, instead of screaming out any of the questions that raced through her mind.

Her mother cracked a smile, her dry lips cracking doubly.

"You need water," Marie said, pushing herself up, but her mother's hand shot out surprisingly fast.

"Don't go," her mother said. "Your . . . uh . . ." She looked at the man beside her.

"Father," said Marie.

"Yes." Her mother sighed. "The words. My memory for them is . . . but your father . . . he's not well. Stay."

Her father stared at her without speaking. His eyes were rimmed with red and his blue veins ran wild all over his face and bare head. There were angry red patches where he'd scratched himself furiously.

"You need water," Marie repeated. She told Syd and Liam to stay with her parents, as she rushed down the long aisle, past the groaning invalids and the blank-eyed dead. She didn't stop until she'd gone out the back door and found the pump off the water tank. She filled a jug, noticing that the giant tank itself was nearly empty. She knew the regulations. It should have been refilled every week. It should never get this low. Something had gone wrong. Someone had not sent a hovercraft to resupply the co-op. Someone had decided all these people were not worth saving.

She rushed back inside with the water, ignoring everything and everyone until her parents were able to take a drink. Syd and Liam just stood there, dumbly. It hadn't occurred to either of them to say a kind word or take the hand of a suffering person. Marie shook her head.

Her mother helped her father wet his lips before she drank her own water. He coughed and choked, but swallowed a few sips. Marie could hardly bear to look at him.

"How long has he been like this?" Syd asked.

"It came quickly," her mother said. "A few days ago, we were fine. Maybe a little tired, but we assumed that was because of the work and the hunger. Others fell first. Their thoughts jumbled. We began to see their veins through their skin. We didn't think it would affect us. But it had already."

She scratched an itch on her face, then the back of her hand. Then her face again. She started to scratch with both her hands, faster and faster, raised red lines on her cheeks, and Marie reached out, stopped her as she had seen her mother do before. "It itches at first," her mother smiled meekly. "Then the blood begins to . . ."

"Burn," her father gasped out the word.

Marie's mother drifted her eyes to Syd. "I know who you are," she told him. Liam tensed and looked around. Marie put her finger to her lips, urged her mother to stay quiet.

"Keep my daughter out of trouble," she told Syd.

"She's better at staying out of trouble than I am." Syd smiled. He felt stupid smiling in a place like this, but he didn't know what else to do. Liam didn't know what to do either. He looked like he wanted to hit something, but then, he always looked like that. "Can you tell me what happened here?"

"It spread so fast," Marie's mother repeated. "As people showed signs, the Purifiers shouted and beat them, but it didn't matter, tried to make them work harder, faster. They slowed. Their bodies—our bodies—could no longer do the job." She read the worry on Marie's face. "No one beat your father or me. I think your friend provided us some protection there." She smiled back at Syd.

Did she realize that not long ago all her fine clothes, her

jewelry, her fancy home had come from the company that profited off Syd's torture? Did she realize that he was the reason she'd lost it all?

"The guidance counselor for our cadre of Purifiers fell ill too," her mother explained. "He tried to hide the signs, but his assistants saw the beginning, they saw the lines beneath his skin, like the Guardians', like ours . . . they threw him in here. They began throwing all the sick in here. They told us if anyone tried to leave, he or she would be killed on the spot."

"They're gone now," Marie said. "They all left."

"We know," her mother said. "They left that one boy of theirs, the youngest, behind. Told him they'd report him if he abandoned his post, even as they abandoned theirs. Told him they'd kill him if they saw him before relief arrived. We all heard him whining." She smiled at the thought. Marie found it comforting to see her mother could still hold a grudge, even as she struggled to hold her head up. "But there he stayed. I think it's obvious to all of us but him that no relief is coming. Your colleagues . . ." She shook her head, looking at Marie's uniform. "We would have fled, a whole group of us, but by the time we realized that boy was the only one standing guard, we were too weak to run. Besides, where would we go?"

"Do you know where this disease came from? How it started?" Syd asked.

"The nopes? Did it spread from them?" Marie wanted to know.

"They showed the first . . ." Her mother's eyes moved around in her head. She looked lost, searching.

"Symptoms?" Marie suggested.

Her mother nodded.

Marie's father let out a pained groan. He pushed himself up onto his elbows and tried to speak. "Not . . . your . . . fault . . . ," he said.

"Shh." Marie's mother stroked his head. "Rest, my love. She knows. She knows it's not her fault."

"My fault?" Marie leaned toward her father. "Why would I think this was my fault?" Her father tried to answer. His lips moved, but no sound came out. She grabbed his hand. "Why would it be my fault?"

"It isn't, Marie." Her mother rested her hand on top of theirs. "He's not thinking clearly. He didn't mean anything by that."

"He meant *something*, Mother. Tell me."

"He's been like this for days," her mother said. "I have no more idea than you do."

"The Machine," her father said.

Syd leaned down. "What was that?"

"Nothing," Marie's mother replied quickly.

"He said 'the Machine,'" Marie repeated. "Why would he say that?"

"I told you, he's been like this for days."

"Brindle," her father said. "Talk to Brindle."

"Brindle?" Liam wondered.

"That was Knox's last name," said Syd. "He means Knox's father?"

The man nodded.

"He knows more about the Guardians than anyone," said Syd. "If this started with them, he'll know what it is. He'll know how to stop it."

"He's in prison awaiting execution," said Liam. "We can't just walk in there."

"We have to," said Syd. "Look at this. We have to find out what's going on."

Liam shook his head. "You don't think the Council will have their own doctors working on it?"

Marie stood up from her parents. She spoke in a whisper. "We have to take this to the Council. We can't handle this ourselves. They'll know what to do."

"They won't do anything," Syd told her. "They want these people—your parents—to disappear. Until it starts affecting people they care about, they won't do anything to stop it."

"Counselor Baram is not like that and you know it," she said. "He'll listen."

"You do what you want," said Syd. "Liam and I are going to the prison."

"We're not," said Liam.

"Nothing's changed," Syd told him. "I can still have you reassigned to—"

"Fine," Liam snapped. He didn't want this argument. He just wanted Syd out of here, somewhere safer. A Reconciliation prison would be far safer than this co-op. At least there, Yovel would be respected. At least there, no one would carry this infection. "We'll go. But that's it. After that, we're done taking unauthorized trips. And"—he met Syd's eyes. *Might as well take a risk*—"you'll ask me nicely."

"What?" Syd scoffed.

"You heard me." Liam crossed his arms. "I'll help you, but you can't just order me around. Ask me."

"Ask you?" Syd raised an eyebrow, studied Liam. The bodyguard stood firm, met Syd's eyes, and waited. He might have puppy dog eyes, but he wasn't going to let Syd treat him like a dog. "Fair enough," said Syd. "Will you take me to the prison to visit Knox's father?"

Liam didn't move.

"Please?" Syd added.

Liam's face cracked a smile. "I will," he said, then he gestured for Syd to walk beside him from the stench of the sickhouse, into the sunlight.

Syd looked back at Marie's parents, but couldn't think of a thing to say, so he let Liam lead him out.

"I'll be back soon," Marie told her mother. "Take care of each other. Help will come. I will make sure of it."

She stood to go, making sure to give each of her parents a hug first.

Before she made her way back to the Council and Liam and Syd went to the prison, they needed to have a word with the young Purifier outside.

"We have to get back to the city quickly," she told Tom. "So we're taking your tractor."

"But how am I supposed to get out of here? Walk?"

Syd shook his head. "You aren't going anywhere, Tom."

They explained the situation as clearly as they could: He was going to look after the sick people until help arrived, doing all he could serve and comfort them, or he would wake up from his next nap to Liam's hand on his throat.

Liam clenched the metal fist in front of young Tom's face.

Syd admired his bodyguard's sense of theatricality. He hoped that was all it was, but he realized, despite all the months with Liam watching his every move, he knew almost nothing about his bodyguard. He didn't, however, seem like the type to make empty threats.

"Don't let us down, Tom," Syd added as a word of encouragement. "We're counting on you. Everyone is counting on you."

Tom liked the sound of that, but as they drove away on their commandeered tractor, they heard him calling after them.

"Wait! But . . . I don't know anything about being a nurse! Guys? How am I supposed to help? I don't know how to help."

That makes two of us, thought Syd.

[16]

"SO THE GREAT AND powerful Yovel comes to pay a condemned man a visit?" Knox's father grinned a gap-toothed grin.

Eeron Brindle, the once-towering executive in charge of SecuriTech, looked like a ghost of himself. His cheeks were sunken, his eyes yellowed, and his hands trembled against his thighs. The black web of veins showed through his skin, but he did not scratch at them.

He knelt on the floor of his cell in front of Syd. A chain bolted to the wall attached to a metal collar around his neck. The cell was primitive, a cinder-block room in a building that hadn't been built as a prison, but the door to the cell was new, a pressure-piston-locking mechanism in a reinforced frame. There was a window, looking out over the jungle, crisscrossed with graphene wiring embedded in the plexi. Those little threads made the window even more impenetrable than the door. That was the idea. The condemned should have a view of the world outside, with no hope of ever being a part of it again.

In spite of the unbreakable window, the powerful door, the chain around his neck, and the prisoner's fragility, Liam stood beside Syd with his bolt gun in his hand. He would take no chances.

"Do you know why the Guardians are sick?" Syd asked.

Knox's father snorted.

"Do you?" Syd repeated.

"I know why everyone is sick," he said. "But I do not know why you've come out here to see me."

"Do you know how to stop it?" Syd continued.

"I get so few visitors," Knox's father talked over Syd. "I never realized how much I enjoyed conversation until I was denied it. I was never a people person, not like my son. I guess you don't know what you've got until it's gone. Isn't that what they say? Or do they say you don't know what's gone until you've got it? That hardly makes any sense, no? My memory's not what it was . . ."

He stared back at them, like he'd lost the thread of what he was saying. Liam shifted his feet. The old man had lost it. Syd knew it too, but he didn't dare look at Liam for confirmation. He couldn't bear the thought that this trip out to the prison was pointless, that he wouldn't learn anything, that he couldn't save anyone. That he'd have to crawl to the Council and beg them to help. Yovel the great.

He was not ready to give up yet. He could still fix things.

"Just answer me," Syd said.

"Conversation is an exchange, Syd," Knox's father said. "It's a deal people make with each other. Call and response, verse and chorus, question and answer, action and reaction. It makes the world go round and round and round."

"Do you know how to stop this sickness?" Syd said again.

"What I am trying to explain," Eeron Brindle told him, "is that a conversation is a transaction and each side must have something of value to trade."

"There's no credit anymore," said Syd. "It wouldn't do you any good anyway."

"Not money!" he shouted, rattling his chain and swaying from side to side. "Words! Trade words with me, you glitch-brained Chapter Eleven swampcat!"

"Hey!" Liam point a metal finger at Knox's father. "You are speaking to Yovel and you will speak with respect."

"Apologies. Apologies. Don't knock more of my teeth out. Those I have left I intend to take to the grave." He laughed again.

Liam shook his head. "This bloodsucker is a waste of time."

"I'll trade words with you," said Syd. "What words would you like?"

Knox's father leaned forward so that the collar squeezed his neck, turned his face red. He whispered to Syd, "Tell me about my son."

Syd leaned back. "What?"

"You heard me." Knox's father nodded. "Tell me about my son and I will tell you about this sickness. They complement each other, I should think."

Syd bit his lip. His voice came out hoarse. "What do you want me to tell you?"

Eeron Brindle's eyes darted from side to side, then he looked at Syd. "Did he hate me?"

"Yes," said Syd.

Knox's father nodded. "Only natural, I suppose."

"So . . . this disease? What is it?"

"It's not a disease," Eeron Brindle said.

"But I've seen it," Syd replied. "It's killing Guardians and now it's killing regular people. And it's spreading."

"It's not spreading," said Knox's father. "It can't spread. It simply is."

"What do you mean?"

"Did you hate my son?"

"Tell me what you mean about this *thing* not spreading."

"Answer my question. Did you hate my son?" A black vein on his forehead pulsed. The man winced, but was otherwise still. He waited, a man for whom patience was more powerful than pain.

"At first, yes," said Syd.

"And later?"

"Later, no, I didn't." Syd pointed at the man. "Your turn."

"Have you ever seen a syntholene addict?"

"I said it's your turn," Syd repeated.

"I am explaining it to you, impatient boy! I swear, you are just like . . ." He squinted, strained to find the word. "Knox," he said at last. "Never listens." He paused, shook his head. "Never listened. Listened. Past tense." He scratched an itch on the back of his hand, then froze in place. Muttered to himself and dropped both hands to his side again. They quivered. "So, again. A syntholene addict. Have you seen one coming off his syntholene patches?"

"Yes," said Syd.

"What happens to him?"

"Seizures, vomiting. Rashes."

"Death?"

"Sometimes death, yeah," said Syd. "What's syntholene have to do with the Guardians?"

"Nothing at all." Eeron Brindle laughed again. He licked his cracked lips with his pale tongue. Even it was veined with tiny blue lines.

Liam stepped forward and jabbed his metal finger into the prisoner's chest, hard. "Speak plainly or I'll—"

"You'll what, boy?" Knox's father laughed. "Torture me? There's no new pain left for me to feel. Can't you see that? The blood inside me burns. The moment my son died my own heartbeat turned against me. And killing me seems pointless, as I'm to be executed anyway. So what is it? Make your threats! Come on! Be creative! I'm listening!"

Liam exhaled. He wanted to crack the old man's head open. But he stepped back.

"Good help is so hard to find, eh, Syd?" Knox's father laughed again.

"You were saying," said Syd. "About syntholene addicts?"

"Ah yes." He smiled. "Withdrawal. When you take away an addict's drug, he goes into withdrawal. Terrible sickness. Deadly if he was truly addicted for a long enough time."

"So?"

"Did you love my son?"

Syd didn't answer.

"It's your turn," Knox's father reminded him.

"I know."

"So? Did you love my son?"

"Not at first," said Syd.

"And later?"

"I don't want to talk about Knox," said Syd.

"Oh, nor do I!" Knox's father laughed again. "But we must, one way or another! You see, he caused all of this! When my son destroyed the datastream, he took away the drug. Like I said. When my son died, my own heartbeat turned against me. So did yours. *Everyone* was networked. Everyone had that data in their blood. Take away the data and then . . ." He cocked his head to the side, opened his arms to show off the black veins running up and down them. "The Guardians went down first. They were nothing *but* networked. The older people next, those on the networks the longest, those with the most data installed. Some have stronger resistance than others . . ." He gestured at himself.

"Some will hold out longer. But, young and old, rich and poor, sinner and saint, eventually, it will take down—"

"Everyone," Syd whispered.

"Everyone," said Knox's father. "It isn't in the blood. It *is* the blood. Isn't it i—ire—?" Knox's father had lost the word he was looking for.

"Ironic," Syd prompted.

"Ironic, yes." The man scratched his neck, stopped himself, muttered something quietly. "The only way to save the revolution my son gave you is to undermine the revolution my son gave you."

"We have to reestablish the network," Syd said.

Liam looked back at the door to the room, worried the Purifiers outside could hear. This talk was treason.

"Is it real?" Syd asked. "Is there a machine that can do that?"

"Your turn, Sydney," said Knox's father with a devilish grin. "About my son."

Syd clenched his jaw.

"Why did he do it?" Knox's father wasn't grinning now. "Why did he die for you? Was it to get back at me? Did he love you? Did he hate me so much? Tell me why."

"He . . ." Syd pictured Knox, the moment before he died. They'd kissed, but it was just Knox being Knox. He didn't love Syd, at least, not that way.

"He wanted . . . ," Syd tried.

Syd stood in front of Knox. "What am I supposed to do?"

"Like I know?" Knox told him. "It's your future. Choose."

"Knox wanted—" Syd began again.

The door to the cell swung open and two Purifiers burst in. Liam whirled around and froze. With them was a third figure, his smooth skin gleaming like plastic. Cousin, his face twisted into a frown.

"My deepest apologies, Yovel." Cousin bent at the waist in a theatrical bow. "But your visit must come to an end."

"Who are you?" Syd demanded, stepping toward Cousin. Liam stopped him.

"I am but a servant of the Reconciliation," said Cousin. "And our wise Advisory Council has seen fit that the time for Eeron Brindle's execution is now."

"What? No." Syd looked to Knox's father, then to Liam. "I'm not done yet."

"Unfortunately, you are," said Cousin. He snapped and the two Purifiers rushed past him to grab Knox's father and lift him to his feet.

"Liam, can you stop them?" Syd asked. "Please."

Liam didn't move. "Syd . . . I can't . . ."

"But you heard him," Syd said. "He knows what's happening. We have to make the Council listen to him. We need more time."

"Ah, 'we need more time.'" Cousin sighed and stepped up to rest his delicate hand on Syd's shoulder. "And yet it never comes. The human condition itself, no?"

In a flash, Liam thrust himself between Syd and Cousin, knocking Cousin's arm away and staring him down. "Don't you ever lay a hand on Syd," he snarled.

Cousin grinned. "And now we have the animal condition," Cousin said. "Like a bitch defending her pup."

Three more Purifiers, all of them armed with electromuscular disruption sticks and bolt guns, entered the room. Syd recognized one of them through the holes in his mask. Finch was grinning.

"Syd," said Liam without looking away from Cousin, "we have to go."

"But—"

"We'll take this to the Council," he said. "But we can't stay here."

Syd looked between the two. Cousin unnerved him and his familiarity with Liam suggested a history that went far beyond today. More unnerving.

He looked to Knox's father, who smiled at him. "I'll give your regards to—?" His face fell. He searched for the word as two Purifiers pulled him from the room.

"Knox," Syd whispered as Knox's father was dragged away.

Cousin held up a hand to stop Syd and Liam leaving after them. The white-masked boys behind him raised their EMD sticks. Finch locked eyes with Syd. He pursed his lips, blew a murderous little kiss.

"Unfortunately, I can't let you go," Cousin said.

"You can't hold us here," said Syd. "I am Yovel, the—"

"Save it," Cousin cut him off.

"But . . . this sickness . . . we can stop it," said Syd. "He told us we can—!"

"No," said Cousin. "You can't."

"But he just said"—Syd shook his head—"the Machine. There must be people left who know how to build it, how to restore that network!"

"Treason! From Yovel himself! My oh my!" Cousin laughed. "I can hardly believe my ears."

"Cousin," Liam seethed. "Let us go."

"There's no point, Brother Liam," Cousin told him. "There's only one person left who could've built this fabled Machine, and Dr. Khan, very tragically, was murdered last week."

The color drained from Liam's face.

"You—" Liam began. "She—?"

"Don't hurt that tiny brain of yours," said Cousin. "Thinking doesn't suit you."

"I order you to let us go," said Syd. "On the authority of Yovel and the Advisory Council, I—"

"The Advisory Council has given me command of the Purifiers until this crisis has passed," Cousin explained. "So I'm afraid I will not be letting you go. I am authorized to do whatever is necessary in the interest of security." He smiled.

"The Council will hear about this," said Syd. "You'll be charged with treason."

"Oh, like me?" Finch growled. Syd clenched his fists and Finch noticed with a smile. "I'll be sure to tell the chair of the Council we made up," he added. "Best friends forever."

"Now, Furious," Cousin mock-scolded him. "You know you aren't supposed to enjoy this sort of thing."

Finch didn't take his eyes off Syd. "I know, sir. But I do."

"Well, it'll be our little secret then," said Cousin. "These boys won't tell, will they? They have their own secrets, after all." He winked at Liam and with that, he and his Purifiers stepped back through the cell door and slammed it shut, sealing Syd and Liam inside.

[17]

AFTER THE PISTONS ON the massive door hissed and slammed the air-locked pins into place, the room was silent. The door was sealed. Syd and Liam were trapped.

Liam had the urge to remind Syd that he'd known coming here was a bad idea. He'd known from the start this would lead to nothing but trouble. But Syd was stubborn and determined to defy not only the rules of the Reconciliation, but all common good sense.

Liam wanted to curse and spit and yell, although it wasn't really Syd he was angry at. He never should have allowed Syd to put himself in this position. He never should have allowed Syd to boss him around. If there was anyone Liam should be mad at, it was himself, for letting personal feelings interfere with his work.

And with Cousin, for being a treacherous snake.

Syd stood beside him in front of the door, looking at it. Liam turned to him, hoping he'd at least have a plan for what to do next. Liam wasn't much for planning.

Before he could open his mouth, however, Syd collapsed onto him, his hand clutching at Liam's shirt, crying against Liam's chest. His shoulders heaved with sudden sobs.

This was unexpected.

"Uh . . . um." Liam didn't know what was happening. He stood there with his arms open, too afraid to close them around Syd and wanting nothing more than to close them around Syd. "What's . . . uh . . . wrong?"

He didn't even know what question to ask, but he was pretty sure, given the circumstances, that was the wrong one.

"Why *did* Knox sacrifice himself for me?" Syd pulled away from Liam. He'd left a wet spot on Liam's shirt, tears or drool or both. His cheeks were damp, his mouth twisting in an futile attempt to prevent more sobbing. He didn't look at Liam, didn't look anywhere, really. He sniffed and shuddered and seemed suddenly so very, very young, even though the two of them were the exact same age. He turned away from Liam.

"Knox gave me his life . . . he died and created this new world, where I'm the one with all the power." Syd dropped his head. "He gave me his future and what did I do with it? I let them kill the nopes. I let them kill the sick. I'm letting them kill his father."

"He hated his father," Liam said.

"That's not the point!" Syd whirled around, nostrils flared.

Liam cursed himself. He always said the wrong thing. He'd never had to comfort anyone before, at least, not anyone he didn't intend to kill moments later. He'd never imagined he'd have to comfort Syd. Never imagined he'd get the chance to.

"I'm no savior to anyone," said Syd.

"But . . ." Liam scrambled for a kind word. "But you're trying."

"Am I?" He wiped his face on shirt, tried to regain his composure. He felt ridiculous breaking down in front of Liam. At least his bodyguard did him the favor of avoiding eye contact. "We're stuck in here, while the only person who might be able to stop this sickness is getting executed. You heard Knox's dad. It's my fault everyone is going to die. I should have just stayed in Mountain City and did my time as a proxy. Knox would be alive. My friends would alive. Marie's parents would be healthy. Now . . . everyone . . ."

Liam couldn't say what he wanted to. He couldn't tell Syd it was *his* fault, not Syd's. He'd been so obsessed with protecting Syd, he'd let Cousin use him. He'd murdered Dr. Khan. He'd destroyed the chance they had to stop this thing. If anyone was to blame for the dying that was to come, it was Liam, not Syd.

Instead, he told him: "We'll go to Baram. We'll go to Baram when we get out of here. He'll know what to do."

"Go to Baram," Syd repeated. "All I'm ever good for is getting other people to solve the problems I've created."

"Well, that's what other people are for, right?" Liam

tried. "You can't do it all alone. There are people who want to help you. *I* want to help you."

Syd exhaled. He finally looked back at his bodyguard. "Listen, Liam. You and me? Whatever idea you have, it's not going to happen. I think you should understand that. It's not possible."

Liam didn't say anything.

"I see how you look at me. Guys like us, back in the Mountain City, we were called Chapter Eleven. It was slang for bankrupts. Broke. Guys who couldn't make anything, didn't own anything, and never would. And the eleven?"

He held up both his index fingers side by side, knocked them together.

"Get it? Two of the same thing. It didn't exactly make a person popular. I taught myself to be alone. I thought the whole bankrupt thing was about sex, but it wasn't. It was about ruin, about being the kind of guy who ruins whatever he touches. That's what I was. That's what I still am. You know, everyone I ever cared about has died, violently, because of me. Every connection I ever made got destroyed. So the revolution erased those old labels and gave me this new identity, Yovel, but I'm still the same person. I'm still the Chapter Eleven swampcat who breaks whatever he touches. You think you want that, but you're wrong. You can do your job if you have to. Protect Yovel. But Syd? He's not worth it."

"Syd," Liam said, but couldn't say any more because just then, a holo projection appeared in the air in front of them, glowing brightly in the twilight.

Outside the window, another appeared, hovering over the treetops. Then another a few yards beyond that. More and more flickered on, wobbling in the air as far as Liam and Syd could see. Some floated jumbo-sized above the jungle, some hovered half obscured by broken walls, some inside, some outside, visible only by the glow they cast through the windows of residential buildings in the distance.

Syd had never realized there were projectors all over the jungle city before. The technology was outlawed, but not, it seemed, eliminated. It continued to have its uses by those whom the Advisory Council trusted to use it. It was a closed circuit system, not a network, but if it could exist, then maybe . . .

Syd felt a pang of hope. Maybe everything could be restored.

At first the holos simply glowed, but then, the image hovering in the cell came into focus. All the projections outside showed the same thing: a close-up of the face of Eeron Brindle, former chief of the SecuriTech Corporation, directly responsible for the creation and programming of the Guardians, and the grieving father of Syd's dead patron.

Knox's father looked directly out from the holo, as if he were staring straight at Syd. The hope in Syd's heart curdled. The black veins of Brindle's face throbbed.

"My name is Eeron Brindle," Knox's father said. "I served as director of data security and counter-terrorism operations, and later, chief executive officer of the SecuriTech . . . Corp . . . Corp . . . Corporation."

He cleared his throat. Speaking took effort but he continued.

"I offer my full con . . . con . . . confession. I manipulated the market to favor the terms of creditors. I ignored protocol as . . . p . . . p . . . proxies were punished more severely than necessary. I authorized acts of violence and intimidation to protect the interests of my . . ." His eyes drifted. He was struggling with language. His lips moved without sound and then, he snapped his focus back and spoke quickly. "Clients! To protect my clients at the expense of the people, and I knowingly profited from all of the aforementioned crimes. I do not deny, nor do I repent these things. I have only one regret—" His voice cracked. Sadness replaced defiance. "In my zeal, I sacrificed my own son's life and for that, I willingly submit myself to this . . ."

It wasn't clear if he'd forgotten the word "execution" or simply couldn't bring himself to say it.

The view pulled back to reveal two white-masked Purifiers standing behind him, each holding an electro-muscular disruption stick. They raised their weapons and held them just in front of his ears. He lowered his head.

Cousin was not among them and Liam wondered where the man had gone. Not knowing Cousin's whereabouts left Liam very uncomfortable.

"We can't let them do this," Syd said. "I need to talk to him more!"

Almost as if he could hear Syd, almost as if he knew he was watching, Knox's father looked up, straight out from the holos: "I'll see you all soon," he said, his lips cracking into a grim smirk. "Some of you sooner than—"

The Purifiers cut him off, touching their EMD sticks to his head. Eeron Brindle's body convulsed; his muscles seized and spasmed uncontrollably. He foamed at the mouth. He dropped dead.

Every holo screen went dark, then disappeared. The sun had set over the jungle and the room itself fell into near-pitch blackness. The only light came from an orb on the high ceiling above them, a ring of green pinpoints of light, flashing in sequence, one by one.

Liam stared at it a moment. "We have to get out of here," he said.

"They killed him," Syd muttered. "He could have helped us and they just . . . killed him."

"We have to find a way out of here," Liam repeated.

He looked up at the sequence of lights. As they blinked one by one, faster and faster, he watched them, counted the length of the sequence, then did it again. It was shorter the second time.

Syd slumped down against the wall beside the door, not paying any attention to Liam. "He knew this would happen. All along. He knew we'd all die. He knew it."

"Syd." Liam turned to him. "I need you to focus here. You're good with machines, right?"

Syd looked at Liam now, making out the glint of the flashing lights off Liam's metal hand, the wide pale face staring down at him in the darkness.

Syd shrugged. "I was."

"Well, you need to be again," said Liam. "Because we need to get this door open in the next eight minutes."

"Why?" said Syd. "They already killed Knox's father. Marie's parents are as good as dead. All of those people. There's nothing we can do."

"That'll be true if we don't get out of here." Liam pointed at the orb on the ceiling. "Because that's a bomb and in . . . about eight minutes, it is going to ignite all the oxygen in this room and incinerate anyone still inside it."

Syd looked at the lights flashing on the ceiling, looked at the giant door beside him and the graphene-reinforced window and took a deep breath.

He could give up, stop trying, and let the bomb do its work. He'd avoid the horror that was to come. Or he could stand up off the ground and use the only skill he had to try to save himself, to save Liam, and then, somehow, to save everyone else from the sickness that his own revolution had created.

One of those things was easy, one of them was hard, and one was probably impossible.

It's your future. Choose.

He grabbed Liam's hand to lift himself up and get started.

He'd had enough.

He chose.

[18]

THE COUNCIL'S MEETING POINT was in a second-floor ballroom of what used to be a hotel. None of the fancy fixtures remained—they'd been looted at least a hundred years ago—but the space was still grand and intimidating. It had no exterior windows, which also made it ideal from a security perspective.

The Council's meeting locations changed every day, rotating between a fixed number of places by a complex pattern that was one of the most closely guarded secrets of the Reconciliation. The secret was so closely guarded, in fact, that everyone knew it. So many people knew the pattern and the locations that no one actually believed it could be the real pattern. It was a brilliant tactic, really. Secrecy through transparency. The Council hid in plain sight.

There was a fail-safe, of course. Whenever the Council

met, there was that row of armed Purifiers behind them, warding off unwelcome guests.

Marie, at the moment, certainly felt unwelcome.

"Purifier Alvarez, we did not call for you to attend this meeting." Chairwoman Pei knelt in her usual place at the apex of the semicircle. There were fewer counselors around her than usual. Only three on one side of her and four on the other. Counselor Baram knelt next to her. The bearded old Counselor was scratching the back of his hand, and though his beard covered most of his face, she could see the faint blue shadows of the veins around his eyes beginning to show through. The disease had spread as high as the Council. At least now they would have to hear her out. They would have to do something besides murder the sick.

"I am sorry to intrude on your business of the day," Marie said loudly. "I felt it was my duty to brief the Council on what I have learned in the hope that my knowledge may be of service to all."

"Your knowledge of what?" Chairwoman Pei snapped at her, impatient. At first Marie assumed it was a side effect of the chairwoman not feeling well, but looking at her, she showed no signs of sickness. She looked healthy, stern, and unforgiving as ever.

"The infection among the nonoperative entities," said Marie. "It has spread to the people. At the educational farming cooperative where my parents are"—she cleared her throat, searched for the right word—"studying, everyone has been infected, even the leader of their Purifier unit.

The others fled and the conditions are terrible. People are dying."

"Death is a part of the natural world," the chairwoman said. "It is not easy to be part of a system of which you are not the master. The patrons fooled themselves for far too long that nature existed for their convenience, but it shook them off like a dog shaking off fleas. We are trying to teach them to live as a part of nature again. Suffering, exhaustion, even death . . . these are parts of the process."

"It's past that," said Marie. "This infection is something else."

"We are aware," the chairwoman said. "Thank you for bringing the outbreak at Educational Farming Cooperative Eight to our attention. It will be contained."

"Contained." Marie felt a chill. "You mean—?"

"There is no cure," said Counselor Baram. "I am sorry to say we have suffered a terrible setback in our research. The doctor who was leading our efforts was murdered last week."

"Murdered?" Marie shook her head. "But . . . there have to be others?"

"The program was secret," Counselor Baram said. "We decided it would be better to minimize the risk of a panic by limiting knowledge of the disease. Very few knew of this doctor's work, which we assumed would keep her safe." He glanced at the chairwoman. "We assumed wrongly, I regret to say."

"Enough, Counselor Baram," Chairwoman Pei said. "Purifier Alvarez does not require this information."

"Secrecy has not served us well," Counselor Baram replied. "It is time we discuss Dr. Khan's theories in the open."

"Her theories were treason," the chairwoman replied.

Another counselor spoke up. "Madam Chairwoman, if restoring the networks can stop the infection, we have to consider—"

"It is not an option," Chairwoman Pei interrupted.

"But . . . you can't just give up on curing the disease?" Marie shook her head. "You'd rather destroy the infected than consider a cure?"

"We will do what is necessary to protect the greater good," the chairwoman told Marie. She then addressed the other counselors. "A return to the past would doom generations to come. All we have done would be for nothing. I will not condemn our children and their children to the old systems that enslaved us, simply because you all lack the moral strength to get through a challenging time. Will some suffer? Yes. But suffering is the price we pay to break free of history." She looked back at Marie with a hard stare. "True believers do not have their faith shaken so easily."

"I believe, but . . ." Marie wanted to argue, but what could she say? She had sacrificed so much to help destroy the old system. Others had lost their families because of the revolution. Why should she be exempt? Could she really let her parents die for some abstract idea about her role in history? And how many others besides her parents would die? Would it be worth it? Who got to decide?

"Your objections, Purifier, are noted," the chairwoman

continued. "But we have other business to attend to this evening." With a wave of her hands, Chairwoman Pei brought up a holo projection.

Marie hadn't seen one in months and the sudden glow in the air startled her. With another wave of her hands, a holo appeared along the far wall of the grand room. On the holo was the lined face of Knox's father, Eeron Brindle, looking out, with two Purifiers by his side.

He spoke and his voice echoed from a thousand other holos scattered through the city: "My name is Eeron Brindle. I served as director of data security and counter-terrorism operations, and later, chief executive officer of the Securi-Tech . . . Corp . . . Corp . . . Corporation." He cleared his throat. "I offer my full con . . . con . . . confession . . ."

Another figure entered the ballroom, a bald man in a Purifier's uniform. He nodded once at the chairwoman, who nodded back. Marie noticed a smile creep across the chairwoman's face as she watched the execution on the projection unfold.

"Is this live?" Marie asked.

Everyone ignored her question. She'd been ignorant to think the Council wouldn't have whatever tech they desired at their disposal. It was the one law of history she began to understand: Even an organization dedicated to equality would find a way to privilege an elite few. For all the chairwoman had just said about the purity of their ideals, the flickering image in the air felt like a stab in her back. If even the Council betrayed its own rules about tech for the sake of convenience, why should she stick by them and lose her parents?

"I manipulated the market to favor the terms of creditors. I ignored protocol as p . . . p . . ." While Eeron Brindle spoke, Counselor Baram stood and excused himself.

"I'm not feeling well," he addressed the room. "I will be back in a moment."

As he brushed past Marie, he met her eyes and mouthed a brief word, before he swept past the bald man behind her. She hadn't been paying close attention, transfixed as she was by the last moments of Knox's father's life, so it took her a few seconds to realize the word he'd mouthed in silence to her was "run."

[19]

LIAM BANGED ON THE door, kicked it, slammed his shoulder against it. Then he ran to the back of the narrow room and smashed his metal fist against the window. It didn't so much as crack. He felt the blow through his metal hand, up his wrist, and all the way back to his shoulder. He'd be feeling that in the morning.

If he ever saw the morning again.

He took a running charge and kicked at the door again. It didn't even quiver. He screamed in frustration.

"Force is not gonna do it, no matter how strong that hand of yours is," said Syd, studying the door mechanism. He was sure he could get it open if he had the right tools.

He didn't have the right tools.

He also didn't have much time. Another minute had passed. Less than six remained.

Syd's heart pounded in his chest and he had to focus his breathing to keep his hands from shaking. In spite of that, he smiled. For the first time in a long time, he had a purpose. He had a skill. He was going to save Liam's life.

"I'll need a hand," he said.

"Whatever I can do," said Liam. "I'm yours."

"I mean, I'll need your hand. The metal one."

"Right." Liam's cheeks flushed again. Syd noticed.

"Can you crush that piston there?" Syd pointed at one of the air-locking controls. "The door pins are locked with pressurized air. If we can reverse the pressure back into the system, we might just blast apart the pins and blow this whole door off its hinges using its own locks."

"Blowing up the door to escape a bomb?" Liam wasn't sure he understood.

"Blowing it out," said Syd. "And if you have a better idea, I'd be glad to hear it."

Liam didn't, so Syd directed him where to bend, what to crush, and what to break. Meanwhile, Syd worked on the wiring, shorting out the safety valves.

As he worked, Syd noticed Liam wincing. He knew his bodyguard had hurt himself trying to break the door open. It wasn't the noblest of injuries, but Syd felt bad for him. He knew all about self-inflicted wounds, especially the pointless ones. They weren't all physical.

There was a high-pitched whine, a squeal as the pressure inside the door built and built. Syd hoped it would build fast enough to work before the bomb on the ceiling went off. He hoped the door would blow with time enough left for them to escape the building, and he hoped it wouldn't blow into the room instead of out, crushing them both to death.

At least if that happened, they wouldn't feel it when their bodies were incinerated.

"Move to the back," Syd ordered, and they crouched down together in the corner. Liam turned and put his arm around Syd, covering him with his body.

"Uh . . . ," said Syd.

"I'm still your bodyguard," said Liam. "Let me do my job."

Syd didn't resist. He couldn't have pushed Liam off if he wanted to. Even injured, the guy was stronger, much stronger.

"My ears are popping," said Liam.

Syd worked his jaw, trying to relieve the pressure in his own. Too much air was releasing into the room and not enough into the door itself. Had he misunderstood the mechanism? Had he made the wrong choice? Had he failed?

Liam was counting to himself in whispers. They were running out of time.

Syd tilted his head up and saw Liam looking at him like he was about to tell Syd something. He opened his mouth to speak, he was cut off by a horrible shriek of twisting metal, and then, with a whoosh and painful pop of pressure, the door exploded out into the hallway, taking a large chunk of the concrete wall with it.

It *had* worked. Syd smiled. He'd made the machine backfire. He'd turned the lock keeping them in into the key to getting out. Maybe he wasn't so useless after all.

"Go!" Liam shouted, shoving Syd forward. "Run!"

They ran through the door, turned at a bend in the hallway. There were no Purifiers standing guard, no one to stop them. Cousin had evacuated the prison the moment Knox's father's corpse hit the floor.

There was no sound of an explosion, but the air around them tasted bitter, and then the hallway brightened. They turned to a stairwell, took the steps three at a time. Syd could see the exit ahead. He felt heat on his back, glanced over his shoulder to see a wall of blue and orange flame dance across the ceiling and turn down the stairway, as if it were a living thing, gulping the air as it chased them. He felt its force pulling him backward, sucking him into the blaze.

A hand on his back shoved Syd through the door. He tripped and flew forward, face first, over a root and into a tangle of brush, just as the tongue of flame blasted soundlessly over their heads. It danced in the air above them a moment, then burned itself abruptly out against the night sky.

Liam had dived on top of Syd to cover him and now his weight was crushing Syd. Syd wriggled out from beneath him and sat up from the ground, catching his breath and looking at the blasted-out building.

"Why would they try to kill me?" he panted.

Liam pictured Cousin's face, his skeletal grimace. "I don't know," he said.

"You were right. We have to go to Baram," said Syd. "It's treason for them to try to kill me. Baram will know what to do."

Liam didn't answer. If Syd leveled an accusation at Cousin, Cousin could just as easily turn it back on Liam. Liam had killed Dr. Khan, after all. He'd killed two Purifiers too, just because they had known where Syd was stowed away. If Cousin had become a traitor to the Reconciliation, he had made Liam an accomplice. He had just as much blood on his hands.

On his hand.

Syd was thinking out loud now. "Chairwoman Pei might not care that it's treason. She gave that guy—"

"Cousin," said Liam.

"Cousin? Whose cousin is he?"

Liam shook his head. It was just what the man was called.

"Well, she gave Cousin control of the Purifiers and orders for Eeron Brindle's execution. Maybe she gave him orders to kill me. Maybe she's making a move to take over, staging a coup."

"If that's true," said Liam, "then you aren't safe anywhere the Reconciliation controls."

"Forget about me," said Syd. "Marie was going straight to the Council from her parents. And she doesn't have a bodyguard with her. We have to get her."

"No way."

Syd pushed himself up off the ground and stood looking

down at Liam. "I'm not asking your permission. She's the closest thing I have to a friend and we're going to save her."

Liam looked up at Syd, standing dark as ash against the burning building behind him. Syd was implacable when he got an idea in his head. He wasn't moping anymore. He wasn't sulking. He might be crazy, but he was starting to act like the guy everyone believed him to be.

The guy Liam believed him to be.

He put up his good hand and Syd helped him to his feet.

"No one else dies today?" Syd said.

"No one who doesn't deserve it," said Liam.

[20]

IN THE PAST, LIAM had come to the Council to give them briefings, to receive instructions, or, lately, to be scolded by them. He'd never gone to them to stop a coup.

When they reached the cleared streets and rows of restored buildings in the heart of the city, Liam stopped. He and Syd crouched together off the side of the avenue in a blasted-out building that was awaiting demolition. It was covered in plants and vines, although it was really only two partial walls and a broken second floor above them, completely open to the elements. Syd's school building was around the corner to the left. The hotel where the Council held its meeting—if Liam had the pattern correct in his head—was a few blocks to the right.

Liam went to the left.

Syd stopped. "Why are we going back here?"

"We're going to make sure it's secure," said Liam. "And you're going to gather what you need. I'm going to the Council alone."

"No way," Syd told him.

"There will be Purifiers at the Council, loyal to Cousin."

"But doesn't Cousin already know about this place?" Syd looked at the squat, depressing school building. He had been looking forward to never seeing it again.

"He thinks you're dead from the explosion. I'd like to keep it that way." Liam continued inside ahead of Syd, who followed reluctantly.

When Liam was satisfied the building was empty, they entered Syd's room. It was just as he'd left it, simultaneously messy and bare. Liam shut the door, watching Syd look at his room. Now would be the time to give him that book. Now would be the time to stop being a coward and speak up. He might not have another chance.

"Are you going to stand there all night staring at me?" Syd said without turning around.

Liam cleared his throat. "No. I'm not. Sorry. Just tired, is all. My mind wandered off."

"No, it didn't," Syd told him. "You want to tell something and you're trying to get up the nerve."

"I—"

Syd turned around to look at him. "The moment you shut the door, you took a breath and held it, like you were getting ready to say something planned, but you exhaled when the moment passed. It's what people do before they give a speech. So, go for it. Tell me what you want to tell me. I'm listening."

Liam took another deep breath. Syd raised an eyebrow. It was now or never.

"I found you a book," he said.

Syd cocked his head. Liam finally managed to surprise him. Syd had not expected a book.

Liam stepped into the hall and retrieved the book from the loose ceiling tile where he'd hidden it. When he came back into the room, Syd was standing by the door, eager, maybe for the first time, to see him. Liam knew it was just Syd's curiosity, but he liked the feeling that Syd was waiting for him to come back, instead of waiting for him to go away.

"What is it?" Syd reached out to take the soft leather-bound volume from Liam's good hand. As he held it, a brief smile actually flashed on Syd's face.

"Just something I found," Liam told him, even though Syd would surely sense the evasion.

"You read it?" Syd looked up at him, those dark eyes studying Liam's face.

He had to be careful now . . . he also couldn't look like he was being careful. Syd noticed everything.

But he'd already hesitated. Syd had noticed his breathing a minute ago; of course he'd notice him hesitate now. People with nothing to hide didn't pause for so long to answer a simple question. Why was he still pausing? Now he couldn't stop not saying anything. He'd gone dumb. What should he say? He was definitely hiding something. He had to admit something. It was too late to turn back. Should he blurt it out? *I killed a woman for you. The doctor who might have stopped this sickness, and I killed her for you and then I stole this book and I'd do it again too. I'd burn the world down if it would make you smile.*

Instead, he said, "I can't read it. Never learned how."

The best way to cover a lie was with a truth.

Syd nodded. He thumbed the pages of the book. "Growing up, a lot of guys in the Valve didn't learn to read. There wasn't much point."

So Syd didn't think he was stupid. That was a relief. He watched the boy flip through Dr. Khan's book, his eyes scanning the pages.

"I wanted to give it to you before—well, you know—in case—"

"In case you don't come back," Syd finished his thought for him.

Liam nodded.

Syd looked down at the book in his hand, then looked back at Liam. "Just come back."

It was Liam's turn to smile. He could have stayed there all day, standing across from Syd, but there was no time.

He pulled the bolt gun from his belt and held it out.

"You'll need that," Syd told him.

"I'll be fine," said Liam. "When I get back I'll give four long knocks. If anyone other than me knocks . . ."

Syd took the weapon and held it. It was heavier than he thought it would be from how Liam handled it.

"Syd, I know I shouldn't say it, but I want you to know that I—"

"Don't." Syd stopped him. "It's better if you just don't."

Liam bit down his lip to stop himself from blushing again. He nodded once more and stepped from the room, closing the door and locking it from the outside.

Maybe Syd was right. Maybe it was better this way. By morning, Liam would probably be arrested for murdering Dr. Khan or dead by Cousin's hand. Or both.

He set off for the old hotel, trying to imagine if anyone living would mourn him when he was gone and which of his dead would be waiting for him on the other side.

He didn't expect they'd be forgiving.

Syd stood in the center of the room with the journal is his hands. The leather cover felt good against his palm and he liked the weight of the pages. A holo was just a trick of light and the words it shared were illusions. They could change, appear, and disappear on a whim. Kind of like people. But these words, handwritten in some kind of dark stain, they were real, solid, immutable. The book was more real than Syd was. It occurred to him he hadn't even thanked Liam for it.

Could a simple thank-you really have been so bad? He wouldn't be dooming Liam to a miserable death just by saying thank you, would he? He took a step toward the door, then stopped, took a step back again. It was better if he didn't reach out, better for Liam, better for Syd. They had to focus on staying alive. They couldn't be worried about each other *that* way.

Still . . . Syd had never known another guy like Liam. Knowing someone *that* way hadn't ever been an option before. Why was he so scared of it now?

He sat down on the edge of his bed, listened to the silence of the room.

Nothing to do but wait. He set the bolt gun down on the table beside his cot and opened the book to the middle.

My work progresses, day in and day out, but little has been accomplished.

So someone didn't like their job. Join the club. Pretty brave, however, for the author to complain in writing. Discontentment was a crime in the Reconciliation. He wondered what this job had been.

Syd had never owned a book before. He wasn't actually sure which order one was supposed to read it in. Could you just start anywhere, like a holo, or did he have to start at the front? He turned to the first page of it and a chill ran through him. The owner of the book had inscribed it.

Property of Dr. Adaeze Khan,
Medical High Command.
For her eyes ONLY.
Dr. Khan.

That was the name Cousin had said.

The doctor who was murdered.

Why would Liam have this book?

He pictured Liam's face when Cousin mentioned the murder, tried to remember word for word what he said.

"*Dr. Khan, very tragically, was murdered last week,*" Cousin said.

"*You—*" Liam replied and then, "*She—?*"

How did Liam know Dr. Khan was a she? He couldn't read; he'd just admitted that, so he hadn't read the inside cover. How else would he know?

For the same reason he had the book to begin with, the same reason he and that man called Cousin had shared such a knowing look with each other.

Liam wasn't just Syd's protector.

He was a killer.

Of course he was a killer. That wasn't news. He'd been a soldier since he was a boy. Syd knew that much about him. He'd seen him kill, even.

But why would Liam kill a doctor? Why kill the one woman who could've helped them?

Syd flipped the pages frantically, scanned the words without really absorbing them.

Resilience factors in Nonoperatives unpredictable yet evidence suggests their presence in a percentage of the control group. Negative correlation with affected treatments. Fatality rates inoptimal.

Scientific jargon. Syd couldn't make much sense of it.

He flipped the pages and he saw sketched strands of DNA, a face webbed with veins.

Before her death, she had taken extensive notes about the infection.

He stopped at one sentence, underlined: _No organic cure viable._

No cure.

He kept turning pages. Midway through the book, just before the writing stopped, he found another passage he understood. The understanding quickened his heartbeat.

I begin to understand the fatality of the condition.
Will present my findings to Chairwoman P. next week.
I fear she will not be receptive. My recommendation:
network reactivation. Feasibility of machine: TBD.
    Others have been disappeared for less, but biodata linkage
appears to be the only way to prevent population morbidity.

Population morbidity? Syd untangled the words. It was a lux way of saying what Eeron Brindle had said: Without the networks back on, everyone would die.

Feasibility of machine: TBD.

To Be Determined.

There were drawings, mechanical schematics, programming notes.

So the doctor believed a machine was possible. Not just

the fever dream of anti-revolutionary cultists, but a real machine that could really turn the network back on.

Was that why the doctor was murdered? The chairwoman didn't like her findings, and had Liam kill her?

Syd looked to the door. He didn't know what he would say to Liam when he saw him again. If he saw him again. Liam was shocked when Cousin told him Dr. Khan was dead. Shocked not because she was dead, but because . . . what? Because he hadn't known who she'd been when she was alive. Syd felt sure of it. Liam had been tricked. He had to believe that Liam had been tricked. No one with those sad puppy eyes could willingly kill an innocent person, could he?

Syd kept flipping pages, looking at diagrams—could those be instructions for the machine? Syd understood mechanical things, far better than he understood people. Machines could be programmed, rewired, redesigned. Fixed. People were another matter entirely.

He didn't really understand the schematics the doctor had drawn. They were way beyond him, but at least reading felt like doing something. What else could he do? He was just one person. He wasn't the great and powerful Yovel. He was just Syd.

"Self-pity's pretty easy," Knox scoffed at him, perched on the end of the bed, his light brown hair shining even under the grim lighting, his green eyes twinkling mischief.

Syd was pretty sure he was dreaming. He stood up and looked down at himself sitting in the chair with the book against his chest and a trickle of drool running down his face, sound asleep.

"Charming," said Knox, suddenly standing at Syd's side.

"You're dead," Syd told him. "You don't get to make fun of me."

"Someone has to," said Knox. "You think you can just walk around letting people worship you? Ha!" Syd smirked. He'd missed Knox's sarcasm. "You know what they call you behind your back?"

Syd shrugged. "I must, if you're about to tell me. I'm the one dreaming you."

"So logical," Knox tucked a stray hair behind his ear. "I guess I don't need to tell you then."

"No," said Syd. "You don't."

"So . . . Liam, eh?" Knox's mouth twisted into a crooked smile. "He's cute."

"I didn't think you went that way," Syd grunted at him. "Or is there a shortage of girls in the afterlife?"

"You just said it, I'm *your* subconscious." Knox looked around the room, picked up a shirt from the floor, examined the toilet bucket behind the screen in the corner. "The real Knox wouldn't be caught dead in a room like this." Knox smirked. "'Caught dead'? Get it?"

Syd rolled his eyes.

"He died so you could live," dream Knox said.

"I know that," said Syd. "I'm alive, aren't I?"

"Being alive and living aren't the same."

Syd looked back at his sleeping self, willed himself to wake up. He did not want to stand here chatting with a subconscious manifestation of his own guilt, even if he did miss Knox terribly.

Syd looked around the filthy room. "I don't know what else to do."

Knox shrugged and brushed imaginary lint off his broad shoulder. He was suddenly wearing the uniform of the Guardians. He smoothed the fabric across his chest. "Yes, you do. Fix it."

"I don't know how," Syd told him. "I can't understand this book. I don't even know where to start."

"Start at the beginning," said Knox, with a wink, and was gone.

Syd opened his eyes. He was awake. He wiped his mouth with his sleeve and the book splayed open on his chest tumbled to the floor. He stared at it.

Start at the beginning. Fix it.

"The beginning," he said to himself. He knew.

He was going back to the Mountain City. He was going to fix it. He was going to find the Machine, or he was going to build one himself.

That's who he was.

He fixed things.

If the people wanted a savior, they'd get one, but on his terms, not theirs. No more speeches. No more waving. If he had to betray the revolution and join the Machinists to save everyone's lives, then that's what he would do.

He was going to turn the network back on and reboot the world.

[21]

THERE WERE THREE ENTRY points to the grand ball-room, and four access points to the floor the ballroom was on. Liam had already plotted a half-dozen escape routes, if it came to it. Force of habit. If Syd had been with him, he would have planned a full dozen in his head before setting foot inside. He was glad he didn't have to.

When he did enter the room, he worried he'd gotten the pattern wrong.

The room was empty.

He knew he was in the right building, but was it the right day? Or was he too late? It was night, but not late. The sun hadn't set that long ago. The Council should still be there. Marie should too.

As Liam reached for his light, he stopped short, froze, and listened. Something scurried in the dark on the far side of the room, something small, like a startled lizard.

If it was a lizard, then something had startled it.

He dropped to a crouch and slanted sideways from the door, regretting for a moment that he'd left Syd with the bolt gun.

"Relax, Liam," Cousin's granite-smooth voice slid from the darkness. "I'm not going to hurt you."

Liam pivoted toward the sound, angling his body to make a smaller target. He had no reason to believe a word Cousin said. He stayed low and moved diagonally toward the sound of Cousin's voice.

"You know if I meant you to die right now, you'd already be dead," Cousin said. "Stop all your skulking about. It's embarrassing."

With a loud hiss, a lighting fixture in the center of the floor flared on, casting the ruined old ballroom in an orange haze. Cousin stood beside it with his hands behind his back, watching Liam the way a spider watches a fly in its web, a hunger in his stillness.

Beside him stood Marie, gagged with her own white Purifier mask, her arms bound behind her back.

"Where are the counselors?" Liam demanded, standing up straight.

"There has been a change of leadership," Cousin said. "The counselors were feeling unwell, and limited in their capacity to function. Chairwoman Pei saw fit to dissolve their authority."

"She can't just do that."

"It's already done." The chairwoman of the Advisory Council stepped into the room from a small door at the rear.

"They lacked the vision to see us through this time of trouble. They thought we had a public health crisis, when what we had was a crisis of leadership. Leadership means making the hard decisions. Life and death decisions. Those who could not understand that have been eliminated."

"You ordered that bomb at the prison?" said Liam.

"I did."

"You killed Syd," said Liam.

A whimper escaped from Marie through the gag in her mouth. The chairwoman's eyebrows shot up; a smile broke open her mouth.

"So that Yovel might live on in the people's memory," she said. "He'll be remembered as a hero who died a martyr's death. No one will know the moping degenerate he really was."

Liam clenched his metal fist.

"Unfortunately, Chairwoman Pei," Cousin interjected, "young Liam here is not being truthful. Syd is alive. If he weren't, Liam wouldn't be in this room with us."

"I barely escaped the bomb myself," Liam said.

"You would have thrown yourself on top of that bomb before you'd let Syd die alone," said Cousin. "We both know that."

"Chairwoman," Liam said. "You can't believe a word this man says. He's a liar and a murderer."

"It's bad luck to scold a mirror, Liam," Cousin said.

"I'm no liar," said Liam. "I confess, I killed Dr. Khan. I thought I was acting on the orders of the Reconciliation."

"Oh, but you were," said the chairwoman. "We

couldn't have the doctor advocating for the Machinist cause, spreading their false gospel, and I knew your . . . *fetish* . . . for that boy would make you do anything for him." Liam began to object, but the counselor kept talking over him. "You are not nearly as subtle as you believe yourself to be, young man, but we are grateful for your service in this regard."

"Why would you want Dr. Khan dead? She was the only hope of curing this sickness!"

"Her cure was worse than the disease!" Chairwoman Pei moved behind Marie, studied her profile, and shook her head. "Even if we could just rebuild the network, link everyone up to constant data once more, how would that look? The people would lose faith in us completely. They would turn back to the easy fixes and the quick credits and endless debts and all the old systems would return. Our revolution would crumble. We would have achieved nothing. We would have changed nothing."

"But it will still crumble," said Liam. "We talked to Eeron Brindle. This doesn't just stay with the nopes . . . without the network, it's going to kill everyone."

"Not everyone, Liam," Cousin said. "Only those who had biodata to begin with."

"There were never many people without it," said Liam. "Maybe a few thousand at most."

Cousin smiled. "Then don't you feel lucky to be among them?"

"I do not enjoy the deaths of any of our people," Chairwoman Pei said as she approached Liam. "But we are trying to build a new kind of world and these things are necessary if the society is to endure. All vestiges of the past need to be wiped away. To that end, Cousin has been given command of the Purifiers; the infected will be contained, and I will see to it that the Reconciliation survives this crisis to emerge stronger than before. Under my leadership. It will not be easy, but I will—"

"Excuse me, Chairwoman." Cousin held up a finger to interrupt her. "If I may?"

"What is it?" she snapped at him. The chairwoman did not even deign to look at Cousin, keeping her eyes fixed on Liam. She was a woman used to giving speeches and not used to interruption.

"I have a correction to make to your last statement." He winked at Liam, who tensed, wondering what game Cousin was playing. "The Reconciliation will not, it should be noted, emerge from this crisis under your leadership. To be honest, neither it nor you will emerge from this crisis at all."

Chairwoman Pei finally did turn to look at Cousin, but she did not have time to register surprise, as his hand rose to his mouth with the small silver tube of a blowgun. He puffed and a needle pierced her throat.

The chairwoman gasped, choked, clawed at Marie standing beside her, and fell, dead. Cousin impregnated his darts with a very potent toxin. Chairwoman Pei's lifeless eyes stared up at Marie from the floor.

"Finally!" Cousin exclaimed. "I could not stand that

pretentious windbag and her lectures. I apologize for the offensive things she said to you, Liam."

Liam had already turned to take cover on the other side of the large light in the center of the room, crouched behind it, ready to spring out, his killing hand poised.

"Again?" Cousin laughed. "Calm down, boy! How many times do I have to tell you I am not going to hurt you? I just saved you from that woman, didn't I?"

"You tried to kill me," Liam said.

"Bygones. You really shouldn't hold grudges."

Liam peeked around and saw that Cousin had grabbed Marie and held her in front of himself, the tip of a dart in his sleeve dimpling her neck. Any more pressure and it would break the skin and the poison would enter her bloodstream.

Cousin cleared his throat. "Shall we now talk face-to-face like civilized humans?"

"You aren't civilized," said Liam. "Or human."

"I am nothing but the things I do," Cousin said. "As are we all."

"So do something good and let her go." Liam stood. He met Cousin's eyes.

"You aren't even going to thank me," said Cousin.

"For what?"

"For the gift I am giving," said Cousin. "The gift I am giving to *you*."

Liam didn't answer. He looked at Marie. Her eyes were wide, but not with the normal terror of a hostage. Liam had seen that look plenty of times in his young life. He'd taken enough hostages to know it well. But Marie's eyes were wide in another way; they had the alertness of a predator. She was in danger, but she wasn't surrendering to fear.

She was ready.

Liam didn't let his glance linger on her for long. Cousin was just as alert as she, and more skilled a killer than either of them.

"Oblivion, Liam!" Cousin shouted, his voice echoing off the high walls, bouncing back at them from the shadows. "That's the gift I'm giving. Everyone gets a piece of it. The Advisory Council. Marie. Even your dear, darling Syd. This infection, this data withdrawal business, it will take everyone soon enough . . . except, of course, for a chosen few. Like us."

Liam moved sideways and Cousin turned with him, keeping Marie in front of his body.

"You and I, Liam, we were never linked to anything, were we? Just like the late chairwoman there, we were born apart, stayed apart, and never had that data in our blood. We'll survive, a few others perhaps. The strong. The pure. But the rest?" He brushed his hand through the air, wiping them all away. "This will all be a graveyard. And then, you'll be free. Your responsibility for that sulking, dark, hollowed-out boy you're so fond of? Erased. Your need, that hunger that you cannot put into words, it'll go too. When there is nothing, there is nothing to long for. *That's* freedom. That's my gift to you. Nothing."

"You're insane," said Liam. "You'd let millions die . . . for nothing?"

"Not everything is a transaction, Liam." Cousin grinned. "The Reconciliation has taught us that at least."

"You wouldn't kill everyone and expect nothing in return," Liam said. "I know you better than that."

"You don't know me at all." Cousin studied his fingernails. "Although, the Nigerians made it clear that an end to the Reconciliation would earn me passage to their republic. Passage for two, in fact." He clicked his tongue, letting the thought settle in. "If you wanted to come with me, to the paradise they've made for themselves over there, perhaps we could find you another dark-skinned boy to protect, if that's what you're into. Maybe someone who'd return your affections?"

Liam didn't say a word.

"You realize that Syd will never care about you the way you do about him, don't you? He doesn't know how."

"Not everything is a transaction," Liam parroted back. He scanned the room, looking for anything to give him an advantage.

"I think Syd will be grateful for the oblivion I'm giving," Cousin said. "I imagine he'd thank me if he could. I suppose you are too selfish to let him have it. It's really all he wants, you know? To be erased. It's the only way he thinks he can be forgiven. Protecting him all this time has been a cruelty. I am offering kindness."

Liam looked to the body of Chairwoman Pei on the floor.

Syd had fought to escape the bomb she'd ordered. Syd had chosen to live. Cousin was wrong. Syd did not want to die.

But now he was alone back in his room, armed, but alone. And Cousin knew he was still alive.

Of course, thought Liam. He cursed himself for being such a fool. Cousin's whole speech—all the rambling about oblivion and freedom and desire—had been a delay tactic. Who knew if his Nigeria nonsense was even true? They had sealed off their republic a hundred years ago. No one ever got in. No one ever came out. All Cousin knew how to do was lie.

He was keeping Liam busy until after the deed was done and Syd was murdered.

Cousin sighed, as if he could read Liam's thoughts, as if he knew the ruse was up.

In a flash, Cousin's hand pulled from Marie's neck and flung the dart at Liam. Liam's instincts fired and before even a moment's thought, he'd thrown himself backward in a flip. The dart dug itself into the floor.

At the same moment, Marie rolled her shoulder sideways, and slammed into Cousin with her knee, right in the crotch. He doubled over and Marie delivered a kick to his face.

He dodged it and her boot caught empty air.

As soon as Liam's feet hit the ground, he snapped a blade from the lining of each of his boots, flinging the first one at Cousin and the second where he knew Cousin would dive to dodge the first. Both blades whistled through empty air and buried themselves in the far wall.

Marie whirled out of Cousin's reach as, in the same instant, Cousin extinguished the light, plunging the room into impenetrable blackness.

Liam kept moving, using his memory of the room's layout to make his way to the small rear door through which Chairwoman Pei had come. He hoped Marie would do the same. They didn't stand a chance against Cousin in the dark. Not that Cousin really cared. He had just wanted to slow them down.

"Going so soon?" Cousin called out from the dark after them. "You can't save him! You can't protect him from this. My future has no place for him!"

The steps were crumbling and the railing long gone from the stairwell, but Liam and Marie ran side by side, leaping from one landing to the next, shaking loose the last fragments of moldy plaster as their feet slammed down.

"You're letting me down, Liam!" Cousin called from above. "But I forgive you. Come back to me when you're ready to give up on that knock-off savior of yours. I'll always be there for you, Brother Liam! You and me into oblivion."

When they hit the overgrown alley in the dark, they stopped to catch their breath for a second.

"Nice moves," Liam told Marie.

"You too," she said. "Now what?"

"To Syd."

"Yeah, and then?"

Liam didn't know. Neither did Marie.

"Syd will have a plan," Liam said. "Syd will know what to do."

They ran and hoped Liam was right.

[22]

SYD PACED THE ROOM, one end to the other, and back again. He tapped on the spot behind his ear, he sat on the bed. He stood up. He sat again. He flipped through the journal. He paced some more.

He hated waiting, hating being stuck in this little room while his friends risked their lives.

Friends? Is that what they were? Liam too?

He wondered how Liam would react when he told him they were going to Mountain City. It shouldn't be a surprise. Where else could they go?

Mountain City had been evacuated. The only people left were scavengers hiding from the Purifier patrols and Reconciliation officials determining what of the city's material should be salvaged and what destroyed. The city itself was not meant to be lived in anymore. It was the city that had produced the great injustices of the past, the Reconciliation believed, so the people must learn to live beyond it, off the land, blasted and ruined as the land was. In a generation, maybe two, the people would be ready to return to the city, but now, the goal was that it be emptied.

It made a good place for the Machinists to hide.

It would make a good place for them to hide a Machine.

Syd was wired, jumpy, eager to get started. He hadn't been back to Mountain City since he'd fled it months ago. He wondered what liberation would have done to it. Would the slums of the Valve have been destroyed? Would Mr. Baram's old shop still be there? Syd's old school? Would he remember the streets, recognize the buildings?

"It's just a few months," he told himself out loud. Nothing could be that different.

A knock on the door. He stopped pacing.

Knock. Knock.

He moved to open it, ready to tell Liam his plan, to tell him what he saw in the journal, to ask him if he had killed the doctor.

Would he ask him why? Did he really want to know?

Syd wasn't innocent either, after all. He was responsible for far more death than Liam. Maybe it'd be best just to let it go unasked. He owed Liam his life, after all. He knew Liam expected nothing in return, but maybe Syd's silence would be the kindness he could offer.

Knock. Knock. Knock.

His fingers froze on the handle of the door.

Three knocks.

Syd waited. Liam said he'd knock four times. Why only three now?

Again: *Knock. Knock. Knock.*

Syd held his breath. He listened at the door. There was not a sound he could hear. It wasn't Liam out there.

He rushed across the room and grabbed the bolt gun from the small table, then returned to the door. He listened again.

Nothing.

Time turned to jelly, thick and sticky. He breathed in. He breathed out.

Knox's voice echoed in his head: *Being alive and living aren't the same.*

To stay alive, he should leave the door shut and wait. See if Liam would come back. See if the mysterious knocker would just go away.

To live meant to do something. To seize control of his future. To be the hero of his own story. To save himself.

He put his hand on the handle and raised the bolt gun. He cracked open the door and saw Counselor Baram's gray beard, his pale face, and small glasses perched on the tip of his nose. Relief returned time to its normal thickness, its normal speed.

He lowered the bolt gun and opened the door.

"You are just who I needed to talk to," Syd told him, eager to unburden his worries to a familiar face. "Things have gotten crazy. They tried to kill me, and I think the

Machine is real, and I know it's treason to say it, but if we can find it, if we can make it work and restart the network, we might be able to—"

Something wasn't right.

Counselor Baram just stood there, his mouth gaping open. His skin was waxy and still. Blue lines crisscrossed his forehead. A red trickle crept down his neck just behind his ear. He didn't speak.

The man standing in front of Syd was dead.

A few things happened at once.

Syd tried to shut the door again, just as the old man's body dropped at his feet, and a heavy fist pushed the door open hard, knocking him back. The active end of an EMD stick jabbed forward, slamming him square in the chest, frying every nerve in his body, like a fuse had been lit, burning beneath his skin from the tips of his toes to the backs of his eyeballs. When he hit the floor, the fuse detonated.

Anyone would have screamed like he did.

He clawed for the bolt gun he'd dropped, but his fingers would not obey the fragmented signals from his brain.

A shower of gray powder filled the air above him, and the lights went out. He felt it settle on his skin.

Graphite bomb. It'd blown out every electrical circuit. The windowless room was pitch-black, but at least the EMD stick wouldn't work for a few minutes either.

Syd gritted his teeth and rolled to his side, covering the bolt gun with his body. He felt it against his stomach and reached under himself, locking the spring back as he continued to roll. As he rolled, he released the spring.

He heard the bolt hit the wall with a thud. He'd missed.

Of course his assailants could see in the dark. These weren't amateurs who'd been sent for Syd. They attacked in darkness because it gave them an advantage. All Syd had accomplished rolling around and taking a wild shot in the dark was to look like a fool to the assassins he couldn't see and to use up his one shot. His nerves were too fried to relock the spring.

He scrambled in the direction of the cot, trying to get under it for cover until he could reload the bolt gun, but he felt a hand on the back of his neck and his shirt. He was hauled to his feet and someone pinned his arms behind his back. Another person stood in front of him.

"The great Yovel," the man in front said. Syd tried to force his eyes to adjust to the dark, but he couldn't make out so much as a shape in front of him. He might as well have had his eyes closed. "You don't like that name *Yovel*, do you?"

The man's breath smelled like green onions and the voice was familiar. He used it to pinpoint the exact location of the speaker's face. Then he turned his head toward it and spat. He didn't hear his spit hit flesh, but he knew he hadn't missed. So it was cloth he'd just spat on, a mask most likely. A Purifier's mask.

"Finch," said Syd. "You killed Counselor Baram. The Advisory Council will hang you for that."

"There is no Advisory Council anymore." Finch laughed. "You know, I always wondered, Syd, why old Baram took you in back in Mountain City. We all thought it was because of what you did for him, if you know what I mean?"

"Can we just do this?" the other voice said in the darkness. "Just kill him already."

"No," Finch answered. "This is our reunion! Did you know that I had sponsors before the network fell? I was getting out of the Valve and moving to the Upper City. On my own. No debt. Just the lux life all the way. And then this Chapter Eleven ruined it for me."

"Just kill him," the other guy pleaded.

"He used to love me, you know?" Finch said. "He'd stare at me all the time in class. Pervert."

Syd gritted his teeth. Of course Finch would end up here, in this room. Of course Finch would be the one sent to kill him. Everyone Syd cared about became an affliction, in one way or another.

Syd felt the EMD stick tap him on the cheek. It wasn't reactivated yet. Finch's onion breath was right in front of Syd's face. "So, do you still think of me on those long, lonely nights?"

"Finch," Syd said. "They would've eaten you alive in the Upper City. You'd always have been trash to them."

"My name is Furious now."

"Furious?" Syd laughed in the dark, hoping his face showed his scorn to their night vision. "That really is a stupid name."

Syd felt Finch's breath hot on his ear. "It's the last name you'll ever hear."

Syd jerked his head to the side, smashing the boy in the nose as hard as he could.

"Ah!" Finch stumbled sideways, nearly falling over the small table.

Syd heard the sound of the book hitting the floor. He tried to yank his arms free, but the other Purifier held him too tightly.

"Right." Finch got in front of him again. Syd heard the familiar sound of an electro-muscular disruption stick charging up. "I want this to hurt."

He jammed the stick in Syd's stomach and fired a pulse through him. The darkness of the room turned red; he felt like his teeth had shattered, his fingernails were on fire, his belly button was a blade driven through to his back; and it seemed like the whole world was screaming, though only his voice made a sound. He slumped where they held him because his feet were kicking uncontrollably and his legs could not support his weight.

When the wave of pain passed, Finch whispered again, "Was it as good as you'd dreamed it would be?"

Then, with a bare fist, he punched Syd across the face. The punch twisted him sideways. The blood in his mouth was warm and surprisingly sweet, like the juice of a berry left in the sun.

As Finch hit him again with the other fist, Syd twisted in the other direction. He preferred the flesh and bone of the fist hitting the flesh and bone of his face to the nerve-sizzling silence of the EMD stick. He'd hurt Finch's knuckles.

"Just kill him before Liam comes back," the other voice whined.

"Let that half-wit thug show up," Finch said. "I'll shove this stick just where he likes it."

"Where would that be?" Liam's voice cut through the darkness.

Syd heard a noise, like an overripe mango falling from a tree, the soft thump, the crunch as the pit cracked on a stone. He felt himself released and he fell to the ground. Beside him, his unrequited high school crush groaned and he knew their faces were mere inches apart. Gentle hands reached under his arms and helped him up, leaving Finch and the other one behind. He heard the buzz of the EMD stick charge, the knocking noise of limbs twitching against the floor, then nothing.

It was over.

"Did you kill them?" Syd asked.

"Does it matter?" Liam replied from the darkness.

Syd didn't answer.

"Can you stand?" Marie asked him. It was her hands under his arms.

He nodded, but then realized she couldn't see him in the dark. "Yes," he said.

"The Council is gone," said Liam, without the slightest hint of emotion in his voice. "There's been a coup and we aren't safe."

"Baram is dead," said Syd.

"I'm sorry," Marie told him.

Syd felt Liam's metal hand tugging him through the darkness.

"The journal," said Syd. "We need it."

"That book?" Liam asked.

"It was her book," said Syd.

"Whose—?" Syd didn't need to see Liam's face to know that it dawned on him. "Oh. I . . . I can explain."

"You're going to," Syd told him. "But not right now. We just need the journal. It's our only hope."

"Where is it?" Marie asked.

"Somewhere on the floor . . . I don't know . . . I heard it fall."

There was a crashing noise as Marie tripped over the table.

"We have to feel around for it," said Syd.

"No time," Liam snapped. "Cousin still wants you dead."

"He should get in line," said Syd.

"I think he just cut to the front of the line," Marie spoke from the dark. "I've got the book. What's so important about it?"

"Designs for the Machine, I think," said Syd. "I don't understand all of it, but restarting the networks is our only hope of stopping this sickness."

"Where'd you get it?" Marie asked. "If we can find the person who wrote it—"

"She can't help us," said Syd.

"I killed her," Liam told them. "Cousin tricked me. It was a mistake. I can't make it right, but I can promise you I won't make another."

Syd took a breath and let his silence answer Liam. It wasn't forgiveness he offered, which hadn't been sought, so much as acceptance, which Liam needed.

Liam's metal hand rested on Syd's arm, gently, and he guided Syd through the hallway. As they rounded a corner, moonlight streaked in from a broken skylight. There was a splatter of blood across Liam's pale cheek and flecked in his short copper hair. His face was a mask of determination.

How many people had Liam killed in his short life? How many could Syd accept?

Marie walked behind them with the journal in one hand and the bolt gun in the other.

"Found it on the floor by the cot," she said. "I thought it might come in handy."

Liam nodded.

"Is there a hovercraft we can use?" Syd asked. "We need to get to Mountain City."

"Why there?" Marie asked.

"It was Knox's idea," Syd told her. He didn't need to look at her to see the puzzlement.

"Hovercraft are held at secure depots around the city," Liam said. "They'll be guarded."

"But . . ." Syd cleared his throat. "You can deal with guards?"

Liam exhaled, nodded. His cheeks flushed a bit in the moonlight.

A lot of questions bubbled up in Syd's mind, about how Liam came to be a soldier, when he'd learned to kill and why it seemed to embarrass him. About how he'd lost his hand. Syd surprised himself by wanting to know the answers, wanting to hear the stories. He never had before.

But now was not the time for questions.

"If you can get us inside a hovercraft, I can start it," said Syd.

They followed Liam from the building, creeping through the street toward a nearby vehicle depot. Liam tore brambles and thorns away, grunting with the effort. Watching him work in the nighttime heat, the blood drying on his clothes and on both his hands, Syd wondered when the last time was that Liam had slept. He wondered when Liam would reach the limits of what he could do and what would happen to all of them then.

They stopped at a low wall of crumbling concrete opposite a fenced lot where three hovercraft were stored. Two Purifiers stood guard at the gate, chatting quietly with each other. They were armed, but seemed relaxed. They probably had no idea there had been a coup, no idea that a madman gave their orders now, no idea that they were going to get sick and die if Syd couldn't find the Machine to restore the networks.

"It's not going to be pretty to break in there," Liam warned. The way he said it was like he was asking permission.

"I know," said Syd, knowing full well the permission he had just granted. "If you can avoid . . ."

Liam turned on the EMD stick he'd lifted off Finch. "I'll try." He looked at Marie. "Stay alert." He disappeared over the wall.

"Looks like you're my bodyguard too," Syd told her as they leaned against the wall waiting in silence.

"I'm not doing this for you, Syd," she said back to him.

"I know," Syd replied.

He could picture her parents' faces, the barracks stuffed with the sick and dying.

It's your future. Choose.

"I'm trying," Syd answered out loud and tried not the hear the sounds from half a block away, a stifled shout, a grunt, a gurgle. The silence that followed was even louder.

Liam suddenly appeared over the wall again. "Time to go."

As they made their way to the first hovercraft, Syd didn't ask what Liam had done, if he'd had to kill the Purifiers or not. One way or another, they were taken care of. Syd's silence was a small mercy, but Liam was grateful.

[23]

WITH A FEW WIRES crossed, Syd shorted the security on the hovercraft. A few more wires reconnected and the engines roared to life. The batteries discharged, the hovercraft lifted, and Syd smiled. Machines, unlike people, were predictable.

Liam stood behind him, leaning on the pilot's chair and watching with fascination as Syd worked his magic. "How do you know how to do that?" he asked.

Syd shrugged, feeling the hovercraft come to life. "I studied. I practiced . . . How do you know how to do what you do?"

"I practiced," said Liam.

The controls shuddered in Syd's hands and he felt the power of the machine running through him. He shifted the pitch where they hovered; tweaked the roll to get the feel of it, leaning the hovercraft left and then right.

Liam stumbled off his feet, landing sideways wedged behind the copilot's seat.

"Maybe I should drive," he suggested as he tried to pry himself up and regain some of the dignity he liked to think he still had.

"Not on your life," Syd replied. "Or on mine."

And with that, Syd pushed the throttle and they roared from the depot, smashing through a flimsy fence. Syd rolled hard, taking them along the eastern road out of the jungle city.

"Aren't we headed west?" Liam asked.

"This Cousin guy doesn't know that. I want people to see us going east."

Liam nodded, impressed with Syd's thinking. Liam was good with blunt force, and he was glad Syd had a head for tactics. Together, they made a powerful team. He wondered whether Syd would see it that way. He also wondered how Marie fit in. She'd served the Reconciliation well. What would she do without a cause to get behind? Could they trust her? In the cabin, she began rummaging through the vehicle, taking an inventory of their supplies. She had the bolt gun now, but Liam had the EMD stick. The only one unarmed was Syd.

Syd accelerated, smashing undergrowth out of their path, slicing past the urban farming co-ops where young Purifiers stood idly about, wondering where most of their workers had gone, and past security checkpoints where young Purifiers didn't even move to stop them, unaware that they were a vehicle full of fugitives. These young cadres hadn't yet been told that a hovercraft had been stolen, nor were they yet aware that the Council had collapsed. It was just as well. If they'd tried to stop the hovercraft . . . Syd didn't let his mind go there.

The vegetation thinned. The ruins of buildings spread out and minute by minute they sped from jungle to desert, cruising over an ancient bit of broken blacktop, the same route Syd had first taken into the city with Knox and Marie all those months ago.

He reached over and hit the intercom.

"Marie?" he asked. "How you doing back there? What do we have to work with?"

Silence.

"Marie?" he repeated, casting a nervous glance at Liam.

"I'll go check on her," Liam said.

Suddenly, there was a crashing sound, a shout.

"Marie!" Syd yelled.

Liam rushed back into the cabin. He saw Marie doubled over on a bench, her cheek dripping blood, and standing in front of her, his face bloody, his nose broken, was Finch.

Liam cursed himself for not killing the boy in the dark. He'd been too eager to get Syd away. He hadn't double-checked his work. Two times he'd allowed Finch to live, which was, to his mind, two times too many.

Finch stood in fighting stance, ready.

Liam adjusted his footing, raised the EMD stick.

Finch whirled on him with a high kick. As Liam dodged,

Finch shifted his momentum into a low slide that swept out Liam's legs. The instant he began to fall, Finch jumped, slamming into Liam's rib cage. He hit the hard metal deck of the hovercraft with a thud, the EMD stick pinned between them, humming with life, just a hair's width from his chin. Finch pressed, using the full weight of his body to nudge it closer. One tap against Liam's skin and it would be over. Liam couldn't get any leverage to break free.

Suddenly, the hovercraft pitched hard, and Finch fell off him, crashing down onto the side of the vehicle. Liam caught on to the bench to keep from falling after him, and as the hovercraft spun in a tight circle to land, he hopped to his feet, rushing Finch before the boy could get up again.

But then he froze.

Finch had Marie's bolt gun and it was pointed at Liam's chest. His eyes were locked on Liam's hips. Finch had gotten good training somewhere along the line. A person could fake a lot of movements before a dive to one side or the other, but you couldn't fake with your hips. His first move and he'd get a bolt through the gut.

"I'm taking Syd back," Finch said.

Around them, the engines powered down. Syd stepped into the cabin.

"Take cover!" Liam shouted.

"Finch," Syd said calmly. "Put the gun down. You're outnumbered."

"I can handle this," said Liam.

"Nothing to handle," said Syd. "We're all going to relax and lower our weapons, okay?"

Finch's eyes darted to Syd. In that instant, Liam started to move forward, but Finch shook his head. "Don't move. Drop that stick."

Liam gripped the EMD stick tighter.

"I said drop it!" Finch's finger moved to fire, just as Marie sprang from the bench and charged at him. Liam tossed her the stick, which she caught and swung into Finch's face. It hit him with a full blast of power, knocking him back against the bulkhead. His limbs flailed out of control, and as he fell, his fingers released the bolt gun's spring.

There was a loud crack as it fired. Liam dove and the bolt smacked into the metal wall of the hovercraft with a clang and an ear-popping echo. On the floor beneath Marie, Finch's body quivered and then fell still. A full charge from the EMD stick was enough to stop his heart. He wouldn't be getting up again.

When Liam stood, he felt a sharp pain. The bolt had grazed his rib cage, slicing open the side of his shirt and a thin line of his skin. It bled fast, like a waterfall.

Marie kicked the gun away from Finch's lifeless hand as Syd stepped forward and looked down at the body. The mangled face and lifeless eyes stared up at him. It'd been high school the last time Syd had let his stare linger on Finch. The world had changed a lot since. Looking down on him, Syd was surprised he still felt a clenching in his chest. The boy had hated him, had tried to kill him. Why should

Syd mourn him? Why should Syd be the only one left who would?

He remembered that line from an old book that Baram had muttered to him: *God gives burdens, but also shoulders.* A half-understood line from a mostly forgotten book. Funny what occurred to you when you weren't sure how to feel.

"Are you okay?" Syd turned to Liam.

Liam touched his side and made sure not to wince. "Yeah," he said. "Just a little cut."

"It doesn't look little," Syd told him.

"We need to get moving. Cousin will be after us."

"The sun's going down soon," Syd said. "I can't see in the dark and if we run with lights on, we'll be easy to spot from miles away. I set us down by some kind of rock formation. We'll wait out the night, let anyone chasing us go by, thinking we're still headed east, then we can double back and head west in the morning. We'll make the Mountain City before noon. Right now, we can rest a minute. We can eat." He pointed at Liam's side. "And we can stop your bleeding."

Liam sat back on the bench behind him. He was tired. He felt lightheaded. Hunger, exhaustion, and blood loss. A rest wasn't the worst idea. He nodded.

Syd squatted and pulled out the emergency kit from under the passenger bench. He was glad the Reconciliation kept their vehicles well supplied.

"Don't worry about me," Liam objected. "I'll be fine."

"It's not a problem," Syd told him. "Remember? I'm good at fixing things." He pulled a tube of BioGlue from the kit. It was lux, high-end stuff from before the Jubilee. The Reconciliation didn't manufacture anything nearly this good. All their stitching was done with needle and thread, like ancient cave people.

"The BioGlue's not even expired yet," Syd told him. "It won't leave a scar."

Liam hadn't actually ever had a wound patched with the good stuff. All his wounds scarred.

"Take your shirt off," Syd ordered.

It was Liam's turn to hesitate.

Syd raised an eyebrow. "So *now* you care about privacy?"

Liam glanced at Marie, who busied herself looking out the small porthole at the desert, pink and red as the sun went down. Liam took a deep breath and peeled his shirt off. The movement was agony and he tried to stifle a groan.

Syd froze looking at him. His entire right side, from just under his armpit down to the waistband of his pants, was sliced open, soaked with blood. That, however, wasn't what startled Syd.

On the upper left side of Liam's chest, scrawled across his pectoral muscle just below the collarbone, he had four letters roughly tattooed. The ink was slightly blue, some natural pigment, and there was no telling how long he'd had it, but the letters were clear as day. They were the same letters that were behind Syd's ear, the letters for Syd's other name, Yovel.

"I just—" Liam began, but how could he explain? Syd hadn't put those letters on his body by choice. They were a curse to him, a symbol of all the agony he'd endured and the death he'd caused. On Liam, they represented a promise. Debts forgiven. What he gave, he gave freely.

Syd couldn't take his eyes off them.

Liam felt a moment of relief that he was bleeding so much. It made it impossible for him to blush again.

Marie cleared her throat.

"I should clean the wound," Syd told Liam, snapping his eyes away from the letters. He knelt next to Liam with the BioGlue and the medic's kit, taking out a sterile cloth and wiping down Liam's side. There was so much blood, he couldn't even see where the cut was in order to seal it.

When the cloth touched his side, Liam winced, but not because it hurt.

Syd shot a look up at him and, when their eyes met, he looked back down just as quickly, focused on the task, not on the rise and fall of the rib cage, the tattoo across the side, the way the light through the porthole made Liam's pale skin glow.

No different from fixing a broken machine, Syd told himself.

No different from any other wound I've had patched up, Liam told himself.

Marie went back to organizing the supplies in the hovercraft, inventorying what they had, the weapons, the food, tools. She didn't know what they'd need or why Syd thought they'd find what they were looking for in Mountain City, but it would help to have an inventory regardless. And it would keep her from watching Syd and Liam in the most awkward medical procedure she'd ever seen.

"I—" Syd started to say something.

"I—" Liam said at the same time.

They fell silent again.

Syd located the edges of the wound. He dabbed the blood away gently and Liam sucked in a breath. Syd began to apply the BioGlue and it stung more than Liam would have imagined. He clenched and unclenched the metal fist, reminding himself he had suffered much, much worse than this.

Syd filled the silence between them with things that didn't need saying. "So, uh, I think, in the city, we might find the Machine, or, like, the parts I need to build a machine . . ."

"Uh-huh," Liam grunted through the pain.

"I mean, if there are pieces of tech left that could do it, I think we'll find them there," Syd continued.

"We have to," said Marie. "If we can't get the network back on . . ."

"Your parents," said Syd.

Marie nodded. "Everyone."

Syd sighed. "You, me, Liam—"

"Not me," Liam whispered. Syd looked up at him. "I was never linked to the network, never had biodata installed. I grew up out here. I'm one of the few. I won't get sick, at least not from this." He looked down at Syd. "Not like you will."

Syd went back to applying the medicated bandage over the sealed wound, kept his eyes lowered. He studied his own dark hand pressed against Liam's pale skin, the dried blood on his fingernails, and through them, like a reflection in water, he saw the Guardians with their black veins oozing, their silent groans as they itched their own skin off, bled out, died. Were they a vision of his future? All their futures? All but Liam's?

"You sound like you want to apologize for it," he told his bodyguard.

"I do," said Liam, and Syd finally looked up and saw those sad puppy eyes, Liam's face twisted into a frown. "I don't know how to protect you from this."

"The Council is gone." Syd looked back down at his hand against Liam's skin. He didn't pull it away. "The Reconciliation is over. I'm not their symbol anymore. I'm not Yovel. Your job is done. The Reconciliation doesn't need you to protect me."

Liam swallowed. "I never did it for them. You know I didn't."

"I know you didn't," said Syd.

Liam raised his good hand under Syd's chin, lifted his face up so their eyes would meet again. He felt a chill run through him, heard his own pulse in his ears. There was a reason he never touched Syd with his good hand. He could almost feel himself shaking. "Let me protect you."

"You just said that you can't."

"I'll find a way."

Syd's lips were cracked, his eyes wet and dark. His stubble grew in unevenly. They looked at each other. "I'm not an easy guy to protect."

Liam leaned down, in spite of the pain in his side. His face was just in front of Syd's. He whispered, "I don't need easy."

Syd took his hand off Liam's side, wrapped his fingers around Liam's hand against his cheek, held it, closed his eyes. Then he took Liam's hand away from his face. He turned away.

"You'll need to keep that bandage on for at least twelve hours," he said, standing. He looked to Marie, who was pretending to be absorbed in organizing the tools in the repair kit by size and shape and color. "When we get to Mountain City tomorrow," Syd told her, "I'll need you to navigate for me."

"Okay," she agreed quickly, acting like she hadn't just been listening to their conversation. "Where to?"

"Knox's father ran SecuriTech," said Syd. "If there is a Machine, he would've had it."

"The SecuriTech offices were emptied right after the network fell," said Marie. "I saw it myself."

"The offices, sure," said Syd. "But that's not where we're going."

"Where then?"

"Where you and I first met," Syd said. "We're going to Knox's house." Syd looked at Finch's body on the floor. "But first let's bury my old friend."

[24]

LIAM TOOK THE FIRST watch of the night, letting Syd and Marie sleep. Then they rotated. Syd and Liam didn't say a word to each other as they switched places, just grunts and nods. They were careful not to bump into each other in the narrow cabin.

As the purple of the desert started to show hints of morning red, Liam woke Syd to restart the engines. Syd startled, but then, seeing the metal hand shaking his arm, remembered where he was and what he was doing. He stood, wiped his face on his shirt, and got to work.

"You feeling all right?" Liam asked.

"Fine," said Syd.

"No symptoms yet?"

Syd shook his head. "Marie?"

"Nothing yet," she said.

"How's your side?" Syd asked.

"Fine," said Liam.

"Well, here we go," Syd announced, as the engines growled to full power and the vehicle lifted from the desert in a cloud of yellow dust. He jammed the throttle and they shot off into the morning. Syd focused on driving, Liam scanned for threats on the horizon, and Marie watched the landscape race by, waiting to see something familiar.

Four hours later, she spoke the first word since they'd taken off: "There."

She pointed up at the shining skyscrapers of the city in the mountains, catching the light high above them. Buildings filled the slopes, smaller and more densely packed the lower down they were. A network of roads wound around the mountain, and as they got closer, they saw many of the roads were destroyed, their guardrails and blast barriers ripped down, or the roads themselves, riding high over the slums, collapsed down off their pylons, crushing the tin shacks beneath.

"If we go around the other side, we can come in through the restricted speedway that I know," Marie told them.

"I can't imagine it's restricted anymore," Syd replied.

"Force of habit. It's probably not much of a road at all anymore."

By Marie's route, they came to the southern wall of the city, an imposing barricade of steel and concrete.

The wall had been there when they lived in the Mountain City, ringing the entire thing, but neither of them had ever seen it. There was a no-man's-land on the other side, a mile-wide strip of open concrete, dotted with guard towers and patrolled by robotic sentries. No one could cross it unauthorized, and a proxy like Syd would never have been authorized. A patron like Marie would have left the city by a more dignified route, if she ever left at all, which she hadn't . . . until the last time, with Syd and Knox. And then they'd snuck out. There was no way, however, to sneak into the city driving a hovercraft. They drove around until they found an access gate.

The paint wasn't even faded on the steel blast door and they could see the shining logo of SecuriTech. Someone had tried to etch some scratchiti curses over it, but the door was resistant. It looked brand-new.

Looking much less new, although in fact far newer than the door, was a sandbagged sentry post beside the gate, open to the desert wind. In it stood a tripod-mounted fracture cannon—old tech, but powerful enough that the Reconciliation had seen fit to ignore their rules by placing it there. And manning the fracture cannon, wearing a green uniform, a white hood, and a respirator against the red dust cloud their hovercraft kicked up, was a Purifier, with his cannon aimed straight into their cockpit.

Syd's blood turned to ice. He tightened his grip on the throttle, steadied the craft, but crept closer. No warning came. No order to stop. As they moved, the fracture cannon did not track them. The white-masked Purifier was still as stone.

Syd set the craft down in front of the gate. The figure in

the sentry post didn't turn to look at them. Marie peeked from the side porthole.

"He's . . ." She pointed, unable to find the words to describe what she was seeing.

Syd idled the engine and Liam got up to look.

"I need to look closer," he told them and lowered the rear hatch. "Stay here."

Syd followed him out into the blazing afternoon. Liam shook his head, but didn't stop him.

They blinked at the sun and coughed in the dust. The land around them was barren hardpan. Any water in the ground had long since been sucked into the city and any life outside the wall had long since been killed off. There was only heat and wind and the wall.

Syd caught up to Liam and they walked side by side to the Purifier. Marie followed with the bolt gun in hand.

The Purifier's white mask was tinted rust red from the desert sand and his uniform was coated with the same red dust. His hands were tied to the fracture cannon with rough cord, but the cannon's mechanism was ripped out; all the circuits and pieces that had made it a weapon were gone. It was just a prop.

Just like the Purifier himself.

"At least we know why he didn't shoot us down," Syd observed.

The Purifier's hands were all bone, no flesh, and beneath the white mask, they could see a glimpse of a bare skull—the jagged toothy grimace, the black eye sockets. A skeleton.

"He's been posed like this," Liam said.

"Why would someone pose a skeleton?" Marie wondered.

"It's a warning." Syd reached out and brushed the dust and sand from the front of his uniform to reveal writing in a brown smear of dried blood. The writing was childish.

NO RECONCILATION ALLOWED.

"The Mountain City doesn't belong to the Reconciliation anymore," Liam observed.

"I don't think it has for a while," Syd added.

"The Reconciliation evacuated most of the city," said Marie. "Moved everyone out to the countryside right after the networks fell. They only left a few people behind to gather the stragglers and the resisters, and to organize the salvage."

"Just a skeleton crew?" Syd suggested.

"That's a joke Knox would have made," Marie said back. Syd bit his lip. He would have liked to take it as a compliment, but the memory stung. And in truth, while he lived, Knox's sarcasm had annoyed Syd. Now he held on to it because he was afraid not to. He was afraid of what he'd lose when he let it go.

"Whoever they left behind was clearly overrun," Liam said. "We have to assume whoever still lives in this city is going to be hostile."

"We've got to go in," said Syd. "If it's Machinists who've taken over, that's what we want. We're on their side now."

"I'm not," said Marie. She looked over at the dead body.

She had pledged herself to the Purifiers, wore the uniform, tried to lead the younger ones as best she could toward the better society she thought they were making. She had no desire to turn back the clock. She just wanted to save her parents.

"We're not going anywhere unless we can get that gate open," Liam noted.

"Remember how we got out of the cell?" Syd asked.

"Uh, Syd." Liam shook his head. "This gate is about a thousand times the size of that cell door and a thousand times as strong."

"Yeah," said Syd, "but we'll use the same principle."

Liam stared up at the giant door. "The same principle?"

"Our hovercraft has a solar fission battery, right?"

Liam shrugged.

"It does," said Syd. "I wasn't really asking."

"How is that the same principle as blowing out the air locks on a prison door?" Liam imagined himself bending pistons and crossing wires under Syd's direction. He wasn't sure he had the strength for it.

"Well, not blowing out this time," said Syd. "Blowing up."

"You're going to self-destruct the hovercraft?"

"Uh-huh."

"Guys?" Marie called.

Liam shook his head. "The explosion will tell everyone we're here. Whoever killed that Purifier. Cousin's goons coming after us. Anyone. They'll all come running."

"We'll just have to run faster."

"This is a terrible idea."

"You have a better one?"

"Guys?" Marie tried again.

"Fine," Liam relented. In truth, he couldn't think of a better idea. He wasn't really an ideas guy. He never really trusted complicated plans. He had a bias toward action, even half-considered action. Blowing up the hovercraft certainly seemed half considered. "So how do we do it?"

"If we can open that hatch—" Syd pointed to a metal panel near the rear of the vehicle that looked painfully heavy to Liam. "Then I'll shut off the coolant system. The engine will overheat; I short out the safety catches, we'll create a feedback loop and when we hit critical mass, well, then, we better be under cover and—"

"Guys!" Marie yelled.

The boys turned to her.

"We could just open the gate." She walked up to a large box with a lever in it, swung open the box, and yanked down the lever.

A siren sounded three times and the gate split open in the middle, two halves sliding into the wall.

"Why do guys always go right to blowing things up?" she wondered aloud, walking past them back to the hovercraft.

Syd and Liam stared at the open door, the warning skeleton, and the empty concrete beyond. They looked at each other, then back to the hovercraft, and climbed aboard.

"I'm glad she's on our side," said Liam, and Syd couldn't have agreed more.

[25]

THOUGH BOTH SYD AND Marie had grown up in the city, they recognized nothing as Syd guided the hovercraft along the broken road. Where once the packed jumble of shanties at the base of the city had teemed with life, there were only smoldering piles of soot, the odd retaining wall, or empty concrete storefront. The city looked like the ruins of Old Detroit, without the graceful cover of nature that hid the old disasters. Civilization without humanity was just a graveyard.

Liam thought he saw movement from the corner of his eye, but when he turned, there was nothing there. The city was a security nightmare. Every dark opening looked threatening, every turn held an unknown danger. How could he keep Syd safe in a place like this?

"They must have abandoned the Lower City," Syd said.

"No one would stay down here longer than they had to. Even when the city was alive, people did whatever they could to get out."

He thought of Finch, his body buried in the desert. He'd had dreams of his own and plans that the network collapse had undone. Bitterness, rage, vengeance . . . could Syd blame him? How many millions of plans had been destroyed when the networks fell? How many millions more now that this sickness had begun to take hold? If Syd failed, if everyone died because of him, did all his mistakes die too? Would negation free him or would there be judgment on the other side? Justice or oblivion?

Which did he hope for?

They roared over a broken blast barrier that had separated the Lower City roads from the restricted speedway of the Upper City. Syd was able to move faster there. The ruins had more order to them, as if the lux Upper City even decayed better than the poor districts. The slums of the Valve and the Lower City might as well have never existed, but the Upper City was dug in deeper. Its patterns endured.

They rose and rose, and as they rose, their large vehicle knocked aside the burned and abandoned husks of small transports. Syd didn't look too closely as he smashed them out of the way, in case he saw the bodies inside. The barriers were in better shape the farther into the Upper City they climbed. He figured that once the borders had been crossed, there was no need to tear the walls down. There were richer targets for destruction: SecuriTech depots and

Xelon Corporate Credit Bureaus, fashion boutiques and medical clinics, EpiCure Flavor Emporia and Gamify Data Centers. There were offices and apartments and mansions. There was wealth in the ruins.

The destruction seemed wanton at first glance, but patterns emerged. There appeared to be different sets of motives at work: the spontaneous revenge of the liberated Lower City, the Reconciliation's deliberate destruction of the old mechanisms of power and control, and then the plain old pragmatism of looting.

The scratchiti carved into the walls told the stories. PROXIES ARISE and NOT YOUR SLAVES ANYMORE and BURN THE KNOCK-OFFS ALIVE and THE ONLY GOOD PATRON IS A DEAD PATRON and GREED IS GONE and above them all, REPENT FOR THE MACHINE, CHEY IS WATCHING.

"What is Chey?" Liam asked.

Syd shrugged. Sometimes people just wanted to leave a mark. It didn't have to mean more than that.

Strangely, as they crept into the swanky residential district where Knox had lived, they still hadn't seen any people. Marie pointed Syd along the roads, as Liam scanned the perimeter. Syd slowed the engines; the roar became a whine and they sank closer to the ground.

"I recognize this," Syd said as they approached Xelon Park. "I couldn't believe the beauty of this place when I first saw it."

The park's weeping willows were chopped down, and

even their stumps had been burned up. The grass was trampled, the hedges uprooted, and the scattered remains of campsites were the only evidence that anything had been there at all before, other than dirt.

Ahead of them was the gated drive up to Knox's old house. The gate itself was gone, even the gateposts and hinges hauled away. On one of the remaining sections of wall that had ringed the house someone had scratched YOUR DEBT IS DUE, SECURITECH SKUM.

"The house was more impressive before," Syd noted.

"I like the place how it is now," Liam said.

Syd settled the hovercraft in the front drive. The grand entry door, which had been reinforced graphene covered in antique mahogany, was now little more than splinters. Mold had begun its slow creep into the entry hall, and even from outside, they could see a riot of dirty footprints going in and out through the doorway and the gaping hole where a floor-to-ceiling plexi window had given astounding views of the park and the city below it.

"Let me go in first," said Liam. "To make sure it's secure. Then you follow."

The house was empty, so Liam called in Marie and Syd after him.

"It's been completely looted," Liam said. "I don't know what you think you'll find."

Syd stood in the middle of the great room, looking up to the balcony above, remembering the last time he was here—the only other time he'd been here—when he first saw Knox's father, first saw Marie. When Knox had made the decision to help him escape. Had Knox suspected he'd never come home again?

Syd held the journal in front of him, flipped through the pages, looking for anything that might resemble the pictures the doctor had drawn, some piece of tech, some clue. There was nothing.

Syd moved to the grand staircase that curved to the floor above and stalked up it, sliding his hand along the smooth surface of the metal banister. Mold had painted black spots on the walls where expensive art had hung. He inched along the upstairs hall and came to Knox's old room.

The door had been blown open by a Guardian before the networks fell and it hadn't been repaired. The room itself was bare, stripped to nothing. Even the plexi in the window was gone. The hazy view of the city beyond showed the dark skyscrapers with shattered windows jutting like rotted teeth gnawing on mushy clouds. Everything was ruined. There was no machine here and no clues for finding one. What had he been thinking, following a dream of Knox back to this place?

"Stay back!" he heard Liam shout. He rushed out to the hallway and looked down over the railing to the great room below.

Marie had the bolt gun up and Liam had assumed a fighting stance, Finch's EMD stick raised. A raggedy assortment of figures was climbing up through the open wall of windows. There were at least a dozen of them, and more came in through the open front door, pressing Liam and Marie back toward the stairs. They moved up step by step, side by side, and the figures pressed in on them.

They were all dressed in combinations of filthy lux fabrics, dirty suits, and half-shredded gowns. The remains of formalwear and Upper City chic, most of it too big for most of them. All of them were teens, none much older than Syd himself. Tattoos of ones and zeros looped around their necks, poked from their sleeves, and on a few of them, covered their faces. Machinists, every one.

They did not seem happy to find visitors.

They all carried weapons—sharpened poles, powerless EMD sticks, one or two bolt guns. To the side, a boy hauled an old combat robot on a length of rope. It was missing three of its legs and the barrel of one of its fracture cannons was bent sideways. It slumped on its own weight and had begun to rust. The boy had mounted a slingshot on its back. That appeared to be in full working order.

"I said stay back," Liam ordered again.

Marie fixed her aim on the guy with the bot. "One more step from anyone and he dies," she said.

The crowd stopped. They all looked to the guy whom she'd threatened. He dropped the leash and put his hands up. The guy behind him, holding the band of the slingshot, kept it aimed at Marie. He'd loaded it with rusted metal bits.

Everyone looked back to Marie.

"What now?" she whispered to Liam.

Syd ducked low, so they couldn't see him from the floor

below. He realized he'd hidden here before, in this exact spot, with Knox by his side.

There was a name for the *feeling* of having done something before, but he couldn't remember what it was. Was there a name for the *reality* of having done something before, repeating your own history in stranger and stranger ways, trapped in a decaying version of the past, losing people as you went?

"Who are you?" a girl in the crowd demanded of Marie. The guy with the bolt gun aimed at him bulged his eyes at her and shook his head, but she moved to the front of the crowd and repeated her question. The girl looked Marie up and down. "Purifier?"

"No," said Marie. "Not anymore."

The girl snorted, skeptical. She wore a man's suit with a tie she'd fashioned from a strip of cloth, and her belt buckle was the gleaming ornament of a lux transport. She had three Purifier's masks hanging from her belt, all of them stained with dried brown streaks. Not all of the streaks were mud, of that Syd was certain. Blood dries brown. The girl's knuckles were marked with alternating ones and zeros.

Marie also noticed the bloody masks, the tattoos in binary. "Who are *you*?" she asked.

The girl cocked her head. "You're in our house, outnumbered, and we ask the questions."

"This isn't your house," said Marie. "Property is shared by all."

That sent a laugh through the crowd. Hoots and howls.

"There's no Reconciliation here, Purifier." The girl laughed. "You can shove your knock-off collectivism."

"I told you I'm not a Purifier," Marie repeated.

"You sound like one," the girl said. She pointed to Liam. "Who's your big friend?"

"No lover of the Reconciliation," Liam answered.

The girl smirked. "I like your hand. You got a name?"

Liam opened and closed his metal hand. "Liam," he said. "You?"

"Gianna, acting chief operating officer of the Xelon Corporation." She bent at the waist into a low open-armed bow. When she came up, she produced a piece of plexi with something scratched onto the surface of it. Beside her, a smaller boy whipped out a tiny solar LED and shined the light through the glass. It projected the scratchings on the glass through onto the wall:

GIANNA S. COO, XELON CORP.

She'd made a primitive holo to imitate the business bios executives used to have. It was ugly, but ingenious. She'd improvised her own little piece of the past.

Marie kept her weapon pointed at the nervous guy beside the bot. "Xelon?" she asked, shocked to see the name of her father's company shining against the wall. She hadn't heard it said out loud in all the months since the Reconciliation banned the corporate names, let alone seen it projected on a wall.

"We're all Xelon here," Gianna said. "House is ours, the park beyond. Xelon territory. We care for the brand until the Machine."

"We aren't from here," Liam explained. "We didn't mean to trespass."

The girl smiled. "The Xelon Corporation welcomes guests. We're not like other corporations in the city. We extend credit without cruelty or bias."

Marie and Liam looked at each other, eyebrows raised. Syd, above, stayed hidden. They were very much outnumbered and he did not want to lose the element of surprise by revealing himself. It was their only advantage if things turned bad.

"Credit?" Marie asked.

"If you are worthy of credit, we will offer it on favorable terms," Gianna told them.

"And if not?" Liam wondered.

"You go bankrupt." Gianna held out her hands, palms up, empty. The crowd hooted again and whooped. Some waved stained Purifier masks above their heads. Bankrupt did not sound like something they wanted to be. "So . . . why did you come here? Why do you deserve our credit?"

"We . . . uh . . ." Marie was trying to think of an answer when a shout from above cut her off. She and Liam turned to see Syd, standing with his hands up; another teenager, this one in the uniform of a Xelon security guard, stood behind him and jammed a weapon into his back.

"Found this one up here snooping!" he shouted.

"Espionage?" Gianna raised her eyebrows. "You from the competition? Come to steal our corporate secrets? That's grounds for execution!"

"Hey," the one behind Syd said, jabbing a kind of pointy stick into his back. Syd glanced over his shoulder and saw that the weapon was simply that: a pointy stick. The boy hooted: "This one's got a marking . . . like a logo behind his ear. It's dirty, though; I can't tell if it's—"

"We've come for the Machine!" Liam announced, loudly.

Syd gave Liam a "what are you doing" kind of look. Marie gave him an "are you completely glitched" kind of look.

Liam peeled off his shirt in one quick motion and the crowd gasped, not at the bloody bandage running along his side, but at the letters inked across his chest—letters that, by now, had become legendary.

"Yovel," Gianna said.

"That's right," said Liam. "I am Yovel. I destroyed the networks and only I can restore them."

In the hush that followed, Syd couldn't decide if Liam's plan had just saved them from a bloody death, or ensured they were all going to be killed.

Gianna waved for Syd to come down the steps. He moved slowly, the stick jabbing into his back. He wasn't sure what Liam's endgame here was supposed to be. Marie still had her bolt gun raised and Liam's EMD stick was charged. They wouldn't last long in a fight, but they'd take a few of these cultists with them. The rest would follow soon enough.

Gianna turned back to Liam. She rested her fingers on the tattoo on his chest, tapped it delicately. Even though the room was warm and humid, goose bumps formed on his skin. He began to doubt his entire idea, as much as it could be called an idea. He hadn't really thought past the part where they didn't discover it was Syd who was actually Yovel, Syd who had caused the Jubilee, Syd whom their assassins had so far failed to kill.

The corners of Gianna's mouth twitched and she turned back to the crowd. She had made some kind of decision.

"It was Yovel who destroyed our corporate data!" she told them, her arms raised in the air. She reminded Syd of Counselor Baram giving his speeches. The crowd hung on everything Gianna said.

The power to control a crowd with words could be deadlier than all the weapons in the world. Was that why Baram insisted Syd give all those speeches? Not to make the crowds respect him, but to make him respect the crowds, to see the power they had, the way they could be transformed, called to action, called to change. If he was meant to lead, this would be a skill he needed. He should have practiced when he had the chance. Gianna must have.

"It was Yovel who severed the networks." Gianna pointed at Liam. "Yovel who crashed our markets. And yet, we received no compensation! Is that justice? No payments were ever made!"

The crowd booed.

I spent my whole life paying, Syd thought.

"But now he is here," Gianna shouted. "And with his blood, we will be compensated!"

The crowd roared their approval. They moved forward, murder in their eyes.

Liam braced himself for a losing fight. "When it starts," he whispered to Syd, "just run."

"I'm not leaving you behind," Syd replied quickly.

"You have to," Liam said.

Marie took a step forward, one step down toward the frothing crowd, her finger on the release of the bolt gun's spring.

"This is not how business is done!" she shouted. She turned to Gianna. "Is Xelon Corporation nothing but pirates and thieves now? A murderous mob?"

Gianna swiped her hand to hush the crowd. "How dare you—?"

"We brought Yovel to you in good faith." Marie pointed at Liam. "We could have gone to any corporation in the city, but we came to you, to Xelon, because we knew you to deal honestly, to honor contracts, to offer the highest market yield on investment. Were we wrong to come here? Were we wrong to do business with you? The Xelon Handbook of Profit Directives clearly states that until a transfer of property is formally completed, no asset exploitation may be undertaken lest it expose shareholders to claims of market malfeasance."

Liam sucked in his breath. He had no idea what Marie had just said.

Gianna looked at Liam and then at Syd with her eyebrows raised. She stepped to Marie. "You know the Xelon Handbook of Profit Directives?"

"I do," said Marie, holding her finger on the spring release of the bolt gun, just in case.

"And you abide by its Best Business Practices?"

"We do," said Marie.

Gianna looked at Syd, who nodded. Gianna looked at Liam, who nodded too, because the others had. Gianna thought a moment, then turned back to the crowd.

"We will do business with our visitors!" she announced. "And when a fair price is negotiated, Yovel's blood will pay his debts." Her face broke into a smile, turning back to Marie. "You are welcome to the new Xelon Corporate Satellite Offices as honored business associates!"

"You guys hungry?" the guy with the bot asked the moment Marie lowered her weapon. "We don't have much, thanks to the corporate restructuring—"

"May the Reconciliation go bankrupt and die," Gianna interrupted, spitting on the ground.

"But what we have, we are happy to extend to you," the guy continued. "With low interest rates."

"We'd love to eat with you," said Marie, smiling. "We can discuss the terms of our exchange and the structure of our agreement after we eat."

She tucked the bolt gun into the waistband of her pants and motioned for Liam to lower his weapon. Everyone relaxed and the room soon erupted in excited chatter.

"Don't mind them." Gianna waved her hands at the crowd. "It has been a while since we've engaged in a good-faith transaction. We've not been in an ideal business environment for some time, you understand?"

"I do," said Marie. Gianna cleared a path for them through the crowd. Syd and Liam were still staring at Marie, dumbfounded.

"What is going on?" Liam whispered in Syd's ear.

"We've just agreed to make a deal with them," Syd said. "To sell you."

"They can't kill someone else's property," Marie explained. "We've bought some time."

"Yeah, but how much?" Liam wondered.

"We still have to work all that out," said Marie. "How much they'll charge us for dinner; how much we'll charge them for you."

Liam looked at Syd.

"Everything costs." Syd shrugged. "We might as well eat."

[26]

"I'M SORRY THE FOOD is so . . ." Gianna searched for the word. "Organic."

Marie shrugged, stuffing a roasted turnip into her mouth. They sat around in the empty great room. The breeze blew through the giant window, cooled the humid air. It also stirred around the stench of over thirty bodies that hadn't washed in months. Syd sniffed deeply at the charred flesh of whatever root he was eating. The burned smell masked the putridity.

"We harvest from the park." Gianna explained their dinner, shaking her head sadly. "A shame what we've been driven to. *Farming*. It's like we're primitives. Xelon Park was once beautiful, you know? I went there as a child. Now . . . well, we'll restore it. With the Machine, when the networks return, the corporations will rise again. Balance, freedom, sponsorship . . . it will follow. Until then, we eat like this. The Reconciliation"—someone behind her cursed and spat—"left seeds behind when they were driven out. We've made use of them until we can get more efficient nutrient production online. Unfortunately, everyone at Epi-Cure Incorporated is a miscreant, a syntholene addict, or a Chapter Eleven."

Syd glanced at Liam, who didn't seem at all bothered by the insult. There were things Liam felt ashamed of in his life, but that wasn't one of them.

"You came to the right corporation," Gianna continued. "We have good credit. We can secure financing for this one." She pointed her chin at Liam. "We at Xelon know how to profit with our partners. We were one of the first to incorporate again after we drove out the green uniforms."

"What happened?" Marie asked. "I mean, how did you drive out the Reconciliation? How did you . . . 'incorporate' . . . Xel . . . Xelon?" She faltered on the company's name. She thought of her father, standing in his suit, leading a meeting of shareholders, proud, powerful, certain of the future. She thought of him now, dying in a squalid barracks.

"When the networks fell, there was confusion at first," Gianna said. Her eyes narrowed; she swayed slightly and the others leaned in to hear. She told of things they themselves had witnessed, but they sat rapt as she spoke, as if the past became real not through the living of it, but through the telling of it. "It was morning and I was in school. Many of us were. Suddenly, the teacher's holo from EduCorp vanished from the front of the classroom. Our datastreams went blank. Some worried their assignments for the day hadn't been transmitted. Others cheered, because a network outage meant no school."

Gianna looked up, scanned the faces watching her. She addressed them all: "Do you remember?"

"We remember," they said in unison.

Gianna continued. "We waited, of course, many of us, but nothing happened. Some tried to look up the outage on their datastreams . . . but they couldn't. In minutes, there was grumbling. No one could figure out why they couldn't look up why. Then the malfunctioning transports ran into each other in the streets. There were crashes; the sky fell onto the city. The hospitals were glitched . . . they couldn't access records or treatments, couldn't activate the patches or identify their patients. The medibots fell silent. They couldn't treat even the simplest conditions. Our biodata was cut off. My father . . ." The girl shook her head. "By the time I walked home from school, an old case of malaria had laid him low. He died within days. Anyone with an old condition relapsed. Do you remember?"

"We remember."

Gianna locked eyes with Marie. "And then the Reconciliation came."

Someone in the crowd cursed. Someone else spat.

"They swarmed up from the Lower City, from the Valve and its rotted slums and they overran our beautiful neighborhoods. Our schools and businesses. Our homes. They had no uniforms then, but they came and they looted. They told us *we* were criminals even as they burned executives in the streets. Our parents. Our families. There were no Guardians to stop them and the personal protection bots no longer functioned."

"My father was burned alive," the guy with the broken bot said flatly.

"My mother was beaten in front of me," a girl in a flame-orange gown said. "They left her lying in the street. They told me if I wanted to live, I would put her out of her misery. I did." She wept into her hands.

Syd bit his lip. This was his Jubilee too, the side of it he hadn't seen, wasn't ever supposed to see. It wasn't all rallies and farms. This was done in his name.

Marie's face was frozen, impossibly still. Inside her stillness, there was a hurricane swirling. She had come from this group; if it weren't for Syd, her parents would have met the same fate as theirs. She could have been one of these lost kids, playing pretend corporation in the ruins of her own home. Syd slid his hand across the mildewy carpet where they sat and rested his fingers on hers. He understood.

"I saw my own proxy on the restricted speedway that first week," said Gianna. "She, of course, didn't know me, but I had seen her on holos a few times, when I broke my curfew. The punishments she received for those things were never too harsh and my offenses were never too severe. She only had two years of debt left before she wouldn't be a proxy any longer. She was part of a mob tearing apart a Xelon transmitter. A group of managers had come out to protect it, in case the network came back online . . . it wouldn't work without transmitters. She kicked the teeth out of one of the men, after he was on the ground. The proxies wanted revenge, and they took it. Many of us hid, in the parks, in the offices. Anywhere we could hide, we hid. Do you remember?"

"We remember."

"Then the Purifiers came in uniforms. The white masks," Gianna said. "They established order. They stacked the bodies of the executives and of the criminals in the windows of empty shops, like new shirts on display. To the Reconciliation"—another curse, a splatter of spit—"they were all the same.

"The Purifiers told us all debts had been erased, and all wealth too. Our possessions were no longer ours. Our tech was banned. We could submit to evacuation, go to learn work and be productive, or be killed. They went door to door, searching, gathering our families, splitting them up, sending everyone away. But we stayed hidden. Some were found. Some were not. For a month, we hid, half starved, full frightened. No one knew what to do. The Guardians, who we thought would protect us, had become useless. They wandered aimlessly. They turned into monsters. We kept our distance. We fought amongst ourselves for scraps, even to eat the zoo animals. We made the polar bear extinct again. Some gave up, surrendered to the white masks and vanished. The gangs returned, like swamp gas rising from the sewage. They hoarded supplies, bribed the Purifiers, enslaved those of us they could catch, and made the children of the city into their pleasure dolls. I had a sister . . ." Gianna shook her head. "We would not have made it much longer, but then, one night, we took shelter in a club, a place I had danced before, Arcadia, it was called. There were others there; they had made it a home. And they had a leader. She told us the truth, the saving truth that turned us on to the righteous path. The Machine. Do you remember?"

"We remember."

Syd remembered too.

Arcadia.

That was where he had found Knox and Knox's friends. That was where he'd kidnapped Knox and gone with him back here, to this house.

Arcadia.

That was where all this began.

Gianna smiled. "Chey is her name." Liam made eye contact with the Syd. The scratchiti. *Chey is watching.*

"Chey taught us that the network went down because we did not serve it well," Gianna said. "She taught us that there was a Machine that could bring it back, but only if we committed ourselves to serve it. We organized, we rebuilt the corporations our mothers and fathers had failed to preserve, and she made a deal with the Maes gang to retake our city. Together, we rose up against the Purifiers. We drove them away and we gathered all the tech that remained, that had not been destroyed, and now, we prepare. We prepare for the Machine. When all will be restored."

Liam, Syd, and Marie looked over the room, the crazy outfits, the imitation holo projectors, the fragments of this or that device or bot the kids pretended to make work. The devotional tattoos honored a programming language surely none of them understood.

Again, Syd had that feeling, the past as an echo, repeating itself as it faded. The poor had longed for Jubilee to save them from the powerful, and now the one-time patrons longed for the Machine to do the same. Every revolution believes it can return something that had been lost, but nothing is ever the same. The only thing that endures are people. Syd saw that clearly now, and perhaps so too did Marie. You could serve a revolution, an idea that ended up an echo of itself, or you could serve people, with all their maddening contradictions. You couldn't serve both. You had to choose.

"We are not insane," Gianna said, seeing herself through their eyes. "We know the tech is broken. We know the network is not back yet. But we must be ready. We use what we have so that we're ready. Chey will build the Machine and everything will come back." She glared at Liam. "And those who stand in the way will be destroyed."

"So there is a Machine? It's real?" Marie asked.

"Of course it's real!" Gianna said. "Chey has showed it to me herself!"

Syd had an idea. By the look on her face, Marie had the same one. Liam still clutched his EMD stick. His only idea was to get out this place, fast. All things considered, it was as good a backup plan as any. But first, Syd had to try something.

"We cannot sell Yovel to you," he said.

The room grew quiet. Gianna's eyes narrowed. "You are backing out of our deal? Or you are beginning negotiation from an aggressive position?"

"Call it negotiation," said Syd, leaning closer. "It is in your interest that we do not sell Yovel to you. You cannot kill him."

"We can do what we please with him once he is our property," she replied. "And if we cannot reach an agreement on the terms of this sale, we'll simply kill all of you."

"That's not very good business," said Marie.

"We're in a challenging economy," Gianna said back.

"But wouldn't it be better if you had to spend none of your own resources on this transaction?" said Syd. "He would still die. And you could still get paid."

"Explain yourself," Gianna said.

"Yeah," Liam added. "Explain."

"We'll sell him to Chey. Think how it will please the Machine to have the blood of Yovel spilled directly before it."

Gianna suppressed a smile. Syd had her. She liked the idea.

"And you would get a finder's fee for bringing Yovel to it," Marie added.

"What is in this deal for you?" Gianna asked, suddenly skeptical. She was wise to mistrust any idea that was not her own, but Syd knew he had to convince her. They would get to the Machine. Once they were there . . . well, then Liam could do what he did best. They would seize control of the Machine by any means necessary.

"Chey is wealthy, right?" said Syd. "Wealthier than Xelon?"

Gianna nodded. "She runs the Benevolent Society. Every corporation makes donations."

"We're businesspeople like you," Syd told her. "We want the best price for Yovel we can get, and we didn't bring him all the way from the headquarters of the Reconciliation to sell him at a discount."

"We do not buy on discount!" He'd offended Gianna. Good.

"You could be a broker or you could be a buyer," said Syd. "I guess it's up to you."

"Strangers don't go to see Chey," said Gianna.

"We would be in your debt," Syd added, sweetening their offer. "Indebted to you."

The crowd murmured.

"We would be your patrons?" Gianna asked. "You, our proxies?"

Syd took a deep breath. "Yes."

Gianna broke into a broad grin. She stood and urged Syd, Marie, and Liam to stand.

"Contracts!" she called out, and another girl stood. She held a plate of plexi and the same small boy shined a light through it so it glowed on the wall. It was filled with tiny scratched-out writing, edge to edge.

"These are your terms, a standard proxy agreement," Gianna said. "You will each sign and become our proxies for a term equal to the cost of your food and your admittance fee to our district and the processing costs for the Xelon Corporation. Yovel"—she pointed at Liam—"will remain in your possession, but serve as collateral until such a time as we broker his sale."

"Uh—" Liam hadn't understood a word Gianna had just said. He stared at the shadows on the wall, knew them to be words, and was amazed at the effort it must have taken to make such a thing and the impossibility of reading it even if he knew how.

"Everything will be spelled out in the Xelon actuarial tables available from your local sales representative." Gianna rolled her eyes.

Local sales representative. Actuarial tables. These were the old words of an old system. They were all playing make-believe.

"How do I sign?" Syd asked. He would play too, if that's what it took.

"Biodata," Gianna said, and someone handed him a small knife. Gianna gestured to the wall and Syd stepped forward. He looked back at Marie, pricked his finger with the blade, and dabbed a dot of blood into the projection on the wall. He stepped back, looking solemn. He never imagined he'd agree to become a proxy again, even if it was make-believe.

Marie stepped forward and went through the same motions, leaving a drop of her blood on the wall of the abandoned mansion. She wondered what her father would think if he could see her now.

Liam stepped up to do the same. But Gianna stopped him. "You are not a proxy," she said. "You are the product."

Liam stepped back beside Syd.

A product. He understood this was a ploy to find the Machine, but still, it made him uncomfortable. People lived and died—he knew that well enough. Products, on the other hand, were used and disposed of. He wondered if Syd saw him that way too: useful for now, but disposable when he'd been used up.

"Excellent." Gianna clapped. The light snapped off and the shadow of the contract vanished. Only the two dots of blood remained. "We will have to determine a system by which you serve as proxies to each of us for an appointed time . . ." She tapped her finger on her chin, thinking. "Of course, you're not actually supposed to know your patrons . . . We'll have to form a working group, conduct meetings on the best way to allocate your debt and maximize efficiency. Also, the method of enforcement for infractions . . . So much to consider."

The room was abuzz in chatter now. Syd overheard words like "synergy" and "cost-benefit analysis" thrown around. Watching them perform their faith so convincingly, he had a momentary fear that he really had made himself a proxy again.

"Can you explain to me what's going on?" Liam whispered.

"You made them think you're me," said Syd. "So we are selling you in order to gain access to the Machine, and until the sale is final, Marie and I are in their debt."

"This is crazy."

Syd didn't disagree. "It will get us where we need to go."

"Now." Gianna turned back to them. "What do you charge for a drive in your hovercraft?"

Marie had to laugh. "They respect private property, I'll grant them that."

"Yeah," Syd replied. "But we're their private property now too."

He turned to go to the hovercraft and stopped. A tingle raced through his limbs, up his neck, like he'd suddenly been swarmed with spiders. He scratched his arm where it itched, which only amplified the itch. He looked at the palm of his hand where the skin was palest. His legs wobbled.

In a flash, Liam was at his side, holding him up. "You okay?"

Syd nodded. "Yeah. Just something I ate. I'll be fine."

He closed his hand, hiding the little blue lines, visible for the first time against his skin.

He looked at Marie, and then at Gianna, at all the kids around their age. On the paler ones it was the most obvious, a web of lines, their blood vessels showing through. Some of them were already scratching at their skin.

It had begun.

The blood of the young was turning.

[27]

WHEN THEY REACHED THE squat warehouse build-
ing on the edge of what had been an industrial district, Syd
settled the hovercraft down in front of a barricade the Machinists constructed. It was a wall of old transports, robotic
parts, and scraps of furniture. The place bore little resem-
blance to the club as he remembered it. The glamour was
gone.

A line of guards, all of them teenagers, stood along the
top of the barricade. A large piece of etched plexi had been
mounted in the ground in front of a bonfire to cast a large
shadow along the width of the barricade. The flickering projection read BENEVOLENT SOCIETY. PRIVATE PROPERTY. TRES-
PASSERS EXECUTED.

The guards wielded EMD sticks like clubs. Others held
crossbows and bolt guns and blades of various sizes. They

may have been playing businessmen, but their invented economy didn't yet have the illusion of civility. They understood what had really held the market together before. Violence. After all, what good was a debt if the creditor couldn't compel it to be paid?

The guards along the barricade were dressed in a mixture of styles—some just like the Xelon kids, others in white jumpsuits, some in casual robes and sandals. Each so-called corporation, it seemed, had their own dress code, and each had their own people standing guard on the wall.

Syd saw the veins on some of their faces, saw others scratching at phantom itches on their skin. If he was going to save them, it would have to happen soon. He had no idea how fast this sickness moved. Knox's father said it affected people differently . . . He wondered how long he had before it took him down.

Liam looked at Syd. He could tell something was wrong. The web of veins didn't show as easily through his dark skin, but they were there, just faintly, and they would get worse. Liam wished he could mitigate that terror for Syd, erase the knowledge that with every heartbeat he got closer and closer to dying.

Then again, wasn't that true for everyone? It was just a question of timing.

Gianna left the hovercraft first and spoke with the guards. A select group of her people followed, and she told Liam, Syd, and Marie to follow.

As he came down the ramp of the hovercraft, Liam tore

open his shirt so that his tattoo was more visible. A few people cast wary glances at Marie's green uniform, but they were mostly fixated on Liam and on the word across his chest. None of them paid Syd any attention, which was exactly what Liam had wanted. As long as they looked at Liam, no one would notice the word behind Syd's ear, or think to question who was who.

Inside the old club, the air was thick with sour body odor, mixed with rusting metal and the chemical stench of burning plastic. Syd was amazed how the place looked like a demented nightmare of the club he'd seen the last time had been there, when it was still a playground for the rich patrons of Mountain City.

Old cars were crammed up against each other, side by side and bumper to bumper, filling the entire space from the back wall forward, with just a small ring around them creating a path along the edges toward the doors in and out. Before, these cars had made up the dance floor. Now, they had turned into a kind of encampment. Figures huddled in the open cabins of old convertibles, while fires simmered inside other vehicles, casting shadowy light throughout the room, silhouetting the forms standing on the hoods.

The holos that had been projected all over the walls the night of the original party were gone, but the cultists living here had painted some on, still images in mysterious pigments substituting for the once vibrant—and loud—holo projections that were timed with the pulsing music. Some had been scratched onto windshields and projected onto the walls by the flames inside the vehicles. The crude shadow logos flickered and shifted unevenly.

The music itself had been reproduced too, a sad simulacrum of the party that had been. Half a dozen forms on a metal catwalk above the dance floor banged and pounded on improvised drums and tubes, making a syncopated beat while a chorus of voices tried to reproduce digital sounds with their mouths. Most of them didn't have a talent for it, but they all had enthusiasm. The effect was not something a person would be tempted to dance to, and yet, throughout the space, small groups danced in jerky, writhing motions.

"They're dancing," Marie stated the obvious, more to remind herself that this was real, that she hadn't gone totally insane.

"They're going through the motions," said Syd.

"Why?" Liam wondered.

"They've built a knock-off world to bring back the one they lost." Syd looked up. The old neon sign still hung over the space, its buzzing glow long since extinguished.

ET IN ARCADIA EGO

He had first seen that sign just moments before he'd met Knox. He didn't know what it meant then. He didn't know now. A nonsense language or an extinct one, it didn't really matter. The past was past. The future was all they had to cling to now, and if they failed to get the networks back on, there wouldn't be a future at all.

There was a bitter taste in Syd's mouth. He felt cold, in spite of the heat of the room. One look at Marie told him she wasn't faring much better. None of them were.

He scratched at his neck, tried to strip away the spidery feeling beneath his skin, let his nails dig deeper, just a little deeper. Relief didn't come, but if he could just scrape a little deeper into the flesh . . . He stopped himself. Remembered the nopes. Scratching wouldn't help him. Focus. He had to focus.

Wires ran around the edges of the room, networks of cables and cords webbed across the ceiling. It struck Syd how much the networked wires looked like the web of veins across the skin of the sick. The disease was an echo of the networks' destruction.

"Who are you?" A form came toward them from the darkness, flanked by several others. Liam shifted himself in front of Syd, his metal fist clenched.

"They are our proxies!" Gianna exclaimed, causing a stir of murmurs from the dance floor and the catwalk above.

"Proxies?" The form stepped into the light. It was another teenaged girl, about Marie's age. Anglo, with her head shaved. She wore a crisp white outfit, perfectly tailored, perfectly clean, with a red silk scarf around her neck.

Two boys flanked her. They too had shaved heads and white suits, although their suits didn't quite fit them and they'd gone shiny and gray at the elbows and knees. Unlike the girl, they were armed.

Bolt guns.

Liam nodded politely at them as they approached. He'd already thought of four different ways to kill them.

A ring of differently attired cultists flanked this trio. Syd understood they were all guards from different "corporations," each vying to stay close to this girl. She was the one who mattered here, the only one.

Chey.

Syd's heart beat faster. He had come to the right place. The Machine was real. He could save them. He could save everyone.

The girl strolled forward, confident in her command, and her escorts helped her down from the hood of an old car so that she stood just in front of Liam, Syd, and Marie.

"There are no proxies anymore," she said. "Not until the Machine wakes."

"We've entered into an agreement with Gianna from Xelon," Marie explained. Chey looked her up and down, taking in the green Purifier uniform, lingering on Marie's face. She pursed her lips, nodded.

Gianna rushed up the Chey's side and began explaining. "They fled the Reconciliation and they entered into an agreement with us and they brought—"

"Yovel," said Chey.

"Yes," said Gianna. "For the Machine. For a fee, we will broker a deal for Yovel. His death will please the Machine?"

Liam stiffened; he puffed his chest out slightly. Chey turned to the guards by her side, whispered with them, then she stepped up to Liam.

"Yovel?" she said. "The one who did all this?" She waved her hand around the club, as if it was somehow the revolution that created a cracked mirror image of what these patron kids used to do for fun.

"He will give himself freely to the Machine," Syd said. "If you will take us to it."

Chey looked to Syd. She brushed Liam aside with a graceful wave of her hand and stepped directly in front of Syd's face. Syd saw Liam tense, his muscles ready to uncoil.

"Why would he do this? The hero of the Reconciliation allow us to sacrifice him?"

"The Reconciliation is bankrupt," Syd said. "Something new must take its place."

"We do not want something new," she said. "We want something back."

Syd looked closely at the girl. Up close, he could see every vein in her face, the tiny capillaries around the mouth, the pulsing arteries in her neck. She projected confidence, but she was not confident. There were sores on her neck, at least half a dozen of them from excessive scratching, and they were poorly concealed by her white suit and red scarf.

She, like him, like all of them, was in the process of dying.

"He wants the network restored," said Syd. "He too wants things to go back. He believes in the Machine and that the Machine will save us."

"Yovel believes?" Chey looked back at Liam.

Liam nodded.

Chey looked back into Syd's eyes. She leaned to his side and lifted her hand up to stroke his cheek. She walked her fingers back to his ear, bent it forward, and looked at the word emblazoned there.

She turned back to the two boys who had been at her side. "You were right," she said. "Syd."

In a flash, Liam whirled around, knocking Chey's bodyguards aside and yanking her away from Syd. He held her in a headlock, his metal hand wrapped around her throat. Marie drew the bolt gun and pointed it straight at Gianna's head.

"Stay back!" Marie shouted.

"Liam! No!" Syd yelled at the same instant.

"Where's the Machine?" Liam demanded. "Take us to it."

A circle formed around them; Marie turned and pointed the gun from person to person to keep them from rushing forward. They'd been in better shape during the standoff back at Knox's house. At least there they'd only been outnumbered ten to one.

"Did you kill Knox?" Chey asked Syd, her voice squeaking out through the vise grip Liam had on her.

Syd stepped close. "What?"

"That night," she repeated. Liam loosened his grip slightly so she could talk. "When you left here . . . did you kill Knox?"

"You . . . you knew Knox?"

"He was my friend," Chey said.

Syd glanced at Marie, then back to Chey.

He gestured for Marie to lower her weapon.

"He was my friend too," he said.

Chey studied Syd, her neck bulging where Liam gripped it. "Lower your weapons!" she called out. "Let them be."

Syd nodded at Liam.

"You sure?" Liam asked.

"I'm sure," said Syd.

Liam released Chey, who gasped and stepped back, rubbing her throat. There were deep impressions of Liam's metal fingers in her skin and she would certainly bruise. The crowd encircling them stood still, their leader in the center, with Liam, Syd, and Marie.

The two boys in white suits stepped forward to stand with her.

"Nine," one of the boys introduced himself. "And this is Simi."

Syd looked at them closely. They were familiar. They'd met before . . . in this very club. Knox's friends. These were Knox's friends. The other one put his hand out for a fist bump. Syd ignored it.

"I'm Cheyenne," the girl in the center said. She turned to Marie. "And I recognize you too. I didn't at first . . . your hair, your eyes . . . they're different. But you're Marie? The girl . . . with Knox."

Marie nodded.

"We were in school together."

"For a little while," said Marie.

"You were supposed to have died," Nine said.

"I know," Marie answered.

"You need to explain this me," Cheyenne said. "What did you do to Knox? Why have you come back here?"

"I didn't do anything to Knox," Syd explained. "He did all of this. He gave his life to shut down the networks and the Reconciliation didn't want to give a patron credit for it. They told everyone I did it. But it was a lie. It was Knox."

"That doesn't sound like him," Cheyenne said.

"He surprised us all," said Syd. "People do that."

"And now you've come here for what? To make amends?"

"To stop that." Syd pointed at her hands. She hadn't even noticed that she'd started scratching her stomach furiously. She stopped.

"This is our punishment!" Gianna stepped into the circle. "Our punishment for serving the Machine without proper zeal!"

"Be quiet!" Cheyenne snapped at her. "We don't require your input here."

Gianna ground her teeth and sniffed, tried to act as if she hadn't just been publicly insulted.

"It can be stopped," Syd to Cheyenne. "Your Machine . . . if we can get it working . . ." He pulled the journal from the pocket on his leg, flipped through to the illustrations.

"You can do this?" Cheyenne asked him.

"I can try."

Cheyenne took the journal from his hand and studied it.

Her brow was furrowed, her lips pursed. Syd could tell she didn't know what she was looking at it, but he didn't dare offend her by speaking up. She handed the journal back.

"Come with me," she said.

"Wait!" Gianna shouted. "We brought these three here on good faith. We were promised compensation!"

"Compensation?" Cheyenne looked at her two associates and back at Gianna with her ragtag cultists. "What compensation do you want?"

Gianna pointed at Syd. "The blood of Yovel . . . or whoever this is."

"No," Cheyenne said.

"But—!"

"Not yet." She looked between Syd, Liam, and Marie. "But if they cannot bring back our networks, I promise you, there will be blood."

Reluctantly, Gianna gave her consent. Not that she had much choice in the matter.

"I don't like this," Liam told Syd as they followed Cheyenne onto the hoods of the cars and weaved their way across the dance floor to the rear of the club. They were surrounded by over a hundred armed figures now, coughing and spitting and scratching and eyeing Syd. "They all hate you."

Syd looked around at the ruined club, the desperate dancers, the army of teenaged cultists, all of them beginning to die, all of them hoping they could be saved.

"Maybe they do hate me," Syd told Liam. "But I'm going to save them anyway."

[28]

A DOZEN LOCKS SNAPPED, a dozen guards stepped aside, and a dozen pairs of hands pushed a heavy door open.

In the small room that had once been—Syd couldn't believe it—a bathroom, the air smelled like burning hair and old fruit, so powerful that Syd could taste it. In the center of the floor, swaying in the hazy smoke, sat a cross-legged figure on the tile. She—or was it "he"? Impossible to tell—was wrapped entirely in wires from the top of her head to the tip of her toes.

Marie leaned in for a better look and gagged. The wires weren't wrapped around the figure. They were threaded into the figure's skin. With flesh and fiber optics woven together, the figure was simultaneously clothed and naked; her eyes were a smokey blue and they stared out unseeing through the haze of smoke in the room. Something about the eyes looked familiar. Syd had seen them before. He had seen them countless times.

"A Guardian," said Syd.

Cheyenne nodded. "She is the gatekeeper, made by the network, a being of pure technological creation." Cheyenne stepped up to the figure, bowed her head, and took a knife from her belt. She pricked her finger and let the blood drip into the fire.

"Something organic must be given, so that something inorganic can be made," she explained. Then she stepped around the terrible Guardian on the floor as if she weren't even there. Syd, Liam, and Marie followed her, trying not to stare.

They stood in front of an open bathroom stall and Syd's heart sank. Inside was a pile of machine parts, discarded projectors, scraps from combat robots and transports, cables and wires running every which way. Not only did it look nothing like the drawing in the dead scientist's journal, it looked nothing like any sort of machine. It looked like a junk heap.

"Is there a transmitter?" Syd asked.

Cheyenne pointed to the fire on the floor behind them.

"A receiver?"

She gestured at the crowd gathered in the doorway behind them. "We are the receiver."

"She's just as crazy as the rest of them," Liam whispered.

Marie sank back against the outside of the stall. She'd gone sallow and sweat beaded on her face.

"You okay?" Liam turned to her.

"It's hopeless," she muttered. "Me. My parents. Syd . . . we're all dead."

Cheyenne stepped up into Syd's face. "You can't turn it on? The great Yovel can't do anything? Because if you can't turn it on, we have to take . . . other steps."

Liam shoved himself between Cheyenne and Syd, stared her down, his metal hand balled once more into a fist. This was the part he knew; this was the part he understood.

"Your machine is nothing but junk," Syd said.

There was a gasp from the watching crowd. Their faces crowded the doorway to the bathroom, a many-headed monster, all its heads crying out for blood.

The mutilated Guardian on the floor swayed in place and Syd's disgust rose up in him. He swallowed and braced himself to keep from vomiting. He let Liam stand in front of him so he could lean on his bodyguard's shoulder. It was hard to stay standing. His legs tingled; the itch was growing hot, like his skin was trying to peel itself off of him. He wanted to jump out of his body.

Syd had been a fool to think this cult of tech-worshipping teenagers would hold the solution to a doomed world.

"Do any of you even know how this tech works?" he exploded at the crowd. "No transmitter? No receiver? No connections at all? You organized your whole freakish lives around this thing and you don't even know what a network needs to network? In all this time, did you ever even try to understand it? Did you ever question anything at all? Did you just expect someone like me to come along and save you from your glitch-brained knock-off lives?"

"You watch how you speak to us, *proxy*." The boy called Nine stepped forward, jabbing an angry finger at Syd.

Without even looking, Liam shot his metal hand out, grabbed Nine's finger, and twisted it back, using the boy's own pained contortions to toss him sideways to the floor.

Crossbows and bolt guns came up. Marie, however, didn't move, didn't even reach for her weapon. There hardly seemed a point. The revolution she'd fought for had led only to death, and her betrayal of it had done the same. She'd wanted to bring justice to all. She'd brought only oblivion.

"Your death will bring the networks back," Cheyenne said without a hint of emotion in her voice. "One life for all our lives. A good price."

"No," said Syd. He fought the urge to dig his nail into his own face to stop the itching. He couldn't believe how fast this was happening. "I know how this stuff works. Killing me won't do a thing and you'll all still die."

Syd looked at Liam, who was ready to fight for him long after fighting could possibly matter, and at Marie, so close to giving up on what she thought she'd known, all her good intentions to make a better world boomeranging back at her.

Syd had to find a way. For her. For Liam. For the living.

It's your future. Choose.

"We can build something. We can do this," he said. "There must still be other tech in the city. Who has power? Who has transmitters? One of your gangs?"

"Corporations," corrected Cheyenne.

"Whatever. Do they?"

"Everything that matters has been given to the Machine." She pointed at their trash heap again.

"How about . . . others? There are others here, right? Not everyone is in one of your corporations."

Cheyenne didn't answer.

"There is Maes," Gianna called out, squeezing through the bodies in the doorway and popping into the hazy bathroom like a bubble breaking the surface of a sewage pond. "The Maes gang," she repeated. "They have tech."

"Maes," said Syd.

He knew the gang. Before the Jubilee, they had been smugglers and killers, running every illicit business in the slum where he grew up. They were the ones who'd killed his best friend, Egan. They'd been hired to kill Syd and he'd barely escaped. He'd murdered one of the assassins. It was the only life he'd ever taken, at least the only one he'd ever taken on purpose. He wondered whether this was how he'd pay for it, returning to Maes on his hands and knees.

Another echo.

Repeating the past was his only hope of escaping it.

Of course, if Maes and his thugs were also sick, maybe he wouldn't have to beg for their help.

Maybe he could negotiate.

Maes was a businessman, after all. He wasn't a cultist and he wasn't an idealist. He was practical, and perhaps he could be convinced that it was in his interest to cooperate.

Syd took deep breaths, tried to push the tingling beneath his skin out of his mind. He couldn't stop himself from feeling it, but he could stop the feeling from mastering him. Knox's father had managed to keep himself together until the very end. If he could stay focused through the final stages of the sickness just to torment Syd, Syd could stay focused now to save the lives of . . . well . . . he felt crazy thinking it: everyone.

"I'll need your help," Syd told Cheyenne. "All your help."

"Maes doesn't allow us into his part of the city," Cheyenne said. "It's how we keep the peace."

"Peace is a luxury we can't afford right now," Syd told her. "Instead, we're going to do some business."

[29]

AFTER EXPELLING THE RECONCILIATION from Mountain City, Kaspar Maes had moved his gang into the former headquarters of the Oosha Panang Chemical Supply Company. It had been one of the grandest skyscrapers before the Jubilee, which meant it had been quickly looted afterward. What remained, however, still impressed.

Its curved steel frame twirled from the base of its own plaza, and the building seemed to corkscrew into the polluted haze. Maes had ringed the plaza with a barricade of concrete and razor wire, and he used a horde of hangers-on as guards. His own enforcers strolled the perimeter and took what they wanted from the squalid encampment.

He had transformed the skyscraper itself into a vertical farm, growing food for himself and his followers up and down its exterior. In the early days of the revolution, slave labor had been easy to come by. When the Guardians were no longer able to work, he started using regular people for the dangerous sky-high planting and harvesting.

Entire ecosystems developed in the smog and he'd quickly found that some of the strange mutations that occurred in his crops caused euphoria and hallucination when ingested. He'd launched a new business in the ruins of the old. He'd thrived.

People like Maes always thrived.

His success, as Cheyenne explained it, eased Syd's mind as they approached the plaza on foot. A man with success had interests to protect. A man with nothing was far more dangerous. Syd hoped they could simply negotiate and walk away with what they needed.

If not, however, there was a backup plan.

"I don't like it," Liam had said when Syd laid it out for him. "I shouldn't leave you alone with them."

"You're the only one of us with military experience," Syd told him. "You've led this kind of attack before."

"Never from a hovercraft," Liam said. "Never with a band of untrained kids."

"We don't have any trained kids for you," Syd said. "We use who we've got."

The plan couldn't be too complicated. They only had a few hours to put it together. Liam would take a group of each corporation's best in the hovercraft. They would wait for the signal nearby and, if called on, they would launch a surprise attack, evacuate Syd and the others, and, if possible, take Maes hostage. Then they would negotiate with his men for their boss's life.

"It's crazy," said Liam. "It's not even elegant."

Syd scratched at his arm. He couldn't help it. "We don't have time for elegant," he said. "We go first thing in the morning."

"Why wait until morning?" Nine asked. He winced when he spoke, like the effort hurt him. His veins had begun to turn black.

"When I was a little kid, my friend Egan and I would rob Upper City construction sites and sell the stuff to Maes's goons," Syd explained. "Morning was always the best time to visit criminals. Their thugs are usually still sleeping off the night before."

Nine agreed, reluctantly. Liam too.

"Promise me," Liam said. "Promise me that you'll send the signal at the first sign of trouble. I'll be there."

"I know you will," said Syd.

"Do you really think this will work?" Marie asked.

Syd didn't answer. There were times that silences were exactly the same as confessions.

Syd's theory about thugs sleeping it off in the morning was a good theory . . . if only it had been true.

Though the concrete barely shone orange in the first light of the day, a dozen sentries blocked the plaza entrance, all of them wide-awake, jumpy, and all of them armed with bolt guns. They pointed their weapons at Syd, Marie, Cheyenne, and the small entourage they'd brought with them. Syd had to hold his hands up in the air and urged the others to do the same, walking slowly. He doubted whether splitting up from Liam had been a good idea after all. He knew he couldn't send the signal yet. It was too soon. They weren't even inside.

"Don't shoot," Syd called out, which wasn't part of a well-thought-out strategy. It was just the first thought that occurred to him while staring at the business end of twelve spring-loaded bolt guns.

"What you want?" one of the sentries grunted. He wore the uniform of a Purifier from the Reconciliation, even the white mask, but the uniform was filthy and frayed. He was either a deserter or had taken it off a dead Purifier. It hardly mattered. He was the one pointing the weapon at them, and his personal history wasn't really the issue at the moment.

"We're here for Maes," Cheyenne said. "We have business to discuss."

The sentry swayed on his feet. Through the holes in his mask, Syd saw his eyes were cloudy. Drugged or sick or both. He was on edge. One of the other sentries, a light-skinned girl half Syd's age and a third his height, stood on her tiptoes and whispered to the boy in the mask. He nodded. "You do business with us first," he snapped.

Syd sighed. *Everything costs.*

A bribe paid—it cost Cheyenne's guards three precious

bolts apiece from their weapons—and they were inside the perimeter.

"It's—" Marie gasped. "It's everywhere."

The plaza in front of them looked exactly like the co-op where they'd left her parents: row upon row of the sick and the dying, black-veined semi-humans suffering loudly. Smoke from countless fires mixed with the smell of every bodily function imaginable and the sounds of groans, coughs, and whispered conversations, all carried on the hot breeze straight at them. The entire plaza assaulted the senses.

Younger people, still on their feet, wandered through the rows, rummaging in the pockets of anyone too weak to resist, scavenging weapons and food and whatever else they thought could be of use. Cheyenne's guards did their best to look intimidating so no one would get too close.

"Move quickly," Syd suggested and they all picked up their pace. He wished he had Liam at his side. Was it just Liam's talent for violence he missed, or something else?

The door to the Oosha Panang Chemical Supply Company had long been torn off. Two catatonic nopes were chained in front of it, staring mindlessly ahead, hairless and black-veined, toothless mouths gaping. They were, however, alive. As he went past, it occurred to Syd that the only dead nopes he'd seen were the ones the Reconciliation had slaughtered themselves. The others he'd seen were . . . well, not exactly living. But alive.

They crossed through the lobby, bright with the morning

sun. People were lying around on the floor, leaning against walls, smoking and murmuring. They fell silent as Syd, Marie, Cheyenne and her small entourage passed them, watching the group with blank stares. The people might as well have been nopes themselves. None made a move to intercept them, which was a relief. None made a move toward the large winch that controlled the elevator either, which was less of a relief.

"What floor is Maes on?" Syd asked.

"One hundred and eight," said Cheyenne.

Syd felt weak in the knees. No way could he make it up 108 flights of stairs.

Cheyenne motioned to three of her entourage. They took up positions on the winch. One more took up a position to protect them.

"Now you've only got one person left," said Marie.

"Then I'll have to rely on you two to protect me," Cheyenne said. "You'll do a better job than you did with Knox, I hope."

There was no clever reply to that, so the three of them boarded the elevator with Cheyenne's bodyguard, Nine.

Syd looked at him as the elevator made its stuttering way up the building. The last time they'd met, Nine had been partying at the club, selling fake ID patches and joking around about everything, even as Syd was running for his life.

Now there was no joking for Nine. His hands shook as he fought the urge to scratch at his skin. The veins were swelling, black, and Syd could only imagine the pain that was to come. He tried to calculate the pace of this; how much time did he have left himself? It seemed impossible to predict. Some fell apart fast, others struggled on for days. The terror was in the randomness. What made Nine suffer so much worse, so much faster?

Nine saw Syd looking at him and spat on the floor, then cursed into Syd's face. "Chapter Eleven knock-off glitch-brained swampcat."

Syd ignored him. Pain made people say all sorts of things they didn't mean. Or, at least, that they would normally keep to themselves, even if they meant every word.

"Quiet, Nine," Cheyenne snapped at him. "We're on the same side now."

"If this doesn't work I want to kill him myself," Nine said.

"Try it and I'll put a bolt through your balls before I put one through your head," Marie told him and Syd felt a little better having her around. You'd have to be pretty crazy to mess with Marie. Then again, Nine looked pretty crazy.

"His parents were killed by the Reconciliation," Cheyenne explained. "Among the first to be executed."

"I'm sorry," said Marie, without thinking. She looked away, out of the open elevator shaft to the sloping Mountain City beyond. She didn't want them to see her tremble. Her parents—far guiltier in the old system than Nine's entertainment executive mom and dad—were still alive. At least, they had been when she left them at the co-op. Was that the last time she saw them? Suddenly she couldn't remember. Her thoughts jumbled. She started scratching at her skin, until Syd reached over and stopped her. She steadied herself. Told herself not to fall apart, not to be the first one to fall apart. She looked at Nine and Cheyenne and decided that she would outlast them, at least. It felt good to have a goal, a little competition, even if she actually had no control over its outcome. The sickness obeyed its own rules and, so far, it had shown itself to be merciless and thorough.

They rode up without talking anymore. Syd thought through what he would say to Maes when they got there, wondered whether the old crime lord would remember when he'd sent his thugs to kill Syd in the desert. If they'd succeeded then, none of this would be happening now. The old system would've gone on, Knox would've gone home, been assigned a new proxy, and no one but Syd would know what had almost been and he'd be a nameless corpse, forgotten, and buried in the desert.

Instead, that was Finch.

The elevator lurched to a stop, swinging and creaking out of sync with the building, which also swung and creaked. In front of them, the elevator doors slid past each other and then back again the other way, like a pendulum, giving them about a two-second window when they lined up.

"I guess we're here?" said Marie.

"We go one at a time," said Syd.

"You first," Nine told him.

"Such a gentleman." Syd gave him a toothy grin and

he noticed Cheyenne sigh when he did it. The sarcasm reminded her of Knox.

Syd pulled open the grate on their side and waited for the doors to line up so he could catch the outer one. When he grabbed it, the momentum almost pulled him off his feet and dragged him into the elevator shaft, but he kept his grip and yanked the outer door open. He let go and let the elevator swing again. The next time the doors lined up, he jumped.

The 108th floor did not look how he had imagined the lair of a gang lord. He was standing in a bland reception area with frayed industrial carpet from wall to wall in a color that could only be described as "none." The furniture was gone, and where once there had been a reception desk, there were now just scraps of wood. Everything had been salvaged.

Behind the desk were two glass doors, both of them cracked. After the others got off the elevator, Syd wondered aloud which they should take.

"They lead to the same place," said Cheyenne, so Syd chose the one on the left, which he decided was luckier, and swung it open to a giant room, where ergonomically designed, injection-molded employee workstations were tossed around as if a hurricane had ripped through. The outer ring of the grand room was lined with offices, which took up every bit of window, giving all the light and air to the higher-up executives who would have occupied them. Now, luckily, they were mostly empty and doorless, so the light from outside streamed in.

At the far end of the great room, however, there was a set of double doors in the corner. Those double doors were flanked with two more nopes chained to the wall, like guard dogs, except they didn't make a sound, just stared as Syd, Marie, Cheyenne, and Nine walked up to them. The veins on their faces bulged and pulsed, webs of gruesome blue.

Not black.

Blue.

Syd wanted to look closer, but before he was even half-way across the desert of workstations, the double doors swung open and the real soldiers of Maes's army streamed out, lining the entire opposite wall and blocking the door-way. As if they'd coordinated with the lobby below, at that exact moment, Syd heard the elevator that had brought them up whistle back down the shaft in a free fall, no doubt crashing to pieces in the lobby. So much for Cheyenne's loyal entourage. They were almost certainly dead.

Maes was not known to take prisoners.

"You will surrender your weapons immediately or be killed," one of the guards shouted. "You are now prisoners of Kaspar Maes."

Well, thought Syd, there's a first time for everything.

[30]

KASPAR MAES, THE MOST dangerous man in Mountain City, could not lift his head.

The gang lord lay entombed in lux blankets and pillows on a grand bed in the center of what had been a giant conference room running almost the entire width of the building. He was surrounded by armed teenaged guards. His hair had fallen out unevenly, his eyes were milky white, and his skin sagged off his jagged skull, like wax melting off steel. The veins through his skin were knobby and twisted. Their throbbing was visible from across the room.

"Mr. Maes," Syd began, trying the humble approach. "We've come to make a business arrangement with you. I believe we can cure this spreading sickness and I would be glad to explain how . . . if we were to become partners."

The dead-eyed gang lord wheezed.

"He can't even hear you," a little boy said, stepping from behind the legs of the older boys standing around the bed. He stood no higher than Syd's hips. He wore shining silver pajamas and a flowing golden robe of the most lux fabric Syd had ever seen. Cheyenne gasped when she saw it, and Marie stiffened, still unsettled by the persistence of luxury in the world she had tried to remake without it. The boy's bright blue eyes looked Syd up and down, and his coils of blond hair, arranged in neat dreadlocks, swished as he approached. He couldn't have been older than eight, but he moved with the self-assurance of an adult who was used to obedience from everyone he met. "Grandpapa is blind and deaf and dumb," the boy said.

"You're—?" Syd began.

"Krystof Maes," one of the guards snapped at Syd. "And you will show him respect when you address him!"

Syd looked from the guard to the little boy. "Respect is too valuable a resource to be given away to strangers for free," he said. "It has to be earned by friends."

The boy smirked. "You're the one they call Yovel."

Syd nodded.

"You used to be called Syd."

"I still am," he said. "By my friends."

"I will call you Syd."

"I'd like that." Syd smiled.

"But we will *not* be friends," the boy added and turned away, walking back toward the bed.

"We won't?" Syd moved to follow him, but the guards raised their weapons.

"You aren't the kind of friend I'd like," said Krystof Maes. "But you don't know me."

"Grandpapa told me all about you." The boy hoisted himself on the bed, flopping across his grandfather's legs without a thought to the agony he caused. Kaspar Maes lifted an arm, but could hardly move to shoo the boy off him. "He'd tried to kill you before you could ruin everything, but that didn't work. And then you became his enemy."

"But I'm not *your* enemy," said Syd. He felt like a fool, arguing with the child. His voice had gone up a register, squeaking on the word "enemy." He never really knew how to talk to children. He wasn't sure if he should coo at them or scold them. He certainly had no idea how to talk to children who commanded armies of criminals and who held his life and the lives of everyone on the continent in their tiny, sticky hands. Should he tell a fairy story or something? Did he even know any? He remembered one, about a frog and a princess and an unpayable debt. It probably wasn't the time for stories.

"Do you want to hear a story?" Krystof asked.

"Uh . . ."

"We'd love to," said Marie, making her voice sound as nurturing as it could. Which wasn't very nurturing at all.

"It's about a group of people who came all the way here after my grandpapa told them never to come to his part of the city." The boy grinned at Cheyenne. "Do you know what happened to them?"

"We came here to—" Nine said, but the little boy cut him off with a piercing, high-pitched shout.

"SHUT UP! I'M TALKING!" He made a quick flick of his

wrist and one of his guards fired a bolt. It cracked through the air as the spring released and, before Nine could even close his mouth, it had passed through his throat.

Nine dropped to the floor, gagging, bleeding. Cheyenne dropped to her knees beside him, held him as he gasped and choked his final breaths. It didn't take long.

"You—" Cheyenne shouted at Krystof, but Syd yanked her to her feet and held her close at his side as her faithful follower, her old friend who was not even old enough to grow a mustache, lay dead below her. Syd pictured Nine before, months ago, laughing with Knox, dancing at the club. He didn't look down at the body.

"We are very sorry to interrupt," said Syd, fighting the urge to scream. The little boy had a temper and, if they had any hope of getting out of there alive, of saving everyone else's life, the boy had to be humored. He had to be appeased. There would be time to grieve later.

Cheyenne gritted her teeth, fought back her own tears. Syd knew she wanted revenge. In murderous times, even little boys had to pay for their crimes.

"Please," Cheyenne forced herself to say, "tell us. What happened to them?"

"I will." The boy nodded. "But only because I want to tell you, not because you asked. They all got thrown out the window." He laughed and jumped to his feet, twirling in a circle and making falling noises.

Marie's hands moved toward the bolt gun on her waist and the flare strapped to her back, but Syd met her eyes, shook his head a tiny bit.

He mouthed the word "no." They'd be dead in seconds if she tried to move for her weapon. And it was too soon to send the signal. Syd wasn't ready to be rescued just yet. He was sure he could get them through this himself. He had to get them through this himself.

"I heard that story with a different ending," Syd said. "I heard they had a good time together with a very smart young man and helped him make his grandpapa feel better."

The boy stopped twirling.

"You can make him better?"

Syd nodded.

"How?"

"We need tech. We need transmitters and processors and control consoles. We need to build a machine to restart the . . ." Syd couldn't find the word. There was a blank spot where his tongue reached for it.

"Network." The boy finished his sentence. "I know that word. I'm smart."

"Yes. Network," said Syd, his tongue unlocked again. "You are smart. If we can work together, I bet we can build a network and get everyone's datastream back and I bet that would make your grandpapa feel better."

"You bet? You don't know?" The boy frowned.

"I only bet when I *do* know," said Syd.

Suddenly, the boy smiled. "I like to bet!"

"Good." Syd nodded, smiling with him. "So let's bet together that this will work!"

"No." The boy shook his head. "I have a different bet for you."

He weaved in and out between his guards. All of them struggled to ignore him bumping into their legs as they kept their weapons trained on Syd, Marie, and Cheyenne.

"If you win, you get all the tech you want!" Krystof declared.

"And if I lose?"

"I watch you get thrown out the window!" The boy made the falling noise again and acted it out with his fingers, Syd plummeting, his legs kicking. The boy made the sound of a scream, then spread out all his fingers. He looked at Syd. "Splat."

Syd took a deep breath. He wanted to throttle the kid. He could picture Liam's metal fist smashing the boy's skull. The thought gave him pleasure. He exhaled slowly to steady himself. He wasn't feeling well. His thoughts jumbled. His blood chafed inside him. He had to get out of here. "What's the bet? What do I have to do?"

"Fight," said the boy. "You have to win a fight."

Syd looked at the line of teenagers guarding Krystof Maes. Some were bigger than Syd, some weren't. He was sick, but so were they. The boy was sick too; he just didn't know it yet.

Syd wasn't a stranger to fighting. A guy like him from a place like he was from . . . he'd grown up fighting. Some of the guys he'd fought had even worked for Maes. He didn't always win, but he never lost bad enough that he couldn't walk away. He figured his odds weren't terrible here. He knew how to fight dirty and he wasn't afraid to do it. It wasn't like he had much of a choice.

"One on one?" Syd asked.

The boy smirked. "Sure."

Syd looked down the line of guards once more. He'd already sized most of them up, identified strengths and weaknesses in each one as best he could. It was a rule of thumb for growing up the way he had: Be humble, be polite, and be prepared to fight with everyone you meet.

"Fine," Syd agreed. "Who's it gonna be?"

The boy giggled. "Him." Krystof pointed to a small door on the side of the office. It opened to what must have once been a conference room. The doorway was empty. "I said *him*!" the boy repeated with a shout.

"Sorry, boss," someone called from inside the other room and then shoved Syd's opponent through the door.

Liam.

And he'd had the hell beaten out of him already.

[31]

LIAM STUMBLED AS THEY shoved him into the room. They had tied his hands behind his back. A cut above his eyebrow dribbled blood down the side of his face, and his lip and cheek were swollen. His shirt had been torn from the collar to the shoulder, and the redness of his chest would turn to black and blue and brown soon enough. There was a cut across his tattoo, like someone had crossed the word out with a blade. It wept red.

"We took care of his friends," the guard who shoved Liam announced. "All of them."

Cheyenne cocked her head to the side, raised an eyebrow, like she'd just heard an intriguing new idea and was considering its merits, weighing the pros and cons. She made a tiny, high-pitched whine and then she simply sat down beside Nine's body, resting her fingers on the back of his head, running her fingers through his hair. She didn't make another sound.

Everyone had a breaking point. Cheyenne had finally reached hers.

Syd let her be. He couldn't comfort her and he couldn't apologize. Those were her followers he'd led to the slaughter, most of them no older than he was. In fact, most of them were much younger. But there were others, still alive, thousands of others, and they were all counting on him now.

Liam looked at Syd. He wanted to say something but there were no words here. Liam knew he'd failed, catastrophically. The Maes boys had swarmed the hovercraft as soon as it settled on a nearby street, like they had known he was coming. There had been too many of them; they'd moved too fast and they were too well armed.

"How?" Syd began, but Gianna stepped into the room through the same small door. She was not a prisoner.

"I couldn't let you just walk away without compensation," she said. She looked at Cheyenne. "That's not our way. I will be paid."

Cheyenne clenched her fists, but looked at the bolt guns and didn't move.

"You're only killing yourself," Syd told Gianna.

Gianna shrugged. "I did what I did."

"I'm sorry," Liam finally mustered, speaking only to Syd. The rest of the world could be damned for all he cared, but he needed Syd's forgiveness. Of course, Syd had been right to keep Liam at a distance, to tell him to forget his feelings. He should have listened to Syd and killed any part of himself that was tender, that was loving, that could imagine a better life, together, for the two of them. That wasn't the world they lived in.

He couldn't shut off those feelings, but he hoped, against all the hope he'd felt before, that Syd felt nothing good for him now. It would make this easier. Liam knew the terms of the bet Syd had just made, and he was glad for them.

Syd was going to win this fight.

Liam had been a soldier since he was old enough to lift a weapon. He didn't fear dying and, in this case, he knew he deserved it. He was glad it would be Syd to do it. Those dark, sad eyes would be the last ones he ever saw. He knew Syd had killed someone once before, out of anger, but it hadn't made him a killer. He hoped Syd could do it again. He hoped in doing it, he wouldn't kill the part of himself that Liam treasured.

"Untie him," Krystof Maes ordered, and Liam's hands were untied. "Now if you try anything, big boy, we'll shoot everybody down and toss your bodies out of the window, okay? I want you two to fight each other."

Liam stood at attention and looked at Syd. Syd just stared back at him in disbelief.

"Fight each other!" the little boy shrieked. "If you don't—"

"Hit me," said Liam.

"I won't do this," said Syd.

"Then you won't get your machine parts," the boy said.

"And you'll all die. You have to do it. I said so and you promised!"

A guard shoved Liam forward into the open floor at the center of the room. Syd stepped up to him.

"Go!" the little boy yelled.

"Hit me," said Liam. "You have to hit me."

"I'm bored!" the little boy whined. "This is boring."

"Do it." Liam shoved Syd's shoulder with his good hand. He kept the metal one lowered at his side.

Syd raised his fists, but he didn't throw a punch. How could he fight Liam? Liam had protected Syd, had confessed his feelings for Syd, had stood at Syd's side even when Syd tried to push him away. Even now, he understood the look on Liam's face. Liam was going to give his life for Syd's, just like Knox had. Syd couldn't bear it. Not another life. Not again.

"I can't," he choked out.

"You can," Liam whispered. "Please."

"Boooooring!" Krystof shouted. He turned to signal his guards.

Liam shoved Syd again, hard. "You will!" He kicked Syd in the shin.

Syd stumbled, but didn't fall. He didn't retaliate.

"You hate me," said Liam, pushing him again. "I know you hate me." He flexed his metal hand, but fired a half-powered jab at Syd's stomach with his good hand. It would hurt, but not very badly.

Syd didn't block. He grunted at the punch. He would not kill Liam for this boy's amusement. The world, the murderous disaster of a world he'd made, would not unmake him. He knew who he was. He refused to turn into something else.

Liam saw it on Syd's face. Syd wasn't going to do it.

Liam was going to make him.

"Are you glitched?' Liam shouted. He swung an uppercut with his good hand, catching Syd across the chin. He had to make Syd mad. He had to draw some blood. The little warlord was going to lose patience. Liam had to protect Syd. He punched Syd again in the stomach. "You know I watched you all the time?" Liam grunted. "I watched you sleep. I went through your things. I saw when you cried for poor dead Knox." He stomped on Syd's foot, and put him in a headlock.

He hoped Krystof Maes was entertained. Syd still wasn't fighting back.

Liam twirled Syd around and yanked him up by his shirt, lifting his feet off the ground with one arm and held him there, free fist clenched, their faces just inches apart, so close Liam could kiss him.

Liam couldn't kiss him.

He tossed Syd onto his back on the ground.

"If you won't fight for yourself, why even live?" Liam kicked him in the ribs. Syd just lay there. Liam kicked him again, willing him to get up, to fight back. To make Liam stop. Every kick was killing Liam, but to stop would kill Syd faster.

"You stopped living after Knox died," Liam grunted at him. "I know you cried like a baby every night in your room. Cried for a dead boy who never could've loved you the way I could. Who never would've."

Syd looked up at Liam, seventeen years of regret written in his eyes and Liam knew he had to hit him again.

Amazing how the loss of a hand wasn't the worst pain a person could feel.

Another kick.

Please, Syd, he thought. *Get up. Make me stop.*

"Knox died to escape his own guilt." Kick. "He didn't die for you." Kick. "You're fooling yourself." Kick.

Please.

Liam glanced at the little boy watching them, his chin resting on his hand. He still looked bored.

Liam bent down and lifted Syd off the ground by his shoulders, rushed him across the room and body slammed him against the floor-to-ceiling window. He felt a puff of air knocked from Syd's lungs. He held Syd up there, pressed him against the window with a forearm against his chest, metal fist raised. He looked Syd in the eyes, nothing behind him through the plexi but dirty sky. The fist could punch the plexi out, send them both plummeting together 108 stories, arm in arm. The fist could crack Syd's skull or crush his throat.

The fist was a lie. He wouldn't do it. They both knew he wouldn't.

Syd looked back at him, and Liam noticed that spark in his eyes, a peculiar fury that came to Syd when he'd made a choice. He wasn't passive. He wasn't playing dead. There was rage in those eyes. There was fight in those eyes. The fight wasn't with Liam.

"Well? Finish him, then," Krystof Maes said, and then sighed. "This is dumb."

Liam's fist drew back. The light through the window glinted off it.

"You think Knox would've died if he knew you'd live like this?" Liam said. "You might as well be dead . . ."

Sometimes the best way to cover a lie was with a truth.

"I would've done anything for you," Liam whispered. "And I still will."

His fist flew forward. Syd's head twisted, dodged out of the way and the metal fist smashed into the window, shattering a spiderweb into the plexi. Syd dove to the ground and rolled away, popping up to his feet, hands balled in fists.

Krystof Maes cheered. He didn't care who won. He just wanted some good old-fashioned blood sport.

Liam charged Syd, swinging.

Syd was faster than the big bodyguard. He dodged to the left and delivered two snapping jabs into Liam's side. He spun around him and kicked Liam forward from behind.

Off balance, Liam stumbled into a line of guards, who caught him and shoved him back into the center of the room, where Syd was waiting, rushing forward. Liam didn't have time to block or to dodge. Syd punched him across the face, sent him sprawling back again into the guards. They caught Liam again. He'd been dazed, lost his balance, and

Syd rushed at him, ready to deliver another devastating punch to Liam's head.

Krystof Maes cheered. "Hold him up," he ordered the guards.

They lifted Liam up. He was heavy and limp, and lifting him up took all of their hands.

That was their mistake.

Before any of them knew what was happening, Syd had turned his momentum away from Liam and spun his fist at the guard standing next to Krystof Maes. The punch dropped the guard onto the bed, on top of the frail body of the old man.

Before that guard had finished falling, Marie had her bolt gun up and fired into the shoulder of another one. He screamed and dove to the ground, crying out in surprise and pain.

Liam, not dazed at all, whirled around and knocked out all four guards holding him with a wide right punch and a perfectly placed head butt.

Cheyenne, with a scream of rage and vengeance, a goddess of fury reborn, charged across the floor, tackled Gianna. She savaged her with her fists and fingers, gouged and kicked, and when she was done, she turned on one of Maes's henchmen, and then another, and another, sending them shrieking for safety.

Syd, by this point, had grabbed Krystof Maes in a choke hold.

"Put down your weapons and surrender!" he shouted.

The guards who had not fled, those who were still standing, didn't move. They looked to one another, unsure.

The little boy in Syd's grip started crying. Sobbing. Kicking and screaming. "No no no no no no no!"

Syd held on.

The boy's guards watched the temper tantrum dumbstruck. They lowered their weapons.

"You done yet?" Syd asked, his hold unrelenting.

The little boy whimpered. He squirmed. Finally, he gave up and nodded.

"I'll kill him!" Cheyenne charged at the boy, her hands and face red with blood, none of it her own.

"Ahhh!" the boy screamed.

Syd spun and put his body between Cheyenne and the boy. "No," he said.

"He killed my people!" Cheyenne yelled. "He killed Nine!"

"And you have more people back at Arcadia that you need to protect," Syd told her. "He can help us."

"You need me!" the boy shouted.

"Where are the transmitters?" Syd asked him. "Where is your tech?"

"Downstairs," the boy said. "It's all just one floor down . . ." He looked over his shoulder at Cheyenne, who stood behind Syd, panting. She picked up a bolt gun that one of the guards had dropped. "Don't let her hurt me!"

"Why shouldn't I?" Syd spun around, so that the boy was facing Cheyenne again, directly in front of her.

Cheyenne raised the bolt gun. The boy turned his head, twisted in Syd's arms. Soiled himself. "You wanted me to kill my friend," Syd told him. "And you killed *her* friends. Why should you live?"

"You're . . . you're Yovel," the boy said. "The savior! You wouldn't let her hurt me!"

"I'm just Syd," Syd corrected him.

Cheyenne locked the spring back. The boy squealed.

"Stop it!" Liam said. "Enough!"

"He deserves it," said Cheyenne.

"If everyone got what they deserved, where would that leave anyone?" Liam told her. He looked at Syd. "He's just a child."

"He's a killer," Syd said. The boy's fingernails dug into his forearm.

Liam reached out and rested his metal hand on top of the boy's tiny fingers, so he stopped clawing at Syd. Then Liam looked Syd in the eye. "So was I."

"Was?" Syd asked.

"I'm trying to change," said Liam. He eased the kid from Syd's grip, turned him around, and squatted down in front of him. He pointed his finger in the boy's face. "We're not going to hurt you. You or your grandpapa. Just tell your guys to help us carry some of the tech down the stairs. We're trying to save everyone. Even you. Get it?"

The boy nodded.

"Do it," the boy ordered his guards. Those who were still able to move scrambled from the room, rushing down the stairs . . . 108 stories down and straight out of the building. The little boy didn't know it, but they weren't feeling well, and they had decided their employment was at an end. They wouldn't be sticking around to help with anything.

Liam let go of the boy and stood. "You okay, Syd?"

Syd nodded.

"Marie?"

Marie nodded, even though the blood in her veins felt like acid. She wanted to scream. Instead, she bit the insides of her cheeks.

"Okay," said Liam. "Let's go build ourselves a machine."

And they would've, if at that moment, the plexi window behind them hadn't shattered open to the sky.

A hovercraft rose in front of it, spun around, and dropped its rear hatch, settling it on the tile of the 108th floor.

Cousin strolled down the ramp with a squadron of Purifiers at his side and a small orb in his hand, glowing in his delicate fingers.

"Oh yes." Cousin's smooth face bent into a smile as he tracked Liam's glance at the orb. "It is a bomb and it is armed."

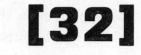

[32]

COUSIN STROLLED ACROSS THE floor tossing the bomb from hand to hand. He looked at the blood smeared across the floor and the bodies strewn about, their clothes flapping in the engine's wake. The veined old man in the bed, staring at the ceiling. The little boy was dumbstruck by the sudden arrival of a slim, hairless figure surrounded by white-masked Purifiers.

The Purifiers all held EMD sticks, humming with power. They all scratched at their uniforms, at their masks, at their skin. Liam wondered what they'd been told, if they were even aware they were serving a man who intended to let them all die.

"My my my," Cousin clucked. He stopped in the center of the room and cracked his neck. "And . . . how is everybody feeling today?"

Liam shifted his feet, prepared to throw himself at Cousin or tackle Syd out of the way, whichever seemed necessary. He had a terrible feeling one of them would be.

Marie had her weapon pointed straight at Cousin.

"Young lady, do you really think that's a good idea?" Cousin cupped the explosive in both hands, presenting it to her as if it were an injured bird. "You wouldn't want me to drop this by accident, would you? Do you know what it feels like to have the air inside your lungs set on fire?"

Marie stared him down. She didn't lower her weapon.

"Nor do I." Cousin laughed. "I'd hate to find out. But please, keep pointing that thing if it makes you feel better." He turned his back on her. "Now, Syd. I think it's time we cleared up a few things." He waved his hand in the air and brought up a holo projection. Cheyenne gasped. The little boy went slack jawed. No one in Mountain City had seen a real holo in months.

This one showed the Nigerian doctor, Dr. Adaeze Khan. She was hard at work, then turned to look out of the projection. "My name is Dr. Adaeze Khan," she said. Though the projection wobbled, it did not cut off like it had the night Cousin had first showed it to Liam. "And if you are receiving this message, it is most likely I am dead. I served as the chief medical specialist for the Reconciliation's immunology project. While I was able to develop organic cures for a variety of resurgent ailments, from malaria to TB, the emergent hematic pathology that has rendered the Guardians nonoperative has resisted all treatment. Survival factors are unclear, yet evidence suggests physiological collapse is a symptom of biodata deletion."

"We know all this," Liam said. "If you're just trying to waste our time—"

"Shh." Cousin didn't even bother to look at Liam, just kept his eyes fixed on Syd through the holo floating in the air between them. "This is the good part."

"I have come to the conclusion," Dr. Khan continued, "that the only possible cure would be a reconstruction of the network linkages and a universal reinstallation of all biodata software in every previously networked individual. While this is not ideologically consistent with the stated goals of the Reconciliation, it is the only way to prevent the nonoperatives' pathology from continuing its course through society at large. I regret to say, however, that any method for reestablishing a network at this point is completely theoretical. I would need at least twelve to eighteen months to develop a system of relays, transmitters, processors, and the manpower for a large-scale medical intervention on the entire population. My requests to the Advisory Council for the necessary resources have been denied. I only hope my successor in this role fares better."

Cousin shut off the holo. "Understand?" he asked Syd.

"There's no such thing as the Machine," said Syd. "We don't even have a way to build one."

"That's right," Cousin said.

Cheyenne approached Cousin slowly, her eyes fixed on the tiny projector on his belt. "No Machine?" she said.

He looked at her curiously. "You're one of those cultists, aren't you? Oh, I've heard about you. Fascinating what people can convince themselves of when they're desperate, no?"

"No Machine," Cheyenne repeated. "This . . . was for nothing?"

Cousin shrugged. "Looks like you'll need a new religion."

Cheyenne clenched her fists and ran at him.

"Don't!" Liam shouted, but it was too late. Cousin didn't even flinch as one of his Purifiers sent an EMD pulse straight at her. She collapsed in a seizure mid-stride.

"Did you really think it would be so simple?" Cousin yelled at the twitching girl on the floor. "Just a machine to get back what you'd lost?" He turned to Syd, pointed his long finger. "You could flip a switch and undo all your mistakes?"

"There was one machine that destroyed the networks," said Syd. "One could've restored them."

One of Cousin's Purifiers moved forward with the EMD to give Cheyenne the killing tap, but Marie turned her bolt gun on him. He stopped moving, looked to Cousin for guidance.

Cousin shrugged and the Purifier backed away. Cheyenne stopped twitching and lay on the floor, her eyelids fluttering, her chest rising and falling with rapid breaths.

"It really is too bad you're learning such important life lessons at the end, my boy." Cousin sighed. "It is so much simpler to destroy than to create. Did you *really* imagine a bunch of teenagers could rebuild a complex system developed over generations out of a some spare parts in a ruined skyscraper? There is no reset button on history. It only goes in one direction."

Syd stayed quiet.

"I've seen that journal you've been carrying around," Cousin continued. "It's just her notes, you know? Passing ideas. They've no more substance than a fart. But it was sweet of young Liam to steal it for you, even if he had no idea how cruel a gift it was. I suppose it's reasonable. He gives you false hope; you give him false hope. A fair transaction. You know how he came to possess the journal, don't you?"

"I know," said Syd.

"And you forgave him?" Cousin looked at Liam and winked. "Maybe he's got a chance, eh? His hope not so false? I almost feel bad interrupting young romance."

"Shut it," Liam said.

"You made him kill Dr. Khan," said Syd. "She *could* have stopped this."

"Don't be so naive. I didn't make Liam do anything. He *chose* to kill Dr. Khan. And she wasn't the first. Not by far! She's one on a long list of corpses that your lovelorn friend made with his own hands. Or, rather . . . hand."

"Shut it!" Liam yelled.

Syd addressed the Purifiers directly. "He'll let you all die." He wished he had better powers of persuasion over a crowd. His head felt cloudy. He couldn't think of the right words to say. "Whatever he's told you is a lie. You saw that holo."

The soldiers scratched at themselves, shifted nervously on their feet, but they held their ground. Cousin smiled at them.

"Everyone makes their choices, Syd, and they make them for their own reasons." He rolled the explosive around in his hands. "That's all life is, really. A collection of choices. My boys have made theirs. Little Marie here"—he pointed at Marie, still aiming her weapon at him—"she can believe all the high-minded dogma of the Reconciliation she wants, but she made her choices too. Coming here, betraying the Purifiers, betraying her oaths and her revolution in a futile attempt to save her parents. That's who she is. All her talk about equality and unity, yet she loves her parents more than she loves her ideals. Her intentions don't mean a thing. Just her actions. My boys value their oaths."

He smiled at his Purifiers. Through the mouth holes in their masks, none smiled back. Maybe he could peel away their loyalty, thought Syd. Word by word, maybe he could take away Cousin's army.

"What do *your* actions mean?" Syd asked.

"I am the end of action," Cousin told him. "With this little ball here, I can do what you can't, Syd. I can undo the past. I can erase your mistakes. Just say the word, and I'll drop this little guy at your feet. It won't hurt much and then, all is truly forgotten. Oblivion is the purest forgiveness, don't you think?"

Liam watched Syd. Marie watched too. The hovercraft churned the air that howled through the open window high above the city and time seemed to whip away on the wind. None of the Purifiers moved.

Syd closed his eyes.

There was no Machine. There was no way to stop this sickness. There was no way to undo what he had done.

Knox's face hovered in the dark behind his eyelids. *It's your future. Choose.*

He opened his eyes. He saw that everyone was watching, everyone was waiting for him, for Syd, to choose.

He looked at Cousin's smooth face, lit by the glow of the bomb, patient as death. His blood burned. He saw Knox there, in the daylight, standing beside Cousin, and he saw the assassin Liam had killed; he saw Finch too. He saw Nine, even as Nine lay dead on the floor just a few feet away.

He felt sick to his stomach. His heartbeat screamed his pulse. His eyes ached. He could end it all right now, end his suffering, end everyone's suffering. He shook his head, and Knox was gone, all of them gone. His vision wobbled.

Syd had had enough.

He swung with his left, swatting Cousin's hand and sending the incendiary orb in a high arc out of his grip straight toward the window. Toward the hovercraft.

At the same time, Syd shoved little Krystof Maes in front of himself and rushed toward the stairwell door in the opposite direction.

Liam and Marie turned after him. Cousin's Purifiers,

taken by surprise, didn't even discharge their weapons. They watched the arc of the bomb through the air, then dove for cover where they could find it.

Cousin dove after the bomb, trying to catch it.

He had been bluffing after all. Cousin wasn't ready to die.

He might have caught the bomb too, had the old man, the decaying gang lord, Kaspar Maes, not rolled himself off the bed and tripped Cousin as he dove.

The orb bounced once and rolled right up the ramp of the hovercraft.

The explosion lit the sky over Mountain City for miles.

[33]

AS SYD JUMPED TO the landing below, the door to the stairwell burst inward; debris smashed into the wall just above him. The boy crumpled under Syd like a doll. Marie was right beside them and Liam, larger than all three, covered the trio with his back.

Sizzling chunks of metal clanked down the half flight of stairs, and from above they heard the sound of the wrecked hovercraft crashing down the side of the building. They were too high up to hear its impact with the concrete below.

In the quiet after the blast, Liam told them to stay where they were. He stood.

"What are you doing?" Syd asked him, which wasn't really what Syd was asking. He was really asking Liam not to go.

"I have to check," Liam said. "I have to know."

He took the cracked stairs two at a time. His shirt had been shredded and burned by tiny flaming shrapnel. He'd kept it from hitting Syd, but the burns on his skin looked painful and the cuts oozed. Liam might not be getting sick, but he was getting the hell beaten out of him.

When he reached the top of the stairs, Liam peeked around the hole in the wall where the door had been and he saw the wreckage. The wall that had separated the office they were in from the rest of the floor was blown away. The exterior wall had been mostly window to begin with, but now the entire thing was open to the elements. Wires, cables, and insulation dangled from above the newly exposed steel beams. The building creaked, swayed, and threatened collapse.

And there, on the floor, in a tangle of burned and broken bodies, was the withered old figure of Kaspar Maes. He lifted his head to Liam and their eyes met. He was no longer the zombie in the bed, but a man with some vitality in him. The veins on his body were blue, not black, and his eyes were clear. He opened his mouth to speak, but a piece of metal had sliced into his neck. His eyes moved sideways, bulged, and his head slumped back to the floor, still. His finger was pointing.

It took Liam another fraction of a second to realize why.

Cousin's dead body wasn't there.

Cousin's living body was right beside Liam, raising an EMD stick.

Liam ducked and punched with his metal fist. The stick swept over his head and his hand connected with Cousin's knee.

The thin man stumbled and Liam headbutted him, breaking the shining smooth nose.

Cousin slumped to the floor. He didn't fight back. His clothes were shreds and he was speckled with cuts, but the old mobster had blocked most of the blast from him. He was hurt, but alive. Cousin was a survivor.

Not this time though. Liam raised his fist to deliver a killing blow. He'd done it so many times to so many people who'd deserved it so much less than this man. But still, he hesitated.

Through bloody teeth, Cousin grinned at Liam. "You never change, my boy. You're still fighting for no reason. They're all going to die anyway. You're just fighting for the love of violence. You know that, right? You'll be nothing without other people's blood to spill."

"I am fighting for something," Liam said, his fist hanging in the air.

"He doesn't want you to fight for him."

"I choose my own fights. And *I* want to fight for him."

"You're a romantic, Liam." Cousin coughed. "I suppose everyone your age is a romantic. You should thank me. I'm sparing you a world where you'll have to grow out of that. Once they're all gone it'll just be you and your memories. You can mourn your whole life away. That's what you want, isn't it? Oh, I know you so well, Liam. You love the longing."

Liam didn't answer. His hand wavered.

"The silences." Cousin sighed. "I always enjoyed your silences."

A flicker of movement from the corner of his eye. One of the Purifiers was up, peeking from behind the overturned bed in the center of the room, a bolt gun aimed.

Liam dove just as a bolt smacked into the wall above him. Another hit the floor at his feet. He scrambled toward the doorway. He saw Cheyenne, on her feet again, kick the gun from the first Purifier's hand.

"Go!" she shouted at Liam, as three more Purifiers emerged from where they'd taken cover and tackled her. She fought back hard, and Liam was tempted to stay and help her, but he had to get back to Syd. As Liam dove into the stairwell, he saw Cousin stand again, pick up his EMD stick, and come after him, ignoring Cheyenne fighting with his soldiers.

Why did Liam let Cousin talk? It was *always* a delay tactic. Was Liam really so desperate for someone to know him?

He had been.

He would not be anymore.

He burst into the stairwell and jumped down three steps at a time to the landing where the others were waiting. "Up," he ordered as he jumped down the stairs. "We have to get out of here."

Syd had his hand on Marie's back. She was doubled over, scratching at her neck. When she looked up, the lines all over her face told the story. She was in bad shape. Syd was too, not as bad, but still, Liam understood.

He'd have to be well enough for all of them.

"Where's my grandpapa?" little Krystof Maes demanded.

"Dead," Liam told him. "Just like the rest of us if you don't help me."

Argument flitted across the boy's face. He was not used to being ordered around and threatened, but he understood the rules of violence well enough. Liam was bigger and stronger.

Together, they guided Syd and Marie down the stairs, just as Cousin and his Purifiers came after them through the doorway above. Cousin moved slowly, leaning heavily on the broken wall, wounded. His Purifiers flanked him. They were still quick.

They raced down the stairs and Liam turned, braced himself to fight. He was woefully outnumbered and they were coming down on him fast.

And then they were running right past him, down the stairs without a second glance his way.

Liam looked back up at Cousin. The bald man shook his head and spat on the ground.

"Fair-weather friends," Cousin said. He still had five Purifiers flanking him. Those five were still armed and still intended to kill Liam. They moved down more cautiously. One of them limped and one of his eyes was swollen nearly shut. At least Cheyenne had gotten her licks in.

Liam couldn't outrun Cousin's five, so he shoved Syd and Marie and the little boy through the door to the 107th floor to hide.

Liam didn't know how to save Syd from this sickness, but he had one set of skills that would be useful right now. Under cover of darkness on the 107th floor, he would put his hand to work, one last time.

[34]

THE 107TH FLOOR WAS filled with old tech, just as Krystof had said it would be. The little boy was brutal and impulsive, but he was, it turned out, not a liar.

As soon as Krystof's grandpapa had seized this building, he began collecting all the tech he could find. With the Reconciliation destroying whatever they seized, he saw an opportunity. He was a businessman above all and understood that whatever was banned would fetch a very high price, even from those who'd banned it. The Reconciliation had to get their spare parts from somewhere, after all, and the cultists in Mountain City would do anything to get their hands on old processors and robot arms and whatever else he had. So he built a stockpile and waited for the world to turn. He never had the chance to unload it all, and now it sat, a massive junkyard hovering in the sky above a city that had no use for its garbage.

It gave Liam a lot of places to hide.

"Just stay here, and stay quiet," he told Syd, Marie, and Krystof, settling them into a dark nook between a disabled Arak9 combat robot and some kind of defunct network relay station that had had its entire processing system torn out. He made sure Marie's bolt gun was locked and loaded. "Can you shoot?"

"Yeah," she whispered, resting the weapon on her knees to steady it. Her jaw was clenched. She was suffering, but she was fighting it. That would have to do.

"Okay," Liam said. "Anyone but me comes back here, you shoot them."

Marie nodded.

"I'm going to get us through this," Liam promised them.

"And then what?" Marie whispered.

"We'll go home," he said. "We'll get you back to your parents."

"And then?" Marie pressed him.

He didn't know. None of them knew.

The little boy beside them wept quietly for his grandpapa, tears his grandpapa had never shed for his own victims. Liam found comfort in those tears. Even monsters could be human.

Syd leaned his head against the hard steel of the combat robot's base. The burn grew stronger, like a welding torch firing beneath his skin. Even in the dark, he saw the veins running along his hands and forearms. Every beat of his heart scorched against the inside of his body, and still, he sensed the worst was yet to come. He tried to focus on

something other than the pain, on something else. Anything else.

"Syd?" Liam leaned toward him. He placed his good
hand on the side of Syd's neck, felt the pulse thrumming
through the artery. "You holding on?"

Syd's eyes met Liam's. Their faces were just inches apart.
He nodded.

"I'll be right back," Liam whispered.

Syd lifted his own arm, placed a hand on Liam's neck
too. Held him as firmly as he could. "You better be," he
said. Then he pulled Liam forward and pressed their lips
together.

The kiss was no longer than a second, but in that second,
any walls between them fell. Liam's body was Syd's body;
Syd's mind was Liam's mind. Someone's eyelash tickled.
Their lips drew apart.

It was Liam now who couldn't find the words.

"I'll be here," said Syd.

Liam squeezed Syd's neck gently, then stood and slipped
off into the dark.

"Oh," said Krystof Maes, the knowledge of what he'd
nearly made Liam and Syd do to each other dawning on
him. "Oh," he repeated, looking at his feet, and it sounded
almost like an apology.

Syd cast a glance at Marie. He tried not to let the agony
show on his face. He could tell she was doing the same. She
reached over and rested her hand on his. Together, they
waited.

"Ah!" They heard a shout in the darkness, a groan, and the thump of a body hitting for the floor.

Liam? Marie mouthed.

Syd shook his head no. Liam wouldn't die that quietly. Not now. Syd had given him a reason to fight. Liam was doing what Liam did best, one Purifier at a time.

In the dark, Syd and Marie waited as the bodies fell one by one by one.

Liam crouched atop an old generator, about six feet above the floor. The first Purifier with the swollen eye had been easy. He thought he was a predator, not prey, so he stalked through the rows of junk heavily.

Now the rest had figured out that they were being hunted even as they did the hunting. Streaks of light from doorless offices along the perimeter of the building cast long shadows through the central floor. The white masks of the Purifiers lit like candles when the light caught them. One passed directly below Liam and he looked down as she approached.

He assumed it was a she. The mask and the green uniform made it hard to tell. She could also have been a young boy, like most of the Purifiers were, but she was, perhaps, too curvy.

Not that it mattered.

She'd thrown in her lot with Cousin. She could have run, but she chose to stay, so Liam would do what he must.

It was nothing personal. This was war, and this was what happened in war, what always happened in war. The young and strong and the young and brave and the young and weak all died the same. Other young people killed them. Pretty simple, really, a fact as old as time.

As the Purifier passed below him, Liam brought his fist down and smashed it on her head. She fell without a noise and a small black tulip blossomed on the white of her mask. He pulled it off, saw the blue lines running along her skin, quickly fading as she bled. Perhaps he'd spared her a worse death to come. Perhaps he was an angel of mercy.

He wanted to believe that.

He knew it wasn't true.

Liam climbed down from his hiding place. He moved along the floor, back pressed against the jumbled metal. He moved like a snake, coiled to strike.

Three left.

Plus Cousin.

And then his work would be done.

Another Purifier ahead, an EMD stick wobbling in his hands. This one was a big boy. Hair on his knuckles, shoulders bulging against the uniform, neck as thick as a tree trunk.

Trees get chopped down.

Liam kicked low, swept the leg. The guy fell, loudly, crashing and thrashing. He turned and swiped with the stick, but Liam cut the distance and pressed the guy's arm against his body, pinning the stick between them. Untrained fighters pull back from a weapon like this, but training teaches a person to step into the attack, move for the weak spot that a swinging weapon opens.

Liam lay on top of the guy, trying to press his elbow up so the tip of the EMD stick would hit the guy's own chin. This one was too strong, though, and pushed right back, inching that tip toward Liam's face.

They lay there in the dark, grunting and pushing on top of each other for what felt like ages, neither able to make killing progress on the other. Their eyes were locked. They had to be about the same age, both of them put here through Cousin's mad machinations. Only one of them would walk out.

It would be Liam.

He stopped resisting and rolled off the guy, dodging the tip of the stick by a hair's width as it sprang forward. The Purifier hadn't been expecting the sudden release, and he nearly threw the EMD stick across the room. He lay there on his back for a fraction of a second, both his arms hyper-extended. He was about to swing around and jam the stick into Liam's side, but Liam was faster. One hard chop to the throat with the right hand and the Purifier gagged, coughed, and spluttered. As a mercy, Liam snatched the stick from him and touched it to his chest, stopping his heart.

He vanished over the top of a junk heap just as the guy's last two compatriots came running to see the commotion. All they saw were the last twitches of the boy's body. He hoped at least one of them would know the dead guy's name. In a different world, that'd have been Liam dying on the floor. He would've liked to have been remembered.

He touched a good finger to his own lips, felt Syd's heat

still on them. It was an illusion, of course, a trick of the mind, but it was enough. He would do whatever he had to to get back to Syd. He heard footsteps and he raised the EMD stick.

The Purifiers who'd come running took one look at the body, cursed, then turned on their heels and ran for the exit, stumbling and scratching at their skin as they fled.

So much for loyalty.

Cousin had to have known his army of teenagers wouldn't stick by him. They were all getting sick and they weren't fighting for any good reason. Liam felt a swell of hope in his chest. Maybe he wouldn't have to kill anymore. Maybe he'd shed the last blood he'd ever have to shed.

Except for Cousin's.

If the man could even bleed.

Syd listened. He heard footsteps, running, cursing, crashing through the door to the stairwell.

"I think they've been scared off," he whispered.

Marie peeked around the edge of the broken transmitter, her weapon unsteady in her hand. Her palms were sweating. She couldn't stop swallowing. Her eyeballs felt like hot coals. The Purifiers had fled. She let out a breath and turned to Syd to tell him the good news. "I think Liam's—"

Her body jolted mid-sentence, the bolt gun fell from her hand. She felt as if her skin were being peeled off, the bottoms of her feet flayed, every hair on her head turned into a live wire.

She'd been hit with an EMD pulse. Her vision turned red at the edges, and she saw Cousin, his stick raised, a smirk on his face. He touched the stick to the little boy and then to Syd and they both crumpled. She saw Liam, leaping over the debris, collapsing by Syd's side, as Cousin seemed to melt away into the shadows.

She heard shouting, running, an explosion that shook her bones. She didn't have time to wonder whether she'd just been killed, whether they'd all just been killed, before her vision went black.

[35]

WHEN MARIE OPENED HER eyes, she was certain she'd died and in death, she'd gotten what she deserved.

All around, there was nothing but fire and the thin black silhouettes of scorching souls. For what she had done to her parents, to Knox, to Syd, to the world . . . this was the kind of death she deserved.

She hadn't expected it to itch.

"Marie!" She felt hands pull her up; her eyes adjusted to the light. Syd knelt in front of her. His face emerged from the flickering fires. "Can you hear me?"

She nodded. Her lips ached and her skin burned. The pain told her she was still alive. The dead couldn't possibly hurt this badly. She scratched at her arms, saw the thin blue veins turning black beneath the skin. The skin itself, red.

"Where—?" Her voice cracked. "Where are we?"

"The roof," said Liam, hovering into focus. Cheyenne stood beside him. Her clothes were torn and burned. She clutched an EMD stick to her chest. Beside her stood three boys in Purifier uniforms, also armed.

Marie tensed, her memory muddled, suddenly certain it had been Cheyenne who'd knocked her out, not Cousin. Or was Cheyenne working with Cousin? Nothing made sense. Heat shimmered off the roof and blurred her vision. She scrambled backward, crablike, scorching her palms on the silver roofing rubber.

"Relax," Liam said. "You're okay. We're safe up here . . . well, kind of."

Marie had crab-crawled underneath the large metal logo of Oosha Panang Chemical Supply Company. The sun blazed at its high point, so even beneath the large sign, there was no shade. Her skin sizzled where it touched the roof.

Little blond Krystof Maes, fair skinned as he was, had already turned red as a thundering sunset. One of the Purifiers pulled his mask from his belt and gave it to the boy to cover his face. Krystof resisted at first, then put it on. It sagged off his small head, like he was playing ghost.

"It's too hot," the boy complained and pulled the hood off again.

Liam was also burning. Each of his freckles darkened like angry pinpricks.

It took Marie another moment to adjust her eyes so she could make out the swaying shapes she had taken for the souls of the damned.

They were nopes.

Three dozen nopes on the burning roof beside them. Syd was watching them, shielding his eyes with his hand. His other hand tapped at the spot behind his ear, then began scratching at the veins on his neck.

"I . . . I don't understand," Marie said. "How did we . . . get . . ." Her words weren't coming. She bit into her lip, hard, to bring his focus back. "How did we get here?"

"Cheyenne scared Cousin off," Liam said. "Fired a few pulses his way right after he knocked you out. Gave me a chance to get the bolt gun."

"Is he—?" Marie asked.

"He got away," Liam said. "Disappeared."

"And . . . them?" Marie pointed at the sweating Purifiers.

"We tried to get out," one of the boys said. "Cousin rigged the stairwell. A trip wire blew out the stairs. Killed Jax and Luxor and King Brat."

The names were absurd; their deaths even more so. They died fleeing from a fight that meant nothing to them, and no one would ever remember their real names.

"A second trip wire ignited the air . . ." Another boy took up the story, shaking his head.

"We ran into these three running back upstairs ahead of the flames," said Liam. "They helped us get to the roof. The stairwell's totally blown out."

"So we're trapped up here?" Marie said. She looked at the nopes again. "We'll just die up here with them?"

"They were here when we got here," said Liam. "They're not dead yet."

Marie tried to wet her lips. "Do you think they get thirsty? Because we will. We'll die of thirst before this"— she held up her hands to show the coal-black veins—"has the chance to kill us."

Liam didn't have a response to that. He was very thirsty himself. He couldn't even recall when he'd last had a drink of water. No matter how tough he thought he was, he couldn't muscle his way through dehydration.

Syd could hear them talking, but he stood watching the nopes, scratching at his head. He couldn't stop scratching. It hurt to scratch. It hurt not to.

Liam, suddenly at Syd's side, reached out a hand, stopped him scratching.

"They *are* still alive," said Syd. "And so are we."

"For now," said Liam. They stood together, watching the nopes walk in circles along the edge of the roof, peering dumbly over the side to the great distance below.

Syd studied them. He saw one point down and another leaned over to look, communicating something to the other one.

Except nopes couldn't communicate.

Syd walked over to the one who had pointed down, stepped right up to her. She turned to him when he approached and he nearly fell back in surprise. Her skin was clear. Red from the sun—the sun burned them like it burned everyone—but aside from that he saw the veins, blue, smooth, fading.

Liam called after him. "Syd, what are you doing?"

"Can you—?" Syd leaned in to the Guardian. She really

did look more like a Guardian than he'd seen one look in months. "Can you understand me?"

She stared back at him, her eyes showing him his own expectant face. Her head cocked slightly to the right.

"Can you hear?" he asked.

She lifted her hand and pointed over the side of the building once more. Syd leaned out, followed her finger and saw, three floors below, where the explosion of the hovercraft had torn open the wall. Wires and cables dangled from the blasted-out side of the skyscraper. Below them, the building's walls turned slightly in a slow corkscrew, sloping outward wider and wider to the ground below. The building was narrower at the top that at the bottom. It wasn't a straight drop down. It was a slope. A very steep slope.

The nope—the Guardian, the whatever she was—pointed at the loose cable and nodded.

"You think you can get down?" Syd asked.

She stared back at him. Her lips, her face, her eyes . . . nothing moved.

"What are you talking to them for?" Little Krystof Maes ambled over, his stubby finger jabbing at the nope. "They're deaf and dumb. Grandpapa used them for labor, like bots used to be, and they couldn't even do that. Not even the work of a vacuubot. They're useless."

He poked the nope in the stomach. She stumbled backward and hit the edge of the roof, lost her fragile footing, and toppled.

Without thinking, Syd's arm shot forward and he caught

her by the wrist. Her skin was hot to touch and she was heavier than he thought she'd be. The momentum nearly pulled him over too. The veins of Syd's arm strained and bulged against the muscle. He screamed with the pressure.

Liam was at his side and helped him hoist the nope back up. Once she was standing on the roof again, Liam squatted down in front of Krystof. "You lay a finger on anyone but yourself again, and I'll toss you over next, got it?"

Krystof nodded.

Marie called out. "Something's happening."

Liam turned to see each of the figures approach Syd one by one. They reached out to him. They touched him on the cheek and each gave a nod. One or two, through broken lips and missing teeth, even smiled. Then they moved one by one to Liam and did the same. They barely showed any symptoms on their skin. No welts and sores. No visible web of black veins, just the faintest hint of blue around their eyes, on their hands.

"They're getting better," said Syd.

"Not all of them." Krystof pointed to the corner of the roof, where eight nopes had fallen, unmoving. Others came over to them and sat beside those fallen ones, touching them on the cheeks as well. Their veins were still black as night, and blood had trickled from their ears, eyes, noses, and mouths. They'd drained and dried there on the roof.

"I think they're grieving," said Syd.

"Nopes can't grieve," said Marie. "Guardians couldn't either."

"But they aren't nopes and they aren't Guardians," said Syd. "They're something new."

The nope he'd rescued walked back to the edge of the building. She gestured for Syd to follow. She didn't open her mouth, even in an attempt to speak. Perhaps she couldn't speak; perhaps she chose not to try. Maybe the nopes understood that words lie, but actions never do. Syd could say all he wanted about trying to save people or make things better, but none of that meant a thing. He'd kept her from falling off the building. *That* meant something.

So it surprised him completely, after all that, when she reached the edge and jumped.

[36]

SYD, LIAM, THE PURIFIERS, and Marie peered after her as she fell, a perfectly formed dive straight down. Some of that old Guardian grace had returned and she hit her target: a hanging cable broken loose from the 108th floor.

She caught it with both hands and, still falling, tied it around her waist. The cable snaked out of the opening above her, pulling loose from the wall. These skyscrapers had been run through with wiring and cables. They were the hidden magic that made the great wireless network run. There were miles of wires inside the walls.

Enough to reach the ground a hundred times over.

Suddenly, the nopes stepped to the ledge in twos and threes, jumping together, catching the cables midair and riding them down.

"No way," Krystof said, speaking aloud what the others were thinking.

As the building sloped out, the nopes rode it like a slide and, as it sloped wider, they stood on their feet, slowed by the cables, and ran down. The haze was too thick to see to the ground below. There was no way to know what happened at the end of the jump.

Each of the nopes grabbed a few wires as they fell, pulled out more than they needed for themselves, making it easier for the next ones to catch on. By the time the first ten had jumped, there were twenty extra wires hanging hundreds of feet down. Some of the nopes missed on their first try to grab, and they could grab others. Some didn't tie on at all; they just caught the previous nope's cable like a vine hanging from a jungle tree, and climbed down hand over fist.

Syd turned to look at the others, while the nopes continued to jump off the building, one after the other.

The dead they'd left behind lay sizzling beneath the merciless sun.

"There's no other way," said Syd.

Liam swallowed. "I don't really like heights."

"Does anyone?" Syd replied.

"I don't mind, actually," said Marie. "I've never been afraid of falling . . . it's the sudden stop that scares me."

Liam shook his head. "You're making jokes now?"

"Might be my last chance," she said. "But one way or another, I'm running out of time and I am seeing my parents again." She approached the ledge, watched the nopes fall, turned back, and looked at Syd and Liam. "You boys do what you want. I'm going home."

And then she leapt.

The boys watched her dive, less graceful than the nopes, but well aimed, one story down. Then two. Then three. She passed the torn-open floor. She fell faster, reached out, and the force of her fall knocked her hand back when she tried to grab a cable. She flipped, plummeting head first.

Syd held his breath. Marie tumbled past wire after wire. She wasn't able to catch on. It was harder than it had looked.

And then a nope from the roof leapt in a perfect jack-knife, slicing through the air. This one didn't reach out for the cables, but rather, dove for Marie and caught her with one hand. The other shot out and caught a wire, snagging it, slowing, and then stopping, hanging in the air with Marie held by her wrist.

The Guardians had been strong enough to do that sort of thing.

The nopes were becoming strong again themselves.

Syd looked down at his arm, the veins throbbing. He felt weaker than ever, agonized. He wanted to jump, but not catch on, let himself fall, let the pain end. Was that how it happened? Would he give up on getting better so he wouldn't suffer through worse? It would be so easy.

The nope below helped Marie to an adjacent cable and they climbed down together, side by side, hand under hand, toward the haze and the ground below it.

Cheyenne suddenly brushed past Syd and Liam and stepped onto the ledge herself. "I've got people waiting for me," she said.

She positioned herself between two of the nopes, gave them each a nod, and together, they jumped. Just like they had with Marie, the nopes caught Cheyenne, then grabbed on to the wires, and helped her to climb. Simply watching them fall turned Syd's stomach. He knew he couldn't stay on the blazing roof. He knew he was getting sicker by the minute. But every instinct he had screamed at him to keep his feet planted where he stood.

One by one, the nopes stepped to the ledge beside him, waited and, when he didn't come, they looked away and jumped alone.

"If we're gonna do this, we have to do it before the rest of them are gone," said Liam.

"No way . . . no way . . . no way . . ." Krystof Maes shook his head, backed away from the ledge.

Syd felt the same as the little boy, but Liam was right. Syd nodded back at him. They didn't need to speak. Liam understood. He instantly scooped Krystof under his arm, held him tightly as the boy kicked and clawed.

"You're gonna live whether you like it or not," Liam grunted as he approached the ledge.

There were eight nopes left on the roof. One stepped to the edge and held out her hand. Syd blew out a sharp breath and stepped up. He looked back at the Purifiers, then at Liam. "See you on the ground?"

"That's a promise," said Liam.

Syd and the nope jumped together.

The air rushed past him as the roof fell away above. He felt his stomach leap into his throat, but after the initial sickening terror, Syd felt a strange thrill. He only had a few seconds before the tangle of wires and cables began to slide past him. He was about to reach out for one when he was yanked backward, his fall stopped short with a bone-rattling jolt.

The nope had caught on for him, just like with Marie, and hoisted him up onto a wire. Their eyes met and the nope began to climb down. Syd looked up. He saw Liam's nervous face peering over the edge. He dared to let go with one hand and give Liam a thumbs-up. Then he looked down.

He regretted it instantly.

His feet dangled over the void. The wind felt stronger than he thought it should; he was acutely aware of the force of gravity pulling at him. He focused on the patch of building directly in front of him, tried not think of the pain of the cable cutting into his palms or the burning in his veins, and he began to climb down.

By the time he got the nerve to look at anything other than the glass wall directly in front of his face, the three Purifiers had all jumped and been helped on to the wires. Syd held his breath as he watched Liam jump with little Krystof still in his arms. He felt almost as if he were falling again too, watching Liam fall. Was it possible to feel something because someone you cared about was feeling it?

Liam caught on to a wire with his other hand, the metal hand, without the help of the nopes. Syd watched him shift the murderous little boy onto his back, where Krystof hung on for dear life, and Liam began to carry the boy down the side of the building. Syd still had the falling feeling in his chest. He knew it was for Liam. It was stronger than the pain in his blood. He began to wonder whether the feeling would ever go away.

He hoped it wouldn't.

Of course, Liam had blood on his hands, a lifetime of murders. But he'd saved Syd and he'd saved Krystof. Neither of them deserved his saving, but Liam did it anyway. Who could say why? If Liam was the sum of his actions, he was a killer, sure, but also a savior. And a romantic. And a thug. And a fool. And a guy just like any other. He was better than the worst thing he'd ever done and worse than the best he'd done too. Like anyone else, his life was somewhere in between.

As Syd watched Liam climb, he couldn't help but want to know that life more, to untangle those knots, to learn Liam's story and to share his own back. He wanted a future that looked nothing like his past, and he wanted Liam to be a part of it. He wanted more time.

If the nopes could heal, maybe there was hope for the rest of them.

[37]

THE TEENAGE PURIFIERS HAD fled Cousin at the first sign of adversity.

He understood, of course.

Cousin had trained enough teenagers to kill that he knew their hearts were rarely in it. Fair-weather soldiers, kids were.

Fickle.

So he stumbled alone through the Mountain City. His mouth tasted of blood from where Liam had punched him, and his shirt was soaked from the wound in his gut, shrapnel from his own bomb. The irony would have been amusing were it not such a surprisingly painful wound. An ironic death was not the kind he had in mind for himself, anyway. He did not intend to die from this.

The streets of the city were empty, its tall buildings

abandoned. Where he passed anyone at all, they hunched over in the shadows and tried to avoid catching his eye. Their skin was webbed with agonizing black. The people lacked the strength to run, to fight, even to ask for help. Who could help them, anyway? The cultists had lost their leaders. The Purifiers too. There were no leaders anymore. There were no movements to lead.

His Purifiers had so enjoyed their brief time without their parents' generation to control them. They took it as quite a shock that the same sickness could lay them low, as if they expected to be made of such different stuff from those who came before them.

He stumbled on, lightheaded, toward the old mansion where he'd parked his own hovercraft. There was a medical kit on board and he could patch himself right up. His fleeing Purifiers would no doubt have stolen the vehicles they knew of by now, which was exactly why he had a backup. That's how he'd survived so long, after all. Always have a backup. Always assume the worst. A pessimist was, after all, merely someone who could never be disappointed.

Poor Liam had looked so disappointed when he saw Syd unconscious. He had really believed everything might be okay after they escaped the explosion. Cousin should have set the EMD charge high enough to kill. He could have spared Syd and Marie the suffering of this incurable sickness. Spared Liam the suffering of watching them die in pain.

But life was suffering, after all, and who was Cousin

to deny his young protégé those last delicious sips of it? He would have liked to have been there when it happened, but not everything could be controlled. That Machinist girl had spirit, Cousin would grant her that. She was truly delusional, but spirited nonetheless.

When he reached the stately walls of a once-grand mansion, he took in the view over the Mountain City. It was the last he'd see of the wretched place. Its ruined buildings, abandoned slums, and silent factories. Fires still burned here and there as the sickly living huddled together, as if togetherness mattered.

Everyone suffers alone, Cousin thought. Everyone dies alone and all of them soon enough. A few days at most. A week perhaps. The older ones were surely gone already.

Strange how the old gang lord Maes had that last fury rise in him, getting in Cousin's way up on the 108th floor. Perhaps that was the endgame of this sickness? Rage?

No.

A ridiculous thought. It had nothing to do with the sickness. People simply died the way they lived.

Maes was a criminal, a man who had lived his life by violence. Of course, his final moments would also turn to violence. Those who spent their lives moping about by themselves—Syd, for example—would mope alone right into their graves. Those who were defiant, like Marie, would defy until they dropped dead. The maudlin would weep and the deal makers would bargain and the jokers would joke, but every last one of them would die.

Every one of them but Cousin.

He lowered the ramp to his hovercraft and strolled up it, hitting the button to slam the ramp shut behind him, like closing the pages of an antique book. He would write its next chapter far away from here. He set his EMD stick down on the bench and moved toward the driver's seat. When it spun around in front of him, he found himself face-to-face with Liam.

Liam didn't say a word.

He'd learned that lesson.

He hit Cousin in the stomach so hard that the man doubled over. Liam had used his good hand, the one that was still flesh. It came away red.

Cousin rose to fight back, but other hands caught him tightly from behind. He looked left and looked right, and saw that Syd and Marie had grabbed him under the arms, pinned him in place.

The two of them were showing all the signs, heavy veins popping through the skin, dark lines, no doubt screaming out in agony with every thump of their eager young hearts. In a few hours, maybe days, they'd wish they'd just let Cousin kill them, of that he felt quite sure.

"So"—Cousin tried a smile at Liam—"you'll murder me and then what? Watch your new friends die? Can't you tell they're in pain? Did you go through all the trouble to escape that roof, just to get some pointless revenge against your old friend?"

"I wouldn't call us friends." Liam punched him across

the face, again using his good hand. "And I wouldn't call this pointless."

Cousin spat out a tooth, smiled a bloody grin. "Everything is pointless in the end, Liam."

"Good thing this isn't the end, then, huh?" He kneed Cousin between the legs. He'd always wanted to do that.

Cousin grunted. Exhaled. Kept on his feet. "Syd will disappoint you, boy. That's what people like him do. They take so much more than they give and they grow to hate you for needing them. He'll look at you and always see a killer and a fool."

Liam raised the metal fist. He could crush Cousin's skull in with one more punch.

"Liam?" said Syd. He shook his head. He didn't need to say anything. He saw Liam, and Liam . . . how to describe it? He felt seen.

"Oh . . . now isn't that so very sweet?" Cousin hissed at them.

"You ready to shut this guy up?" Marie suggested.

Liam nodded. Syd nodded.

Marie whistled and the ramp lowered again, letting in a streak of dusky sunlight. Krystof Maes stepped inside. Syd and Marie dragged Cousin backward down the ramp and tossed him to the ground. Cousin said something, but they couldn't hear him over the whirr of the motors as Krystof shut the ramp again.

Syd went to the driver's seat, fired the engines to life, took a deep breath, and set their course to the east.

But his blood boiled. His vision turned red at the edges. He felt dizzy.

He looked at Liam, stared at him. For a moment, couldn't remember his name. "I . . . I think you should drive," he suggested, standing. "I need to lie down."

He stumbled as he stood. Krystof steadied the controls, while Liam steadied Syd, guided him to a bench in the back.

Marie sat next to Syd, felt the fever on his forehead. Or was that her own fever? The adrenaline of survival had been masking the agony of their symptoms for hours . . . everything hurt now, rising from the inside out.

Marie wanted to scream. Instead, she lay down next to Syd and stared up at Liam blankly. Syd felt her breathing, felt the heat of her beside him. It hurt where they made contact, but he couldn't bring himself to move.

You don't look so good, lover boy. Knox winked at Syd, standing just behind Liam.

"Lover boy?" Syd said aloud.

Liam heard him, but ignored it. Syd was delirious.

Knox rested a hand on Liam's shoulder, looked him up and down. Winked at Syd. *A guy like you could do worse.*

"A guy like me could do worse," Syd mumbled.

Liam touched his cheek, just like the nopes had done. It was hot. Very hot. He elevated Syd's legs on a small toolbox and moved Marie to the opposite bench. She groaned and her eyelids fluttered.

"Wake me up when we get back to my—" Marie whispered.

"Parents." Liam finished the thought for her. She nodded. Liam bit his lip and rested his hand on Marie's to stop her from tearing at her neck, where her carotid artery pulsed visibly.

Cousin had been right. His friends were still dying. He had no idea if the healing of the nopes meant they would heal too. He had no idea if the city in the jungle they were going back to would be anything but a charnel ground. He had no idea if Marie's parents would be alive, or if she would wake up from this nap. Or if Syd would wake up.

After all they'd been through, nothing had changed: Liam wanted to protect Syd more than ever, but he couldn't protect Syd from this.

"Drive," Syd mumbled, his eyes closed. "The great Yovel returns."

Liam laughed a little. At least Syd still had a sense of humor. Except, Liam realized, he hadn't really had one before.

Syd was trying to put Liam at ease. Syd himself did not feel at all at ease. Knox was still standing over him. Quiet now. Syd tried to look into Knox's eyes, but his face blurred. He suddenly couldn't recall what Knox had looked like.

Knox was dead, had been dead, would always be dead.

Syd shuddered. He didn't want to forget, but he wasn't ready to join Knox yet. He wanted more time. He needed it. Could Knox just give him some more time? Was there any more time to spare?

He opened his mouth to plead, but no sound came out. Liam placed a finger on Syd's lips, told him to rest, and threw himself into the pilot's seat, gripping the controls to keep from screaming.

"Am I going to get sick like them?" Krystof asked, settling into the copilot's seat beside Liam. "Will it hurt?"

"I have no idea," Liam answered, lifting the vehicle, steadying its pitch, accelerating. He wasn't as good at this as Syd. His hands quivered.

Waterfall, he thought to himself, but it didn't work.

He felt everything.

Yes, he wanted to tell Krystof, *it will hurt. Even if you don't get sick like them. It will hurt.*

But silence was kinder than confession.

He gunned the engines and sped across the desert, straight for home.

Cousin lay on his back in the dust and watched the hovercraft speed away. His hands rested across his stomach, pressing down to stop the bleeding. One look at his crimson fingers told him it was not working. He rested his back against the ground and looked up at the hazy sky.

"I know you're there," he said, tilting his head to the left, where he saw three of his Purifiers standing with that cultist girl. Behind them, a whole sea of faces, tattooed teenagers, watching him bleed. "You come to finish me off?" Cousin groaned.

Cheyenne squatted beside him, shook her head. "We just came to make sure they got away unharmed. And they did."

She stood up and turned from him, trailed by the Purifiers. Her followers parted as she walked, scratching and grunting with their own agonies, but leaving Cousin behind. When they left, however, he was still not alone.

"Oh," he said, seeing the thin figures circling him, staring down where he lay.

Nopes.

They cocked their heads at him curiously and, one by one, they squatted at his side, like Cheyenne had done. They reached out their bony fingers and rested them on his cheek. Cousin tried to turn his head away, tried to move, but found himself unable.

Even as he lay on the ground, surrounded by these silent creatures, he also saw himself from above, like a drone looking down, as, one by one, the nopes touched his cheeks, and then, one by one left him there, until he was alone in the dirt. He watched himself until there was silence.

[38]

LIAM DROVE AT FULL speed all night, lights blazing. Stealth didn't matter now. There was no one after them. There was no one left to be after them. He settled the vehicle down in the early morning dark, just by the side of the grim barracks where they had left Marie's parents. The engines sighed to silence and he sat in the driver's seat, waiting.

The little boy was sound asleep beside him, sunburned, eyes twitching with a dream. What dreams a little monster like him dreamed, Liam didn't know, but they couldn't be so different from Liam's. Violent lives are predictable. It's when the violence stops that everything gets harder.

Everything was about to get harder.

Liam stood up quietly and moved to the back of the cabin. Marie and Syd both slept restlessly, groaning and scratching and turning on the narrow benches. Neither of them was bleeding, which was some relief, but their veins were still black against their skin. Marie's had swollen to create a terrible topography across her body. They were both sweating torrents and the cabin smelled sour.

Liam hit the ramp button, opening it for fresh air. He hoped the noise would wake them. He didn't dare jostle them awake. He'd learned the dangers of that from life as a soldier. Startle someone from sleep and they might attack before they know who you are, or the shock itself could kill them.

Syd sat up slowly. He hugged himself as the dim first light of morning shot like needles into his eyes. Marie winced herself to standing, and her facial expression suggested she was in just as much pain. Liam tried to keep his own face blank, but Syd was too observant. He could imagine what Liam saw. Their condition had gotten worse.

"Where—?" Syd's voice cracked. His throat was dry. He couldn't remember what he wanted to ask.

Liam got them both some water.

"Old Detroit," Liam said. "The co-op where—"

Marie didn't wait for him to finish before she stood and made her stumbling way down the ramp. Not even the agony and exhaustion in her body could stop her. She crossed the distance to the barracks and practically threw herself into the dark doorway.

Liam helped Syd move quickly to catch up.

When they got inside, they saw Marie in the center of

the room, a slash of new sunlight across her chest, like a wound. She wept, body-shaking tears.

The barracks was empty.

"They're gone," she said, swaying in place. "Gone."

Syd and Liam approached her, put their hands on her shoulders, tried to offer comfort. She was unsteady on her feet, so Liam took her weight on his arm and let Syd walk under his own power. They walked with Marie outside.

"That kid we left," she said. She had trouble finding his name.

"Tom," said Liam.

"Yeah." Marie shook her head. "He better be . . . dead, because if not, I'm gonna . . ."

"You don't know what happened here yet, Marie," said Liam.

"He left his post," she said. "All I need to know. I told him to stay. He left. My . . . p . . . parents."

"You told him to look after the sick," said Syd. "Maybe he did."

"Yeah," a voice called from behind them. "Maybe that's *exactly* what I did."

They turned to see the pock-faced boy, no hood on his head, standing on top of a dirt berm that marked the edge of a field on the other side. He only had the faintest traces of visible lines on his skin, a few ruddy patches from scratching.

"How—?" Syd tried to form the question.

Tom shrugged. "Didn't get it so bad."

He'd known Tom before. The kid had barely had any working biodata. Couldn't afford it. That may have saved him. Syd tried to remember what he'd had himself, as if the memory would predict his fate. He looked at Marie. She'd had a lot more biodata than he did. She looked a lot worse off too.

"My . . . parents?" Marie demanded.

"You should come with me," Tom said and turned around, vanishing down the other side of the high berm.

Marie let go of Liam and did her best to catch up with him, scrambling on hands and knees up the high dirt mound and sliding down the other side.

What she saw there took her breath away.

In the field in front of her, there were hundreds of people. Some stood in clusters around mounds dug in the dirt, others stood alone, watching the sunrise or quietly crying into their hands. Among the countless murmured conversations, Marie made out the unmistakable sounds of laughter.

"These are funerals?" she said.

Tom nodded. "Some of them, yeah," he said. "But not all."

He pointed at one large group of people, a mix of Purifiers and people in regular clothes, some covered in the telltale web of veins, others with perfectly clear skin. There were also nopes there, or whatever they were now. They would need a name. They stood together around a low fire where the people were talking and eating. The nopes, too, were eating. Feeding themselves. Living.

"What is going on?" Syd asked when he caught up to Tom and Marie.

"Two days ago, people started standing from the floor," Tom explained. "They were getting better. They went outside. I tried to stop them, but I wasn't feeling so good myself. They went outside and just, like, strolled around. More and more every hour. And then the nopes showed up. And they were, like, well, Guardians again. Strong and a little scary. Intense. But not cruel. They walked right into the barracks and started helping people. Helping people get air. Helping people bury the dead ones, the ones who bled out. I couldn't believe it. I didn't know what to do. I just started helping too. And all night we held funerals and we found food and had feasts. It was like, I dunno. Like what the Reconciliation wanted? Everyone together. Even the nopes. People getting better."

"Everyone?" Marie scanned the field, searching for her parents.

"Well, no," said Tom. "Not everyone."

He pointed at her father, standing at the edge of the crowd, looking at the sky.

"Dad!" Marie gasped and ran to him, stumbling, tripping in the dirt, but still running.

Syd and Liam watched from a distance as she fell into her father's arms. He held her up, lifted her. As her strength faded, his strength had returned. Her father hugged her deeply and said something to her. When he spoke, Marie's legs gave out and she collapsed before he could hold her up. He bent down to hold her, shaking and sobbing on the ground.

"Her mother," Tom told them. "Died yesterday."

"Of the sickness?"

"Not everyone gets better," he said.

"What's the difference?" Liam asked. "Between the ones who get better and the ones who don't?"

Tom shrugged. "Some people die. Some don't. Just the way it is." He started off across the field. "I gotta get some breakfast. Roasted soy patties. You want some?"

Syd shook his head. He wasn't hungry. His hands shook.

"Yovel himself." Tom frowned. "Sick as anyone. Who'd have thought?"

"Just Syd," Syd corrected him, his voice quiet. "I'm just Syd."

Tom looked around the field, at the jungle city beyond it. "Yeah," he said. "You are." Then he wandered off to get breakfast. Marie was still in her father's arms, talking, crying, telling him everything that had happened to her.

And he told her how they were organizing, how they had set up a market for food, a place people could trade for what they needed. How he'd organized everyone into groups with jobs to do, even when they didn't need to be told. How people took care of one another.

"There aren't many of us," he told her. "But I think we can build something here. If you'll help me."

"Not like before?" Marie asked.

Her father shook his head. "Nothing will be like before."

She held him and she breathed his scent in deep. "Of course I'll help you, Daddy," she told him.

"First, you need to get better." He led her to a comfortable spot to lie down, somewhere in the shade, somewhere she could see him as he worked and call to him if she needed anything.

She lay there, burning, but watching her father, knowing that whatever had passed between them, she was forgiven. And so was he.

Across the field, Syd shivered. His hand twitched as he wiped his face, terrified to see a trickle of blood run down from his nose. He stared at his wet finger. He shook it to get the blood off. He tried to wipe it from his pants. It wouldn't wipe away.

"Blood," he shouted. "Blood. Blood." It was all he could think of. He couldn't find other words. He would bleed out. He would not get better. He would die, right here, on the ground . . . He started to hyperventilate.

"Relax," Liam told him, catching his hand, holding it still. "You're okay. There's no blood. Look. Look."

He held Syd's fingers up in front of him. There was no blood on them. He wasn't bleeding. His blood boiled inside him. If only it would come out. Maybe he'd feel better if it would just come out. Syd looked at Liam. He tried to scratch again, tried to rip his arm open. Liam stopped him. Syd wanted to explain. If he could only bleed, the pain would stop . . .

"Let's just sit a minute," Liam suggested, helping Syd down to lean against the dirt mound.

"Who makes it?" Syd asked. "Who decides?"

Liam didn't know. He didn't answer. What good could words do?

Syd looked at Liam, those sad, eager eyes. He searched for the words. He had to explain something. He saw Knox standing in the sun, a hazy shape. He couldn't make out his face.

It'll get worse before it gets better, Knox said.

"It's going to get worse," Syd said out loud.

"You won't suffer alone," Liam told him.

Syd frowned. He spoke slowly, fighting to find the words to say what he meant. "Everyone suffers alone."

Liam took his hands, looked him in the eyes. Made Syd focus, made Syd listen.

"Not you," Liam told him. "Not while I'm around."

Syd looked at his dark-veined hands in Liam's; the one good hand, warm and calloused, the metal hand, hard and hot as sunlight. He looked at Liam's face, expectant, hopeful, wanting something Syd didn't know if he had to give, if he had the time to give. He wanted to know if it would be okay.

Like I know, said Knox. *It's your future.*

Syd looked up for his old friend, snapped his head around, but Knox was gone.

Only he and Liam remained. Only the two of them.

"I don't know what's going to happen," said Syd.

"Me neither," said Liam. "History only goes one way."

Liam put his arm around him, and Syd didn't flinch. He let Syd rest his head on his wide shoulder. The metal hand sat softly against Syd's back. His left hand reached across and laced its fingers between Syd's and Syd squeezed the fingers together.

It wasn't that Liam decided to do it, or that Syd did either, just that their hands knew things they couldn't.

Syd closed his eyes, felt sleep coming on, a pulse of fire in his skin, their fingers laced, all the feelings at the same time, the hurt, the help.

"Tell me your story," Syd muttered.

"I'll be here when you wake up," Liam told him.

Syd shivered and let himself curl closer. "If I wake up," he added.

"I'll be here," Liam repeated. "And I'll tell you then."

Syd might have replied had he been awake, but instead, he slept, and in his sleep, he dreamed and in his dream he dreamed he was awake.

And Liam was still there.